THE CASE OF THE DEFUNCT ADJUNCT

THE CASE OF THE DEFUNCT ADJUNCT

BY FRANKIE BOW

Hawaiian Heritage Press

The Case of the Defunct Adjunct
Copyright © 2015 by Frankie Bow
Published by Hawaiian Heritage Press

Edited by Lorna Collins
Cover design by Deirdre Wait/ENC Graphic Services
Formatting by Eddie Vincent/ENC Graphic Services

Hardcover
ISBN 13: 978-1-943476-01-5
ISBN: 10: 1-943476-01-2

Library of Congress Control Number: 2015959134

CHAPTER ONE

It was another beautiful Mahina morning. A pale mist veiled the lawn; dewdrops glittered on the hibiscus hedges along the walkway; the tall palms by the library building swayed and bounced in the wind. I barely noticed any of it. I had one minute to make it to the old Health building, way out on the edge of campus. I felt so harried and damp that I was tempted to skip class and go home. Unfortunately, as the professor, I didn't really have the option.

A fat raindrop hit me in the eye as I reached the shelter of the language building. A cluster of students chanted their *Mele Kāhea,* the sung request for permission to enter the classroom. As I hurried by, the *kumu* opened the door to let the students file in one by one. Class was starting. I abandoned my dignity and broke into a sprint.

My business communication students had dispersed themselves around the room like gas molecules, expanding to fill their allotted container. The only two who sat near each other were the twins. In the back row, as far as possible from everyone else, was Bret Lampson. As usual, Bret stared through me, focusing on something far beyond the walls of the classroom. From the first day of class, Bret had tripped my internal danger alarm. The Student Retention Office had been unmoved by my concerns, reminding me that it was my job to honor each student's unique learning style.

"Apologies for being late." I placed my stack of papers on the

desk and smoothed my skirt, trying not to let on how winded my hundred yard dash had left me. The air tasted sour and musty. I hoped I wasn't breathing in asbestos particles and black mold.

"No worries, professor." The round young man in the front row pushed up the brim of his red baseball cap. "We all human. Anyway, we can't leave until you're more than fifteen minutes late."

"Well, I certainly hope I never keep you waiting for fifteen minutes." I couldn't imagine getting to the point where I was as cavalier about deadlines and due dates as some of my senior colleagues. I felt bad enough about having ruined my perfect on-time record, even if it was only by ninety seconds.

"Professor Harrison's always late," the girl twin volunteered. "Last semester he kept forgetting we had class. Someone hadda go get 'im from his office." Her brother nodded agreement. They looked like characters from a Japanese comic book, with pale skin, big dark eyes, and spiky black hair.

"Well," I said quickly. "Let's get started."

As instructive as it might have been to listen to my students dish my fellow faculty members, I had to nip this conversation in the bud. My class would happily spend the entire period complaining to me about their other professors. Just as they complained—I was certain of it—about me when I wasn't around.

"Everyone brought in their first-draft elevator pitch? We're going to—yes? Is there a question?"

"Today your birthday, Miss?"

"I'm sorry?"

"You could take the day off," the boy twin said. "No need work on your birthday."

"Actually, my birthday is tomorrow, not today. Right now there's nowhere I'd rather be than here in class, with all of you. Okay, let's see what you have." I started collecting papers, heartened that everyone seemed to have something to hand in. I glanced at the boy twin's paper as he handed it to me. "*Elevator pitch*," I whispered to him.

His sister shoved him triumphantly.

"*Told* you, babooz. No such thing as a *escalator* pitch."

The young man in the red baseball cap twisted around in his chair.

"Eh Professor, you going out wit' Professor Park for your birthday?"

"Oh yah, Miss," a young woman exclaimed. "You gotta get 'im to take you to Gavin's down on Mamo Street."

"Tomorrow is Tuesday," someone else chimed in. "That's when they get all you can eat prime rib night. Like Vegas."

"I'll take it under advisement. Thank you. Now, does everyone remember why it's called an elevator pitch?"

The classroom fell silent.

"Anyone? No? Okay, we did talk about this last time, but just as a reminder." I kept talking as I moved from desk to desk collecting papers. "It's called an elevator pitch because in a tall office building, you may run into someone important on the elevator. You have their attention for about thirty seconds. Only thirty seconds to convince that person to hire you, or invest in your business, or even—"

Out of the corner of my eye, I caught the girl twin shoving her brother again. He pushed her back, and I shot them a look before they escalated to a full-on slap fight.

I had one more paper to collect. Bret Lampson stared through me as I approached the back row.

"Bret." I spoke as gently as if I were waking him from surgery. "Do you have your assignment?"

He blinked, focused, and shook his head no.

"Couldn't put it on paper."

"Well, if it's a matter of computer access, some students prefer to handwrite—"

"'Cause of those people who want my ideas. I already told you."

I lowered my voice to a whisper, aware that the rest of the class was watching us. "Remember what we talked about before? If you want to keep your *best* idea to yourself, then just give me your *second-best* idea."

"It's not that easy. I have to, I have to…"

Now he was staring right at me. I stepped back.

"Bret." My hand was shielding my neck. "Do you have *anything* for me?"

"Uh-huh." Keeping his eyes fixed on mine, he reached down into his backpack and pulled his hand out. He held something that gleamed dully under the fluorescent light. It took me a few seconds to figure out what it was—a *leiomano*, a vicious-looking polished wooden club studded with sharks' teeth. Behind me, students were rising out of their seats and crowding through the single door in the front of the classroom.

CHAPTER TWO

My hands flew into a defensive posture and I stepped back, half-aware of the students stampeding out behind me. Bret remained in his seat, gazing serenely at the weapon, running his fingers dreamily over the jagged teeth. I stumbled backwards until I reached the classroom door. Then I grasped the jamb, swung out, and broke into a run. I reached the emergency call station on the other side of the building and pressed the big silver button. Silence. I looked back over my shoulder. No one was chasing me. I mashed the button again. This time I heard a dead click. The emergency call station was out of order. I reached into my laptop bag for my phone, only to remember that I had left it back in my office, charging.

I ran down the concrete walkway, past the language building, all the way to the College of Commerce building. I passed the out-of-order elevator, sprinted up the stairs and down the hall, fumbled for my keys, unlocked the door to my office, pulled it shut behind me, and stood, hands braced on my desk, wheezing.

The air conditioning in my building was out again. Sucking in the warm, heavy air was like trying to quench my thirst with a milkshake. When I had recovered enough breath to speak, I called security. No one was answering the phone, so I gave up and called Emma.

Emma Nakamura from the Biology Department was my best friend at Mahina State University. She would know what to do.

Unfortunately, Emma wasn't picking up her phone either. I

didn't leave a message on her voice mail, because I know she never checks it.

I pulled a pocket mirror out of my bag, dabbed the mascara smears from under my eyes, and smoothed down the curly hair-tentacles that had sprung free from my ponytail. Then I went down the hallway to talk to my department chair.

I knocked on the door frame of Dan Watanabe's office, and he motioned me in. Dan already looked weary, and I didn't like adding to his burdens. He had to know, though.

I parked myself in his visitor chair, and told him what had happened in class.

"That young man needs to be referred to counseling," I concluded. "And he needs to be removed from my course immediately. For everyone's safety."

"I'm sorry, Molly. I wish I could do something, but I don't have the authority to remove a student from class. For something like that, you'll have to talk to the dean."

"Please, Dan, there has to be some other way."

Dan reached for the gigantic jar of antacid tablets he keeps on his desk, and shook out a handful. I thought he was going to offer me one, but instead he stuffed them all into his mouth.

"Look." He took a few seconds to chew and swallow. "You should give Bill a chance. He'll do the right thing."

"No he won't. He'll just tell me to try to work it out with the student."

Dan shrugged. "I don't know what to tell you, Molly. He's the boss. You'll have to take it up with him."

I thanked Dan and trudged down the hall to the dean's office. Serena, the dean's secretary, looked up quickly when I came in.

"Aw, you okay, Molly? Heard about what happened in your class. Terrible that thing." At least one person seemed sympathetic.

"Serena, it's so frustrating." I propped my forearms on the wood-grain Formica counter, enjoying the momentary coolness. "Dan says I need Bill Vogel's permission to remove a disturbed student from my class."

"Well, don't get your hopes up." Serena swiveled her chair

around to face her computer. "You know the dean doesn't like to turn away paying customers."

"I know. It seems like no one's going to do anything until there's a classroom massacre or something."

"Probably not even then. Didn't do anything after the last one." Serena tapped on the keyboard. "Okay Molly, I got you one appointment with the dean for four o'clock, right after the retreat. It's starting soon, you know. You better get going."

"Oh, I wasn't planning to go to the retreat. I have all those textbook evaluations to do—"

"It's not optional." Serena swiveled her chair back to face me.

"How can it not be optional? It's summer. My paycheck stopped on May fifteenth."

"You're here teaching summer school," Serena said. "And you're working on that other thing too."

"Yeah. Remind me never to volunteer to do that again."

"Sorry, Molly. Student Retention Office told us it's mandatory. Not so bad, you know. You get coffee and free food, and the banquet room has a nice ocean view."

"Where was it again?"

"Lehua Inn ballroom. You better get going. You don't want to miss it when they hand out the campus teaching award."

"No, wouldn't want to miss that."

"And you know who's a finalist this year?"

"Is this going to make me feel better, or worse?"

Serena grinned mischievously.

CHAPTER THREE

Linda Wilson, Acting Associate Dean of Mahina State University's Student Retention Office, presided over the registration table. She wore her blonde hair pinned back by a pink silk hibiscus, which echoed the florid print of her muumuu.

Emma Nakamura nudged me. "Eh Molly, look. It's the Queen Bee—"

"Shh. Not so loud."

Linda from the Student Retention Office was Emma's nemesis. One of them, anyway.

"What? She can't hear us. We're all the way in the back of the line."

A nervous young man, whose crisply-pressed aloha shirt was too big around the neck, assisted Linda. As each attendee signed in and filled out a name tag, the young man handed over a folder and delivered what looked like a practiced speech.

"Aw, this line is gonna take forever. Let's just go to the bar. Look, it's right over there."

"I wish. I bet the Lehua Lounge is nice and cool inside." I shook the hem of my shirt to get some airflow around my skin. "What I want to know is, how does Linda wear those long-sleeved muumuus every day without passing out?"

"She's cold-blooded, that's why. Like a snake."

"I see she has another new assistant. She doesn't seem to keep them very long."

"That's 'cause every full moon, she mates with them, then

devours them headfirst."

"Stop it. Do you think I should tell her about what happened this morning with Bret Lampson? You know, I already tried to tell them that I was concerned about him."

"Wouldn't do any good. She'll just come up with some reason why it's your fault."

"Yeah, you're right. Hey, guess who's a finalist for the teaching award."

"You?"

"Seriously, Emma? You think the Student Retention Office would nominate me?"

"Okay, who then?"

"Your brother's office mate."

"My brother's former office mate, you mean. Jonah's classes got cancelled, remember."

"Oh, that's right. Sorry."

"No way." Emma socked my shoulder to demonstrate her incredulity. "Kent got nominated? Fo'real? Who told you?"

"The dean's secretary."

"Kent Lovely? That stringy little schmuck—"

"Shh. Not so loud. Hang on, I'm going to grab something to read."

We were inching past a polished koa stand stacked with tourist brochures and free newspapers. I stepped out of line and grabbed a copy of *Island Confidential*.

"Ugh. Kent? He's even worse than his buddy Rodge. Seriously, the teaching award?"

"Kent is not worse than Rodge. Rodge is the reason we have to keep our doors open when we have a student in our office. That's why it's called the Rodge Cowper Rule—wait, did you just call Kent a *schmuck*?"

"Oh, maybe you forgot that I earned my Ph.D. at Cornell."

"You would never let *anyone* forget you went to Cornell, Emma."

"It's in New York."

"They say *schmuck* in Ithaca? Seriously?"

We had reached the front of the line. I started to write my name on the sign-in sheet. Emma picked up a glossy flyer from the table and waved it under my nose.

"Look, Molly. *Wowing Your Students with Extraordinary Customer Service!*"

Linda's young assistant recited his lines. "Good afternoon, ladies. Today, you'll learn about some Best Practices to help you generate peak customer satisfaction."

Linda caught sight of Emma and placed a hand on the young man's arm, as if to say, *I'll take it from here.*

"Hello, Emma. Molly. How *nice* to see you two here today."

"Hi, Linda." I smiled pleasantly, finished signing in, and offered the pen to Emma.

"Of *course* we're here." Emma snatched the pen from me. "No choice. They told us it was mandatory."

Emma scribbled her name and phone number on the sign-in sheet, and then we each took a paper name tag and a felt-tip marker. I wrote *Molly Barda—College of Commerce* on mine. Emma wrote *"Emma"* on hers.

"Linda," I said, "this customer satisfaction thing—you know, when we keep telling the students that they're the customers, some of them interpret that to mean the customer is always right, and they can do whatever—"

"The customer framework is a transformative paradigm," Linda interrupted. "New ways of thinking are going to disrupt education as we know it, with improved modalities of engagement. We'll be going over that in our session today."

"Yes, I'm sure it will be very helpful and interesting. All I'm trying to say is—if all I focused on was customer satisfaction, why wouldn't I just, I don't know, throw away the syllabus, let the students miss as many classes as they want, and then give them all As?"

Emma snorted. Linda looked startled. Maybe I had gone too far.

"Why Molly," Linda said. "I'm pleasantly surprised."

"You are?"

"That's very out-of-the-box thinking."

"It is? Oh, no, I didn't mean—"

Linda turned to Emma.

"It would be wonderful if *all* of our faculty were as open to fresh thinking as you are, Molly. *Some* of your colleagues are afraid to give up control in the classroom. They're threatened by change."

Emma folded her sturdy arms.

"Maybe some of us don't want to *change* into Clown College."

"We're not trying to start an argument." I grasped Emma's elbow and steered her away from the registration table.

"Yes we are," Emma protested.

"It was so thoughtful of the Student Retention Office to arrange this for us," I called back. "I know you put a lot of work into it. Thank you, Linda. Thanks, uh—"

I didn't know the new sidekick's name, and hadn't noticed a name tag.

"Have a great afternoon, ladies," Linda said. "Enjoy the retreat."

CHAPTER FOUR

The round tables of the Lehua Inn's banquet room were filling up with Mahina State faculty. The men wore subdued aloha shirts and khaki trousers. The women dressed by discipline. Colorful Guatemalan bags, gauze skirts, and flowing gray hair marked the social sciences. Humanities favored bold eyeglasses and hair colors not found in nature. My few female colleagues in the College of Commerce sported a nonthreatening business-y look that might be described as "Beverly Hills real estate agent." T-shirts and shapeless jeans indicated the natural sciences.

Emma Nakamura was an accomplished biologist, and looked it. Her wavy black hair was pulled back into an indifferent ponytail. Her face, browned and lightly freckled from hours of canoe paddling, was bare. Her idea of dressing up for our offsite retreat was to wear a seed company t-shirt she'd picked up for free at a conference.

I didn't fit in anywhere.

Not surprising, I suppose, for a literature Ph.D. teaching in a business school. At some point I'd have to modify my vintage wardrobe if I was going to survive in humid Mahina. I imagined my heatstroke-reddened corpse, stylish in a vermillion wool Lilli-Ann coatdress and opaque tights.

"Friggin' Student Retention Office." Emma pressed on her paper name tag as she beelined to the refreshment table. "They're about as useful as a MRSA infection."

"You know Emma, Clown College is actually very hard to get

into."

"What?"

"You told Linda you didn't want us to change into Clown College."

"Why does anyone listen to those Student Retention Office idiots? You see Linda was wearing her flower on the right? But she's married, ah?"

"She is married. To Bob Wilson, in the History Department. The way you wear the flower in your hair signals your relationship status?"

"Yeah. Left side means you're taken, like wearing a wedding ring on your left hand. Moron. Her, not you."

Emma glared back toward the banquet room entrance, where Linda and her assistant were still signing in attendees.

"Well *I* didn't know that about the flower placement, Emma."

"Yeah, don't worry about it. You're not the one trying so hard to go native."

"And Emma, you shouldn't antagonize the Student Retention Office."

"Why not?"

"If you get on their bad side, they'll wish you into the cornfield. Like they did with the Philosophy Department."

"They'll what with the cornfield now? What are you talking about?"

"You know that *Twilight Zone* episode? Didn't you ever watch *Twilight Zone* reruns when you were a kid?"

"We only got one channel where I grew up," Emma said. "And that wasn't on it. Are you telling me something happened to the Philosophy Department? I never heard any—whoa."

"What are you—oh my *goodness*."

Through a side doorway, in our line of sight, we could see music instructor and teaching award nominee Kent Lovely. Standing next to him, hip to hip, was our elegant and intimidating vice president, Marshall Dixon. We watched Kent take Marshall's hand and raise it to his lips.

"Classy," Emma said. "He didn't even put down his energy

drink."

"A kiss on the hand? Well, that's sort of charming."

Kent turned Marshall's hand over and nuzzled her open palm.

"Aaah. I take it back. Not charming at all."

"Zero to creepy in three-point-two seconds," Emma agreed. "I thought Marshall Dixon had better taste. Well, that's one way to get yourself nominated for a teaching award. I never would've guessed *those* two were—"

"I'm changing the subject now." I nudged Emma toward the refreshment table. "Look, food."

"*Haupia* cheesecake. Right on."

She rolled up the program, tucked it into her back pocket, and headed for the food line. The Lehua Inn is famous for its *haupia* cheesecake. Haupia is a stiff coconut jelly. Combined with creamy cheesecake and nutty graham cracker crust, it's heavenly.

"Eh Molly, don't look now. Here comes our one-man hostile work environment."

Kent Lovely materialized next to us, beaming, and still holding his energy drink. Kent was well into middle age, and dressed in defiance of the plain fact. His midnight-black hair was gelled to a crisp. His aloha shirt was unbuttoned low enough to show off his wiry physique and his cinnabar tan. A tiny zircon stud sparkled in one leathery earlobe.

"Ciao, Molly." Kent caught Emma and me in a hug, one in each arm. "Emma, *Ai watashi kon'nichiwa.*"

His culturally-sensitive salutations out of the way, Kent released us from his cologne-drenched embrace and pushed ahead of us. He pulled two plates off the stack, and started loading them up. Emma and I took one plate apiece, and followed Kent as he mowed his way through the salads, to the hot dishes, and finally over to the dessert table. He was William Tecumseh Sherman, and the buffet table was Atlanta.

Kent paused his historical re-enactment to turn back and address us. "So, ladies." (Here he paused to lick his fingers.) "Who do you think is gonna get the teaching award today?"

"Who else was nominated?" I asked. "Besides you?"

Kent helped himself to the last two slices of *haupia* cheesecake, balancing them atop the mounds of pastry, roast pork, rice, waffles, and fruit piled on his plates.

"Let's see." One of the slices of *haupia* cake started to slide off its summit. Kent pushed it back up into place and licked his finger again. "It was me, Bob Wilson from history, and that minority chick from the Psychology Department."

Emma stared at him in disbelief.

"Sorry Emma-chan, minority *lady*. Wish me luck, girls. Oh look, brownies."

He set his plates down, grabbed a brownie, stuck it in his mouth, picked the two teetering plates back up, and sauntered off.

"Ucch," Emma said. "I hope he chokes on a waffle. Oh, gross. He left his old soda can right next to the food."

"Well, he only has two hands," I said. "Priorities."

Emma looked around, not finding what she wanted. "So where's the alcohol?"

"The papaya slices smelled kind of fermented," I said.

"How am I supposed to get through Student Retention Office re-education camp without alcohol?"

"I brought Buzzword Bingo."

"Not the same thing."

"No," I agreed. "It's not."

Emma and I scanned the packed ballroom for empty seats. "Good turnout," I said.

"Well, it was mandatory. Eh, speaking of that, where's Stephen?"

"He's probably busy with rehearsals. Those seem to be taking a lot of his time lately. Anyway, he never comes to these things."

"He's gonna get in trouble for skipping this."

"That's my Stephen. He doesn't think the rules apply to him."

I spotted my colleague Iker Legazpi at a table near the raised stage at the front, and waved to get his attention. Iker is a professor of accounting and one of my favorite people, despite his positive attitude. He must get the same underachievers, plagiarists, and grade-grubbers the rest of us have, but he gives each student his full attention and the benefit of the doubt.

As Emma and I made our way toward the front of the ballroom, we noticed people staring at us. Entire tables fell silent and watched us walk by.

"What time was this supposed to begin?" I whispered to Emma. "Are we late?"

"Nah. It's barely started. How come we couldn't just have this thing on campus, like in the cafeteria or something? I'm sure the taxpayers of Hawaii are thrilled to be paying for a banquet room with an ocean view."

"Speaking of views, I feel like everyone's staring at us. Maybe we look really good today or something."

"Nobody here cares how we look, Molly. Don't be a *putz*."

Iker Legazpi stood up to greet us. His side-parted brown hair was lacquered perfectly into place as usual, but the heat and humidity had made his plump face pink and shiny. Dark sweat stains spread under his arms of his long sleeved oxford shirt.

Iker's round face wore a troubled expression. This was unusual.

"Molly, Emma," he sputtered. "This is terrible. Emma, such an injustice for your brother, to lose his job. This thing makes me madder than a wet blanket." English wasn't Iker's first language, and probably not even his second or third.

I had never seen Iker so agitated. In fact, this was the first time I'd ever heard him complain about anything.

"How did *you* know about Jonah getting his classes taken away?" Emma demanded. "Molly, I just told you about that this morning. You told Iker about it, didn't you?"

"No," I shot back, "and I don't know why you always assume *I'm* the blabbermouth. Anyone who bothered to check online can see Jonah's guitar classes aren't on the fall schedule anymore."

"Molly told me nothing," Iker said. "She is as quiet as a clam."

"See?"

"It is in the newspapers," Iker gently removed the copy of *Island Confidential* from my hand and opened it for us to read:

Whistleblower Loses Job: Accused Keeps His.

CHAPTER FIVE

Emma snatched the *Island Confidential* back from Iker and flipped to the center pages of the tabloid. *Whistleblower Loses* was the headline on the left page, and *Job: Accused Keeps His* finished the thought on the right. Featured in the article were photos of Jonah Nakamura, the "Whistleblower," and Kent Lovely, the "Accused." Iker hovered as Emma read, unwilling to take his own seat before Emma and I sat down.

"Hey, look at this picture." Emma pulled the paper closer, making it difficult for me to read over her shoulder. "Kent Lovely had a moustache. I didn't think it was possible for him to look any creepier."

"He looks villainous," I said. "He shouldn't have tried to smile."

"Yeah, he probably thinks he looks real handsome. Ucch, look at Jonah, he looks high."

In the photo, Emma's brother, Jonah, looked dazed and a little sleepy, which is exactly the way he always looks.

"Emma, what is this? Jonah is a whistleblower? What's Kent 'accused' of? What's going on?"

I was hoping she would sit down, and then Iker and I could, too. She didn't, though.

"It was so stupid of him. Jonah, I mean. Well, Kent's stupid too, but I'm not talking about him."

Kent was sitting several tables away, next to his buddy Rodge Cowper and well out of earshot. I wondered whether he had seen today's *Island Confidential.* Possibly not. Kent didn't strike me as much of a reader.

"No, Emma," Iker said. "Your brother was not stupid. He did what was right"

"Okay, my brother was right *and* stupid. But look where it got him. It's so unfair."

"Can I see it?" I was fairly hopping with impatience.

"I'm not done yet," Emma snapped.

Iker quietly cleared his throat.

"The article describes allegations of unauthorized purchases by Kent Lovely, using university accounts. Emma's brother Jonah reported it. I wonder whether this might be related to the investigation you and I have been doing, Molly."

"What investigation?" Emma demanded.

"Oh, right. That. The administration asked Iker to do some kind of audit. Sorry Iker, I know we can't technically call it an audit, an *investigation* of purchases done over the last fiscal year. I volunteered to help Iker out with the write-up."

"Why you?" Emma challenged me. "*You* don't know anything about accounting. You almost called it an audit."

"Oh, like you know all about it? Do you know *why* I'm not supposed to call it an audit? Ha, didn't think so."

"Molly was so kind as to offer her help with my English." Iker fidgeted, uncomfortable with interrupting. "It is a struggle for me to express the right words. Often I do a poor job."

"Your English is fine," Emma said. "You didn't hafta let Molly butt in and take over."

"I do not say this to indulge in self-flatulation. I simply acknowledge my limitations."

"So then, what'd you guys find? With your not-an-audit? Was there anything about my brother? And how come you never told me about it, Molly?"

"I did tell you about it, Emma, remember? When I was complaining about getting stuck on this project, sorry Iker, and you and I swore after we get tenure, we wouldn't sign up for any more unpaid—"

The penny dropped.

"Emma. *You* sent this story in to *Island Confidential. You're* the one who tipped them off."

"I never."

"Yes you did. I know it was you. Just this morning you were telling me how everyone's going to know the real story soon enough about why Jonah lost his classes. Remember? And you were just accusing *me* of being a blabbermouth."

Emma and I glared at each other. Iker averted his eyes and shifted from foot to foot.

"Okay fine," she huffed, finally. "Maybe I sent in a tip. But how was I supposed to know *Island Confidential* was gonna run with it like this?"

"What did you *think* they were going to do? If even half of this is true, what newspaper would pass up such a juicy—"

"You know what? I'm glad they published it. It's disgraceful, and shame on the university for firing Jonah. And now he's lost his job, he's *never* gonna move out."

"Does *your brother* know you did this?" I asked. "Or is he going to find out about it from the paper the way Iker and I just did?"

"He'll figure it out."

"And this Kent Lovely, accused with strong evidence of misappropriating university funds, is nominated for the teaching award." Iker was indignant. "It is a scandal that stinks to Betsy's Heaven."

By this time, most of the attendees had taken their seats. Iker, Emma and I were still standing, and people were really staring at us now.

"These seats are awfully close to the front. I brought Buzzword Bingo." I patted my laptop bag. "Why don't we take our food and sit in the back?"

Iker nodded gravely. "That is an excellent suggestion. This Bingo game that you bring is very helpful for me. There are each time so many new words that I do not understand."

"You and me both, Iker." Emma clapped a sympathetic hand on his shoulder.

We found a small four-top in the back, with three empty seats. I assumed that the man occupying one of the chairs was kitchen staff, waiting for his shift to begin. He didn't look particularly approachable, but there was no other table with room for all three of us. The man's head was shaved down to stubble, and he wore a flannel shirt open with a Dead Kennedys t-shirt underneath. He was going through a stack of papers, which he quickly put away to make room for us.

"Oh, hey. Pat Flanagan." He extended his hand.

"I hope we're not intruding," I said, returning his handshake.

"We're gonna play Buzzword Bingo," Emma added. "You wanna make it a foursome?"

I handed out four Buzzword Bingo cards, and then poured a heap of pennies onto the table.

"This is my first in-service," Pat said.

"You work at the *university*?" I exclaimed.

"In which department are you?" Iker asked.

"English. I teach intro comp. I'm just a part-timer though."

"I thought adjuncts didn't have to do the professional development," Emma said.

"Didn't have anything better to do," Pat examined his Bingo card. "I thought I might even learn something. Oh look. Out of the Box, Silos, Student Centered. Looks like you got all the classics here."

"Shh." Emma waved her hand to quiet us. "They're starting. Oh, Pat, that's Linda, from the Student Retention Office. She always wears that long muumuu. To cover up the tentacles, that's why."

"Emma has some history with the Student Retention Office," I explained.

"Aw right, like you don't, Molly. Hey, did she just say we finished last year with an 'explanation' point? Stop talking you guys, I'm gonna miss my buzzwords."

Linda was succeeded on stage by a woman with short, spiky copper hair and gigantic earrings that looked like mobiles. Pat, Iker, Emma, and I filled our Buzzword Bingo cards rapidly as she talked. I was one space away from completing a row when she said, "…outstanding customer service." I scrambled to find the phrase on my card, but was distracted by an eruption of applause.

"Kent Lovely?" the presenter called out. "Is Kent Lovely here to accept the award?"

Emma rolled her eyes and made a rude noise. Iker sat mournfully silent. Pat watched, his expression neutral.

"Do you know Kent Lovely?" I asked Pat.

"Not well," he said.

I braced for the sight of Kent Lovely swaggering up to the front of the room and claiming the campus-wide teaching award.

Kent Lovely, however, was in no position to swagger anywhere. Kent Lovely was face-down in his *haupia* cheesecake

CHAPTER SIX

The paramedics showed up within minutes. After they'd rolled Kent out on a gurney, the program resumed as if nothing had happened. We finished up right on schedule. Pat Flanagan said his nice-to-meet yous and was gone. I gathered up the Buzzword Bingo supplies. Emma, Iker, and I joined the somber exodus from the Lehua Inn's main ballroom.

"I can't believe they just kept the retreat going," I said. "I mean I know they already paid for the room and the speaker fees, but still."

"Right?" Emma agreed. "That had to be the most uncomfortable icebreaker activity ever."

The crowd shuffled out to the main exit. I'm sure everyone was as eager to get out of there as I was, but it would have been unseemly to sprint. As we inched past one of the ballroom's broad pillars, I heard a woman's voice:

"...our biggest problems are Larry Schneider, Dan Watanabe, and Molly Barda."

I stopped and listened as the crowd jostled around me. Who was talking about me? And whose problem was I? I looked around, but I only saw my glum colleagues, shuffling out into the hazy afternoon.

A different woman spoke next, her voice as polished as a radio announcer's: "I think we're going to need to show a stronger outcome than one additional graduate, if you want to justify scaling up."

Emma was way up ahead by this time. When she realized I was no longer walking beside her, she stopped and pushed her way back. I held my finger to my lips and pointed at the pillar.

"Marshall Dixon," I whispered. Emma's eyes widened, and we both listened.

"You're *so* right, Marshall. That's why we were thinking, now that we've done proof of concept in a small major, the College of Commerce should be next."

Emma punched my arm hard at the mention of my college. Iker had continued walking ahead. Just as well. He wouldn't be interested in eavesdropping anyway, and he'd probably disapprove of our doing so.

Then the voice—not Marshall, the other one—said, "Schneider's a dinosaur. Very inflexible. Hopefully he's retiring soon. Watanabe is department chair, so we can't really do anything with him. But I think we can work with Molly. She doesn't have tenure yet, so she'll be receptive."

Emma made a rude hand gesture. I shushed her and strained to listen. I wondered if Emma and I looked conspicuous, standing in a nearly-empty ballroom with our ears pressed against the pillar. Probably.

Marshall said something I couldn't quite hear.

"Marshall," wheedled the other woman, "the Foundation doesn't want to see *any* failures. Remember, it's not the students who are failing here. It's the teachers."

"*Teachers,*" Emma mouthed, and at that moment we knew who the second speaker was. It was Linda from the Student Retention Office. Sure enough, Linda's chair at the reception table sat empty. The young man in the oversized aloha shirt was manning the table alone, gamely thanking each of the dazed attendees as they drifted out.

"I'm not saying Molly's completely irrefixable," Linda said. "She just doesn't understand our culture. She actually admitted she *won't let a student pass her class if they don't write.*"

"Don't you teach business writing?" Emma whispered to me.

"Doesn't Barda teach business writing?" we heard Marshall

Dixon ask Linda.

"Oh Marshall," Linda chuckled, "could you imagine what would happen if everyone was such a stickler?"

"If everyone *were*," I whispered to Emma.

"Shh." Emma punched my shoulder. I rubbed it and glared at her.

"*You* shh."

"...due one week from today," Linda was saying. "We need to demonstrate positive action to increase student success."

Marshall's reply was too quiet for us to hear.

After a long silence, Linda said, "We've both seen next year's budget cuts."

"And the ledge turned down our request to increase tuition. I hope it works out with Skip Kojima."

"Well, until it happens, Marshall, remember the Foundation's keeping the lights on."

"What about learning outcomes?" Marshall asked. "How did the seniors do on the subject test?"

"Oh, we discontinued the subject test," Linda said. "But our other results are excellent. Student self-efficacy is up two percent, and self-esteem is up three percent."

"Someone should tell the Foundation about this," Emma whispered. "Molly, *you* should do it. They should know how these idiots are wasting their money."

"*Me*? Why me? *You're* the big do-gooder who likes to send in anonymous tips to people. Why don't *you*—"

"Shh." Emma's shush reverberated in the quiet ballroom.

Suddenly Marshall and Linda were standing in front of me. I sprang away from the pillar as if it were made of bees.

"Hi Marshall," I said brightly. "Linda, hi." I looked around, wondering why Emma wasn't saying anything. I caught a glimpse of her disappearing into the Lehua Lounge.

"Molly." Linda gushed so sweetly you'd never guess she had just tried to get me fired. "Did you get enough to eat?"

"Yes, the buffet was wonderful. The Student Retention Office did a *lovely* job putting this together for us. Thank you."

I looked from Linda to Marshall and back again, an idiotic smile pasted on my face.

"Well," I said. "This was a wonderful retreat. Except for what happened to poor Kent, of course. I hope he recovers. I can't wait to put all these useful ideas into practice. In fact, I should probably get back to my office right now—"

"Molly," Marshall said. "I need to talk to you and Iker. Excuse us please, Linda."

CHAPTER SEVEN

Iker hadn't gone far. He was by the door of the Lehua Lounge, talking to Kent Lovely's buddy, Rodge Cowper. Rodge looked like a mess. His thick gray hair was disheveled, and the buttons of his rumpled aloha shirt strained over his belly. Marshall caught Iker's eye and beckoned him over. Iker nodded and patted Rodge's shoulder. Rodge cast a longing look at the dark doorway of the bar and then plodded away toward the parking lot.

Iker greeted Marshall with a little bow, managing to convey respect without being obsequious. I have figure out how to do that without making people think I'm mocking them.

"I read your report." Marshall Dixon didn't believe in small talk. "Very thorough. You must have worked quickly. Thank you for your hard work."

"Oh, Dr. Dixon, that was not the final report." Iker's plump fingers fluttered with dismay. "It was the draft only. Our work is not complete. I have requested copies of the purchase orders, but those have not yet—"

"I appreciate your diligence," Dixon interrupted him, "but it's not necessary to pull the purchase orders."

I watched the last few stragglers file glumly out toward the parking lot. I wished I could escape too. After seeing that affectionate interlude between Marshall and Kent, I did not want to discuss the irregularities we'd found in the Music Department. Now that Emma's brother Jonah was gone, Kent Lovely *was* the Music Department.

"It was Molly who suggested we should look at the Music Department—" I heard Iker say.

Marshall whipped around to address me directly.

"I just gave you that file. What in there points to the Music Department? Did you have advance knowledge of *Island Confidential*'s allegations against Kent Lovely?"

I shook my head no. Marshall Dixon glared at me as if I had done something wrong.

This was completely unfair. Iker and I had been doing Dixon a favor, volunteering to investigate the complaint to her office. The only reason I'd agreed to this thankless project was number one, I wanted to help Iker out, and number two, working for free over the summer is the kind of thing you agree to do when you don't have tenure yet, to show the administration you're a "team player."

"Perhaps you can explain why you focused on the Music Department."

"Kent Lovely was showing off a brand-new sound system," I said. "According to our charge, we were supposed to flag unusual purchases. I have some familiarity with these types of setups. I told Iker we should probably follow up on it. That's all."

"Showing off?" Now Dixon was looking at me as if I were something she'd found stuck to the bottom of her handmade Italian leather pump. "Kent Lovely was showing off for *you*?"

"Not for *me*, personally, no. Definitely not for me."

"Showing off in what way, then?"

Geez, she really wasn't going to let this go, was she? I felt a trickle of perspiration run down my left side. I probably had sweat stains the size of dinner plates by now. Good thing I was wearing a busy print.

"Rodge's office is right next door to mine," I explained. "Kent is in there all the time. The walls are pretty thin, so I hear *all* their conversation. And those two love to talk. You wouldn't believe some of the private—um, anyway, one day there was music coming from Rodge's office. It was *really* loud. I mean, so loud my books were inching off the shelves with every beat. I'm sure everyone in the building could hear it. I went next door to ask Rodge to turn it down."

"And did they?" Marshall demanded. "Turn down the volume?"

"Uh, eventually, yes."

"And on the basis of that single incident, you directed Iker to investigate Kent Lovely."

"Well—"

"Isn't it likely that Kent's playing music was related to his professional responsibilities as a music instructor, and interim chair of the Music Department?"

"Oh, certainly," I agreed.

I did not tell Marshall the minute I was in Rodge's office, Kent seized the opportunity to brag about his new high-end sound system, making sure to work in a few tiresome double-entendres around the "power" of his components.

"Molly was very dutiful," Iker said. "She was right to alert me. And her suspicion was correct. The procurement of that system appeared to have been—"

"Iker," Marshall interrupted, "The current draft of your report will be sufficient. You can cancel any outstanding requests to pull additional documents. We can save the taxpayers a few dollars in copy fees."

"The inconsistencies were not only in the Music Department," Iker protested. "You will see in the draft that there was insufficiently documented activity in Biology—"

"I'm sorry Iker, we don't have time right now."

Marshall checked her watch. The ostentatious diamond-and-steel model seemed at odds with her elegant style. Not that she needed *my* fashion advice.

"You've done enough for now. Please remember this matter is *confidential.* You must understand we have a very sensitive situation right now, with these public allegations and Kent Lovely's medical situation. I need to know this information won't be leaked anywhere. That it will be kept safe."

Marshall Dixon was still glaring at me, her stern expression damning me in advance as a blabbermouth.

"Oh yes," Iker assured her. "As safe as a house on fire."

"Fine." Marshall Dixon turned away and then glanced back. "We can touch bases later. You'll have to excuse me. I'm meeting Skip Kojima at the airport."

"*The* Skip Kojima?" I asked. "Kojima Surfwear? He's coming here? We talk about him in my class. His company is a great example of—"

"Yes," Marshall spun back and cut me off. "That Skip Kojima. We may have an opportunity to name the College of Arts and Sciences."

"Oh," I exclaimed. "Well, good luck, then. Really."

Marshall nodded curtly, shook Iker's hand, then mine, then she was gone. I flexed my fingers and winced as I watched her leave.

"Touch *base*," I said quietly. "Not touch *bases*."

"Pardon?" Iker asked.

"The expression is touch *base*. It's from baseball. Touch bas*es* means, I don't know what it means. I hope we didn't just torpedo our entire music program."

"Yes." Iker looked mournful. "The music is important. It would be a tragic thing for our students to lose the music."

Our legislature had long ago decided the taxpayers of Hawaii should not fund "useless" degrees in disciplines like art or music. Our university responded by cutting music funding to the bone and beefing up the engineering program. The push to graduate more engineers hasn't actually resulted in more engineers, but the College of Commerce, widely seen as the soft landing of choice for the casualties of calculus, has been enjoying record enrollments ever since. Naturally the College of Commerce is a big supporter of the engineering program.

"Iker, did you say there were irregularities in biology? Emma's department?"

"Yes, that is what my investigation showed."

"Is there a question about Emma? Is she in trouble?"

"I do not know." Iker spoke carefully. "Further investigation is required."

"So that's it? We're done with this thing?"

"That is Doctor Dixon's wish, yes."

"Well, good. It's not like I don't have classes to teach and textbooks to review and crazy students to worry about. Oh, that reminds me, I need to get back to campus. I have an appointment with our dean."

Iker didn't seem to share my relief. At all. In fact, he looked downright unhappy.

"Are you okay, Iker?"

"I do not like to do a slap-shod job," Iker said. "I do not believe this thing is finished."

CHAPTER EIGHT

"Why does Marshall Dixon wish to 'name' the College of Arts and Sciences?" Iker asked. "It already has a name. It is the College of Arts and Sciences."

"It means Mister Kojima would give Mahina State a big donation, and in exchange it would become the *Kojima* College of Arts and Sciences."

"Ah, yes. Now I understand. As I say, my English is not so good. I hope that she enjoys success in this endeavor."

"I agree. It would be nice to have someone besides the Student Retention Office calling the shots around here. Now where could Emma be? Just kidding. I know where she is."

The Lehua Lounge smelled like decades of cigarette smoke, with a whiff of chlorine bleach. When my eyes had adjusted to the dim light, I spotted Emma seated at the bar. Except for the dark koa paneling, the décor was undistinguished. The duct-tape-patched red vinyl booths had been there for a generation or more. The dark industrial carpet was a recent replacement.

Emma tried, and failed, to get up to greet us.

"Emma." I rushed to catch her before she toppled over. "You okay?"

"I'm fine," she slurred.

"All right." I maneuvered her back onto the rattan bar stool. It squeaked under her weight.

"Did I really say I hope he chokes?"

"On a waffle."

"What?"

"You said 'I hope he chokes on a waffle.' But you were provoked. Kent took the last of the *haupia* cake. Emma, it's not your fault. Is it, Iker? Tell her that what happened to Kent is not her fault."

"Emma." Iker was stern. "You must not try to escape your conscience by drinking yourself into Bolivia. That only makes another problem."

"Problem? I do not have a problem. *You* have a problem."

"It's time to go," I said. "I have to get back to campus."

Iker and I struggled to ease Emma into a standing position.

"I'll drive," I added.

"Aw, man. Molly, I can't believe I'm saying this, but I hope Kent's okay."

"Emma, you are not responsible for what happened to Kent. If you really had *that* kind of power? The entire Student Retention Office would be a mass grave."

Iker winced.

"Sometimes bad things just happen," I added quickly. "And we don't know exactly what happened to Kent. Oh, Iker, wait. Let's get Emma some water first."

I started to look around for the bartender. But to my horror, Emma grabbed a half-empty water glass sitting on the bar, and gulped down the contents.

We parted ways with Iker at the hotel entrance. He went left, to the covered parking area. Emma and I hurried out to the open lot as raindrops splattered on the asphalt around us, evaporating in little puffs of steam. Even in her impaired state, Emma outpaced me easily. Emma is an avid canoe paddler, and very fit. Becoming very fit is on my to-do list, but it's near the bottom.

I maneuvered Emma into the passenger seat and then drove us back to campus. I found a shady parking spot in the science building lot, reclined Emma's seat as far as it would go, locked up, and left her to sleep it off.

I got down to the College of Commerce building in time for my appointment with Bill Vogel. I checked in with Serena, and then stood at the front counter of our main office and waited. I could see Vogel through the glass partition, feet up on his koa wood desk, leafing through a magazine. When fifteen minutes had passed, Vogel put his feet down and picked up the phone. Serena answered her phone, and then ushered me back to Vogel's office.

I seated myself in the plush chair facing his vast desk. Had the shark's tooth club incident happened only this morning? This had been an eventful day.

"Well, Molly." Vogel glanced at his watch, "What's all this about?"

"There was an incident this morning in class," I said. "A student pulled out a weapon when I asked him for his homework. It was very unexpected. Well, of course it was unexpected. I mean who expects—anyway, sorry, let me start over."

I related the morning's events, willing myself not to stare at Vogel's obvious hairpiece. He'd selected a dark purplish-brown shade I associate more with German punk rock divas than with business school deans. I wondered where in Mahina one would procure a toupee. I'd never seen a wig store in Mahina. Do people buy hairpieces online?

I realized Bill Vogel was talking to me, and I was, despite my efforts, staring at the top of his head.

"I'm sorry, I didn't catch that."

"I said, whatever issue is between you and this student, you should try to work it out among yourselves."

"No, please. Listen."

I scrambled to recall the wording from our most recent campus safety workshop.

"I believe that this student *poses an immediate danger to me and to the other students*," I blurted desperately. "I'm asking you to remove him from my class and refer him to counseling."

"Oh. Poses an immediate danger." Bill Vogel sounded peevish now. "Looks like you said the *magic words*."

"I'm simply describing the situation to the best of my ability." I found my eyes wandering back up to his hairline, so I stared down at my folded hands instead.

"I don't have the authority to remove a student from the classroom," he said.

"You don't? You're the *dean*. Sorry, I mean—"

"You can try, but you have to get it approved by the Student Retention Office."

"I have to ask the Student *Retention* Office to remove a student from class?"

"Talk to Linda Wilson." Vogel picked up his magazine by way of dismissing me. "You know Linda, don't you?"

CHAPTER NINE

So my dean had just fobbed me off on the Student Retention Office. Not that I'd expected him to be helpful. Bill Vogel hates to turn away paying customers. As I left his office I glimpsed Vogel through the glass divider, picking up his phone. Probably calling the Student Retention Office to warn them I was on my way. No, that was silly. The dean certainly had more important things to do than spend his time trying to thwart me.

Serena looked up from her work. "All done already? That was quick."

I nodded. "I'm going up to the Student Retention Office. In case anyone's looking for me. Thank you for setting up the appointment for me."

"Okay. Well, good luck, Molly."

I trudged uphill to the gleaming new glass-and-metal building that houses the Student Retention Office. The glass doors parted with a *whoosh* and a blast of refrigerated air. On the far side of the vast lobby, behind a curved stainless steel counter, sat a receptionist in a fluffy white sweater. I approached her cautiously. With her slight frame and owlish glasses, she looked like a nervous bird, which might start pecking at me if cornered.

She ushered me into a small meeting room (the kind of "closing" room you'd see at a car dealership or an art gallery) and left me to wait. I got comfortable at the little round table and took in my surroundings. The polished wood floor reflected recessed lights. A saltwater aquarium was embedded in the wall, affording a glimpse of the room on the opposite side. Fluffy strands of seaweed swayed in the clear water. Colorful fish darted in and out of sight: watery azure, vibrant magenta and yellow, velvety black tipped with orange. I watched them for a while, and then turned my attention to the inspirational posters on the walls: *Shoot for the moon. Even if you fail, you'll land among the stars.*

That doesn't make any sense, I thought. Stars are much farther away than the moon. But maybe "if you fail, someone will die in a horrible fiery crash" wasn't inspiring enough.

Mirror, mirror, on the wall, there is a leader in us all.

I wondered if anyone in the Student Retention Office had considered what it would be like if everyone really tried to be a leader. It would probably be like the summer internship I did in college at a marketing company. The employees, all MBAs, each thought that he or she should be running the place. Everyone "planned." No one, except for the lowly summer intern (me), actually *did* anything. "That's *implementing*," the MBAs would sneer. "I don't *implement*."

The last I heard, the company had been bought by a competitor, who took over their accounts and fired all the MBAs.

There are no wrong answers. There are only different ways of knowing.

That one would make Emma's head explode. I'd have to make sure to tell her about it.

Linda finally appeared, accompanied by a fellow blonde who introduced herself as Kathy. Like Linda, Kathy wore a muumuu. While Linda's was a high-necked, fussy floral that looked like a Victorian nightgown, Kathy's was knee-length, with a simple yellow on red hibiscus pattern and a square neckline.

"You put on such a lovely event today," I said, hoping to ingratiate myself. "I got so much out of it. I'm really glad I went."

It was true. I'd had a nice plate of the Lehua Inn's famous desserts, and I'd met someone new. I wondered if I'd have a chance to see Pat Flanagan again.

"I mean, what happened to Kent wasn't lovely, of course. Oh, I didn't mean that to be a play on his name. I know his last name is Lovely. Kent Lovely. Sorry. That was terrible. I hope he's okay. Do you know if he's okay?"

"They airlifted him over to Oahu," Linda said. "He's getting the best available care. We just have to wait."

This is one of the drawbacks of living on a sparsely-populated island. A serious medical situation means taking an air ambulance over to one of the big hospitals in Honolulu. A medical emergency plus bad weather? You just have to hope it never happens to you.

Linda actually sounded worried about Kent. Her show of compassion was encouraging. Maybe she was part-human after all. "Anyway, why am I here. I talked to my dean, and he said I should speak with you. This morning, a student—"

"Yes, we know," Linda interrupted me. "Bill called to tell us you were coming."

"Oh. He did? Well, that was thoughtful."

"Molly," Kathy said. "Our mission at Mahina State is to serve *every student.*"

"Even the ones you disagree with," Linda added.

"I don't think I'd characterize it as a disagreement, although sure, I don't *agree* I should sawed into little bits by an insane student."

"We shouldn't judge the students by *our* standards," Kathy said. "We have to meet them where *they* are."

"You teachers can't just come here and impose your mainland values," Linda added. "You have to respect our local culture."

I stared disbelievingly at the two muumuu-clad Midwesterners.

"*Our* local culture? You know Bret's from Marin County, right?"

"We can't approve your request to remove Bret from class," Linda said.

"Bret has been identified by our office as at-risk," Kathy explained.

"We don't say at-risk, Kathy," Linda said. "We say *at-opportunity.*"

"Maybe I should just report this to the police," I said.

"Now, Molly." Linda's tone was one you'd use to calm a tantruming toddler. "We have something to help you improve

41

your classroom presence. Kathy?"

"This complimentary copy of *Be a Rock Star in the Classroom!* was made possible by our Foundation grant," Kathy chirped, handing me a copy of the glossy SRO publication.

"*Be a Rock Star in the Classroom!*," I read from the cover. "*Ten Tips for Generating Excitement and Peak Customer Satisfaction.* Thanks. I'm sure this will be very helpful. But I'd also like to file a Student of Concern form. I know that I have the right to do that."

Linda and Kathy exchanged a look.

"Well," Linda sniffed. "It looks like *someone* was paying attention at the campus safety workshop."

CHAPTER TEN

The strains of Khachaturian's "Masquerade Waltz" jolted me awake. I groped at my night table until my hand landed on my phone. It was Emma calling.

"Molly, are you still asleep? Get up."

I pulled the phone away from my ear.

"Eh. Molly." the phone squawked. "You awake or what?"

"This better be important. You interrupted a very pleasant dream."

"Ah, keep that stuff to yourself, Molly. I don't need to hear about it."

"No, I was dreaming we were back at the retreat. I was just about to bite into a big slice of *haupia* cake, and then this orchestra started playing and we all had to leave. What's so urgent anyway?"

"Kent Lovely is dead."

I sat up, instantly awake. "No. When?"

"He died in the hospital overnight." Emma's voice was tight with panic.

"That's awful. Poor Kent."

"Oh, forget about Kent."

"What do you mean forget about Kent? Didn't you just tell me he died?"

"I mean, don't waste your time feeling sorry for Kent. It's too late for him."

"Well that's not very—"

"They think my *brother* did it!" I moved the phone even farther away. "They think *Jonah killed Kent Lovely.*"

"Jonah? Why? Jonah wasn't even at the retreat. Why on earth would they think your brother had anything to do with Kent's—"

My eye fell on the copy of *Island Confidential* lying on my night stand. *Whistleblower loses job. Accused keeps his.*

"Never mind. I can guess. So why are you up so early?"

"Nine in the morning is not early."

"It's nine?"

I climbed out of bed and pulled aside the light-blocking curtain. A blaze of sunlight hit me in the face.

"It's already in the paper," Emma said.

"It's in the *County Courier?*"

"Nah, *Island Confidential.* It's on their website."

"I guess they know when they've got a good story. So what does *Island Confidential* say?"

I heard clacking noises as Emma navigated to the relevant part of the article.

"Kent was a popular teacher of computer music...cause of death unknown pending further...blah blah, oh, they got a quote from our chancellor. 'A great loss for our *ohana.* He'll truly be missed.' Like the chancellor could even pick Kent Lovely out of a lineup."

"Well, to be fair, neither of *us* could pick the chancellor out of a lineup. I don't think I've ever seen him in person. Have you?"

"I can't remember now. Maybe I've only ever seen pictures. Some people are saying that the chancellor died years ago, and Marshall Dixon's keeping his frozen body in a storage closet and running the whole university herself."

"I heard that one, too. But it wasn't his whole body. It was just his severed hand for when she needs his fingerprints."

"I can't believe they're hassling my brother. Kent probably killed himself with his dumb energy drinks."

As Emma ranted, I made my way into the kitchen and switched on the coffee machine.

"Sorry Emma, I have to put the phone down. I'm going to make coffee now."

I ground the beans, and started the pot brewing. Then I picked the phone back up.

"...and anyway I don't know why they're making such a big deal about Kent," Emma was saying. "We had part-timers die before, you know."

"We have?"

"Sure. Don't you remember that Spanish professor? I forget her name. The one who *plotzed* right in the middle of class? She was like a hundred years old, but she couldn't retire 'cause she didn't have any savings. There wasn't any big deal in the paper about *her*. The administration just let her students have the rest of the semester off and gave them all As."

"Oh I think I did hear something about that poor woman. Anyway, Emma, they have to make a big deal about regretting Kent's tragic death. After that 'whistleblower loses job' story, Kent had such a high profile they had to say something. Otherwise it would look like the university doesn't care about people who die."

"They don't care. Everyone knows it. Ooh, look at this. They tracked down Kent's ex-wife on the mainland."

"What did she say?"

"It says they couldn't print her comment."

The coffee started to trickle into the carafe. I breathed in the aroma and savored it. Sin is like coffee, Iker Legazpi had said to me once. It always smells better than it tastes, and the second cup is never as good as the first. It was hard to imagine my saintly colleague having that much first-hand knowledge of sin, but he's right about coffee.

"...and they wouldn't even tell me what Kent died from," Emma was saying.

"You talked to the police?"

"Yeah. They came over to the house and asked us all these questions."

"What? They can't do that. Can they?"

"They did."

"Couldn't Jonah say he wouldn't talk to them without a

lawyer?"

"That's exactly what I told them," Emma said, "but then they were like, this is just a friendly chat and would I rather they take both of us to the station, so I was real cooperative after that. I do not want the police poking around in Jonah's business."

"Why not in Jonah's business, particularly?"

"I mean, he's not a criminal or anything, but come on. I mean, him and his friends don't exactly end their day with a glass of warm milk and bed by nine."

"Well, maybe *whoever* called in that story to *Island Confidential* in the first place should have thought of that before they pushed their brother into the spotlight."

"How was I supposed to know Kent was gonna get himself murdered? Can't you come up with something constructive, instead of sitting there being a nudnik?"

"Me? What can I do? *I'm* not a lawyer."

"Fine then, don't help."

"Besides, I just learned at the Student Retention Office that there are no bad ideas, only different ways of learning. Wait, that wasn't it."

"Look, maybe by *your* standards Jonah's just some slacker pothead loser, but he's *my* baby brother. And I know he's innocent."

"Emma, I don't think Jonah's a—I like Jonah. And of course I want to help, but what do you want me to do?"

"You gotta use that big fat brain of yours and find out who really killed Kent Lovely."

I held the phone to my ear and poured my coffee one-handed.

"Emma, *I'm* supposed to find out who killed Kent Lovely? How is *that* supposed to happen?"

"Aw, come on! You're smart..."

I opened my mouth to thank Emma for the compliment.

"...and *really* nosy, and once you start on something you *never* let it go. You're like a tick."

I left the thanks unsaid. "Emma, there are people whose whole job it is to deal with crimes. They're called *police*. And if you're trying to flatter me into doing a favor for you, you're not doing a very good job."

I poured the cream and accidentally tipped in too much, forcing me to restore the balance by topping up with more coffee.

"You have good instincts, is what I mean," Emma said. "An' you don't give up."

"That's better."

CHAPTER ELEVEN

"So you think I have good instincts?" I asked Emma. "Since when?"

"Remember that job candidate? For Associate Vice Dean of Handholding and Nose wiping, whatever that stupid thing was called?"

"Oh, our search committee. How could I forget?"

Emma's voice was making my ear hurt. I set the phone down on the kitchen counter and switched on the speaker.

"Everyone else on the committee thought he was a great guy," squawked my phone in Emma's voice. "No one expected him to fail the background check."

"Except me."

"Exactly. That's what I'm saying."

"I have a finely tuned creep detector, Emma. That doesn't make me a murder expert."

"Just keep your eyes open. Watch an' listen. That's all I'm asking."

I sipped my coffee and stared out the back window at the broad-leafed ti bushes and spiky birds of paradise in my backyard. The grass was looking a little shaggy. I wondered if I could afford to have the lawn guy come by more than once a month.

"Eh, Molly. You there?"

"How about this? When I go in to campus today, I'll stop by the Accounting Department and see Iker. He might come up with something you and I wouldn't have thought of."

"Yeah, okay," Emma said grumpily. "And happy birthday, by the way."

"Thanks for remembering." I pressed the hang-up button and rubbed my temples.

My office looked shabby, even in the dim flicker of the ancient fluorescent tubes. The particle-board desk hadn't stood up well in Mahina's humidity. My bookshelves bowed under the weight of my books. These included several textbooks on basic business writing, a stack of copies of *Be a Rock Star in the Classroom!*, and a bound copy of my doctoral dissertation, *Reproducing and Resisting: Hegemonic Masculinities and Transgressive Alterity in the*— actually, it's kind of a long title. You can look it up if you're really interested.

I cranked my desk fan up to top speed, plumped down in my chair, and got to work. I had to select a new textbook for my introductory business communications class. Easy, right? That's what I'd thought at first. But once the publisher's reps figured out I had some decision-making power, the complementary desk copies started flooding in. My desk was now heaped with textbooks. They ranged from weighty tomes, certain to strain both backs and bank accounts, to a slim picture book, apparently a top-seller at universities with Division I football.

I pulled up my evaluation spreadsheet. As I reached for the top book on the stack, my chair made a loud crack. I bounced on the seat a few times, but I couldn't replicate the noise, so I ignored it.

After an hour and a half of reading through *Business Communication: A Contemporary Approach* and *Communicating In The Workplace* and *BUSINESS COMMUNICATION TODAY!*, I was ready for a break. I had read somewhere that sitting for too long was deadly, and if you wanted a chance at a healthy old age you had to get out of your chair now and then. I stood up and twisted my upper body back and forth to loosen up my spine, and went down the hall for a bathroom break.

I returned to my office to find my office phone ringing. *Stephen better not be calling to cancel dinner*, I thought, but it wasn't Stephen on the phone. It was my parents calling to wish me a happy birthday.

The first thing they asked—the first thing they always asked—was whether I was okay.

My parents have mixed feelings about my living in Hawaii. They remain convinced that at any moment I might be swept away by a tsunami, blown out to sea in a tropical storm, or engulfed in a river of boiling lava from an active volcano. I don't know if it has anything to do with my being an only child, but my parents can be a little overprotective.

"Everything's fine," I assured them. "Stephen's taking me out tonight for my birthday. He's—yes, of course he's going to show up this time. No, I really can't. I'm still working. No, it's true, I'm not getting paid over the summer. Why don't you two fly out here? Doesn't everyone want to visit Hawaii? Mom, it's not true. I mean, I know it's not Waikiki—Okay, we might be a *little* off the beaten path, but—oh, they do *not* look like jungle huts."

From my office window, I could see the squat, metal-roofed classroom buildings and, farther up the hill, our weather-beaten dormitories. They actually did look a little like jungle huts, not that I would admit it to my mother.

"Well, we just wanted to say how much we missed you," my mother said. "We do worry so."

"Take care, Sweet Pea," my father added.

"Okay. You too. Thanks for the birthday wishes."

I rolled my neck to get the kinks out and then looked over the pile of textbooks for anything I could eliminate straightaway. One bulky specimen, *Critical Perspectives on Business Communication,* was a clear candidate for the reject pile. At a dense seven hundred-plus pages of nine point type, it was certainly overkill for a lower-division class. I pulled it out of the stack and heaved it onto the chair behind me.

A loud crack made me turn around slowly. My chair wasn't there. In its place was a pile of chair parts on the floor. *Critical Perspectives on Business Communication* was still resting on the seat, which was now on the floor. I grabbed one chair arm and pulled up. The arm came off in my hand.

Great. My office chair had just collapsed, and with the budget situation the way it was, it would probably take days to requisition another one. I'd go talk to Serena. Serena was one of the few people who knew how things really worked around here. She'd be able to help me.

CHAPTER TWELVE

I stood at the entrance of the main office and fidgeted as I waited to talk to Serena. There was no point in going back to my office, with no place to sit. A garrulous young man in a baseball cap had gotten to Serena before me. I didn't understand every word of the conversation, but I gathered the young man hoped to enroll in Rodge Cowper's Intro to Business Management class in the fall. Serena was trying to explain that when a class was "full" that meant it was full. Not that there was one more spot just waiting for a squeaky wheel to roll in and claim it. She said it more nicely, of course.

People who thought the rules didn't apply to them were the worst. Like when Stephen claimed to be exempt from the campus-wide smoking ban because he smoked *clove* cigarettes. This probably wasn't the best time to ruminate on Stephen's failings. We'd be having dinner in a few hours, and there was no point in my showing up grumpy.

My phone was charging in my office, so I had nothing to read as I waited. One copy of the summer course catalog lay on the counter, with OFFICE written diagonally across the cover in black permanent marker. In the event that was an insufficient deterrent to theft, the catalog was tethered to a pen holder with a dirty piece of string.

Just as the conversation sounded like it was wrapping up, the young man launched into a long story about a pig hunt.

I found myself studying the kid's sleeve tattoos, a writing

lattice of alarmingly realistic giant centipedes. I hate centipedes. Have you ever pulled a load of clothes out of the dryer, and felt something drop onto your instep? And you look down to see a six inch centipede draped across your bare foot, its spiny legs twitching their last? Well I have, and I don't recommend it.

At long last, the young man turned to leave.

"Eh, I get 'em now," he said to Serena. "T'anks, Aunty."

"No worries, Davison. Say hi to your dad for me."

I watched him leave and then approached Serena's desk.

"Aunty? He's your nephew?"

Serena laughed. "Nah, he's not my nephew. Plenty students call me Aunty."

"They do? Why?"

"It's a term of affection and respect," she said.

"Huh. No one calls *me* Aunty."

Serena smiled encouragingly.

"One day, Molly."

"If I live that long. This has not been my best week. And it's only Tuesday."

"You stayed around here for the summer is why," Serena said. "Most faculty just take off for the whole time, where no one can find 'em. Eh, terrible, first the thing in your class, and then what happened at the retreat. Maybe you should take few days off and rest, ah?"

"Well *thank* you for saying that, Serena. You're the first person who's expressed any sympathy."

"Nah. Really?"

"Really. According to the Student Retention Office, everything is all my fault, for not being enough of a rock star in the classroom or something. I wonder what they'd do if we all decided to act like *real* rock stars in the classroom. Show up drunk, yell obscenities, and smash all the A/V equipment."

"They gotta take the students' side, no matter what," Serena said. "It's their job. Like the public defender's office."

"I know. And things could be a lot worse. At least I'm having a better week than Kent Lovely."

"Hmm." Serena shook her head. "Shame."

I could see Bill Vogel in his office, behind his soundproof glass partition, talking on the phone. No one else was around. I lowered my voice to a whisper, just to be on the safe side.

"Serena, when you say shame, do you mean shame that Kent died? Or shame on him?"

Serena didn't return my eye contact. Her mouth was a straight line.

"You play with fire," she said, "you gonna get burned."

"So who do you think burned him?"

"You okay, Molly? What's that thing you holding?"

We were on to the next subject. No further discussion of Kent Lovely.

"What's what thing?"

"The black thing you get in your hand."

I realized that I was still holding the arm of my collapsed chair.

"Oh. This. That's right. I need to requisition a new office chair. Mine just fell apart. How do I do that? Do I fill out a form, or do I just tell you, or..."

"Ohhh, I'm so sorry, Molly." Serena scrunched her nose, as if imparting something distasteful. "Cannot."

"That's okay. Where do I need to go? Which office? Just point me in the right direction."

Serena sighed. "No, what I'm saying is, no more money for office furniture."

"What?"

"Not after the latest cuts, you know. You gotta buy 'em yourself. Outta pocket."

"But—"

Bill Vogel was off the phone now. He was leaning back in his chair, his tasseled loafers resting on the koa wood desk. He was picking his teeth with a business card.

"Deans get a separate budget from us mere mortals," Serena said, following my gaze. "I heard Marshall Dixon got a big donor on the hook, but till he comes through, things are gonna be tight. You know what some people do, they get one of those yoga balls to sit on. You know the kine?"

"You mean those things that look like giant beach balls? Really?"

"Oh, yah. Supposed to be really good for your back, and exercises your abs. I had a girlfriend lose two inches off her waist when she started using it. It's like it makes you exercise all day, and you don't even notice. Next thing you know, you all wiwi. Oh, that means skinny, Molly."

I ran a thoughtful hand over my tummy. "Interesting. Do you know where I could buy a yoga ball in town?"

"Check Galimba's Bargain Boyz. You know Bargain Boyz? Not all fancy like your mainland stores, but good prices. You can go right now, won't be as crowded."

"Yeah, I might as well." I turned to leave. "No point hanging around my office without a chair to sit on."

"Oh Molly, wait. You still need to tell me your community organization."

I returned to the counter.

"My community organization?" I asked.

"Remember, everyone's gotta join a community organization? I'm putting together the list. Only need one. Which one did you decide?"

"It's not optional?"

"No, not optional. Dean Vogel promised the Chancellor we would get one hundred percent faculty involvement with our Friends in the Business Community."

"So what do I need to do?"

"Just pick one and join. Rotary, Business Boosters, Japanese Chamber, Podagee Chamber, whatevers. Molly, you Podagee, ah? Barda?"

"No. Barda's not Portuguese. It's an Albanian name. Which one of those groups has the least amount of unstructured social interaction? Making small talk with strangers stresses me out."

"Probably Business Boosters," Serena said. "You show up, sing the Business Boosters Song, listen to one guest speaker while you eat lunch, and leave. And you don't have to have a member nominate you. Just tell 'em you're from the College of

Commerce. Easy."

"Okay," I said. "I'll do it. Put me down for Business Boosters. Thanks."

I pushed back from the counter and headed for the door.

"Eh, Molly. You cannot just tell me the name. You still gotta show up an' join."

"Okay," I called back over my shoulder.

"Oh, and Molly, one more thing."

I turned back reluctantly.

"They're restarting the search for the Associate Dean of Learning Process Improvement. So you're not done with the committee yet. You know the candidate didn't pass the background check."

I approached the counter again.

"Just between you and me," I confided. "I didn't vote for him. But as usual, mine was the minority opinion. So we'll have to start up the committee again in the fall?"

"Cannot wait till then. You guys are gonna have to start meeting right away."

"What? Come on. How can they make us meet during the summer? We're not even getting paid for—"

"I got the information here."

Serena handed me a printout of the scheduled meetings. I noticed one new name on the distribution list: Patrick Flanagan. He had been good company at the faculty retreat, and he appreciated my homemade Buzzword Bingo cards. Maybe meeting over the summer wouldn't be so terrible after all.

"Thanks Serena." I hurried out of the office before she could add anything else to my to-do list.

CHAPTER THIRTEEN

Emma and I sat in her hybrid, becalmed on Holua Street. Several cars ahead of us, a white hatchback was stopped, signaling its intention to turn left into the gas station. There was no break in oncoming traffic. With only one lane in each direction, there was nothing for us to do but wait.

"Are there no left-turn lanes on this side of the island?" I asked Emma. "I don't think I've ever seen one."

This probably wasn't the best time to chat about Mahina's transportation planning. Emma gripped the steering wheel and called down curses upon the driver of the white hatchback, the owner of the gas station, the city council, and finally Galimba's Bargain Boyz, which had the nerve to be located on the other side of our taxing commute.

"That was some magnificent swearing," I said, once we were moving again. "I think I heard Hawaiian, Japanese, and Yiddish."

"Little Podagee too," Emma said modestly.

"Impressive. So what are you getting at Galimba's?"

"They got this coffee machine I want," Emma said. "I tried ordering it online, but I couldn't find anywhere that ships to Hawaii. Oh yeah, speaking of which... When we go inside, don't act like you're shopping."

"What do you mean? What else would we be doing in a store, if not shopping?"

"Nah, nah, nah. What I mean is, not like you're shopping for yourself. Act like you're getting supplies for *work*. Don't look like you're having fun or nothing."

"I *am* getting supplies for work. I have to buy a chair for my office. And I don't anticipate it being much fun at all. Why?"

"'Cause. The old-timers hate it when they see professors walking around not working during the week."

"But we we're not even getting *paid* for the summer," I said. "Why should we be working if we're not getting paid?"

"Yeah, they don't care. One time I went out for paddling practice in the afternoon, no more classes, already had my grading done, saw Mister Shiroma, old friend of my dad, yah? So he acts all friendly when he sees me. Two days later, guess what's in the paper? Angry letter to the editor about how he saw one university professor out paddling in the middle of the day instead of teaching class, and how come we're wasting their tax dollars? Of course Mister Shiroma doesn't see all those times I'm up till midnight grading exams."

"I get it. Look busy and unhappy. Reminds me of a summer internship I had."

"If I really did have a bunch of free time? *I'd* write some letters to the editor about how old busybodies like Mister Shiroma are wasting *my* taxpayer dollars."

Emma pulled into a parking spot in front of a corrugated metal building. A single white vinyl banner with black block lettering was the only indication this was a store and not a warehouse.

"Is this new?" I asked. "They still have a temporary sign."

"Nah, that banner's been up for years. Permitting process for a permanent sign is too humbug, that's why."

"It doesn't look very inviting."

"They got good deals though, Molly. When I was here last week, they had a bunch of those kine boneless bras you like. You should see if they still have some."

"The ones with no underwire?" I picked up my bag and climbed out of the passenger seat. "I do like those."

"The ones they had were all too small for me, but you'd probably fit 'em. What'd you need again?"

"An office chair."

"Oh yah. Come."

I followed Emma through the open bay door. The humid interior was a little cooler than the outdoors, which is to say still pretty warm. In a warehouse with thirty-foot ceilings and metal walls, air conditioning would have been an extravagance.

The bare-bones ambience hadn't deterred Mahina's frugal shoppers. The aisles were jammed with bargain hunters wielding Galimba's oversized carts. Emma and I pushed through the crowd to the back of the store, where Galimba's had a small display of office furniture.

"Aw, ugly," Emma exclaimed.

"It does look kind of cheap. Look, you can see the seams from where the plastic was molded. Maybe I could sand it off."

"Try sit," Emma said.

The fabric was so rough the fibers pricked my skin through my clothes. Some kind of hard object embedded in the back cushion, possibly intended as "lumbar support," poked my spine.

"That doesn't look comfortable," Emma said as I stood and rubbed my lower back. "Probably not worth the price, ah?"

I checked the price tag.

"It's not even that cheap," I said. "Serena told me I should just buy a yoga ball and use it for my office chair."

"Not a bad idea, Molly. You could use the exercise."

Emma helped me pick out a yoga ball from the clearance shelf in the sporting goods section. Then we wandered over to the lingerie bin and rummaged through the bras. Emma thought it would be helpful to hold the bras up to my chest to see whether they would fit. I swatted her hand away and told her to go look for her coffee maker.

Once I had picked out every bra they had in my size, I steered the giant shopping cart over to Galimba's beverage section and loaded it up with a few bottles of wine and a half gallon of the cheapest vodka they had. As I made my way to the cash register, a floor display caught my attention. It was a stack of large boxes, crowned with a gleaming, stainless steel contraption. This turned out, on closer examination, to be a high tech coffee brewer. It was probably the one Emma was after. And I wanted it.

It would be perfect for my office. No more long walks up to the Dining Center for coffee so insipid you could see straight through to the bottom of the Styrofoam cup. No more getting stuck on campus after hours with my only coffee option being the Sputnik-era vending machine over in the Arts and Sciences building, the one where no matter which button you press, everything comes out tasting like a mixture of chicken soup and hot cocoa.

I lifted a box from the display, and was about to place it into the cart, when I saw the label with the price. With a sigh of disappointment, I set the box back down. With my house payments, my student loans, and what I had to set aside for car maintenance, there was no way I could afford it.

Galimba's only had one cash register open. *This must be a way to keep costs down*, I thought, like the informal signage and the nonexistent climate control. I pushed my cart to the end of the long line, and pulled my phone out to check my email as we inched along. I'd lost track of Emma, but I knew we'd rendezvous at the car. I saw nothing from Stephen confirming tonight's dinner. No news, I assumed, was good news. Maybe he was out buying my birthday present. With any luck, it would be a coffee machine.

CHAPTER FOURTEEN

I was able to be productive even as I waited in the checkout line at Galimba's Bargain Boyz. My phone was able to get enough of a signal inside to allow me to check my email. Even in the summer, my inbox needed frequent weeding. Every day I deleted several of the Student Retention Office's cheery reminders that the only problem with higher education was lazy, arrogant faculty members who refused to use the latest tech baubles in class. Then there were the announcements for conferences I could never hope to attend (sure, I'll jet off to Prague in the middle of the fall semester). In my frenzy of deleting I almost missed a message from one of my students:

Aloha Professor, I won't be able to make it to class tomorrow. My brother was supposed to pick up my cat for me at the Humane Society, but he just told me he has a last minute guitar class to teach. I hope this does not effect my grade too much, since it is low already. Please let me know of anything important I miss. Mahalo, Tiffany Balusteros from business communication.

I've seen a lot of excuses for missing class, but the emergency guitar lesson was a new one. I wondered if Tiffany's brother was picking up business from Jonah Nakamura's former students. I typed a quick reply on my phone:

Dear Ms. Balusteros,

Everything we cover in class is important. Please check the course website for the assignment schedule, and best of luck with your cat.

The next message in my inbox was a glowing report of the

previous day's retreat, sent by the Student Retention Office's Media Relations Department. With a chill, I read that Kent Lovely was the winner of the teaching award. There was no mention of Kent's collapse or subsequent death. The press release had gone into the publicity pipeline before the event; the winner had obviously been chosen well in advance.

"Eh, Professor, you all set?"

It took me a moment to recognize him without his red baseball cap. My pleasant and voluble summer student, Micah, was manning the cash register.

"You ready, Professor?"

I cast a panicked look at the long line of people waiting behind me. I was trapped.

"Micah." I stuffed my phone back into my bag. "Hi. So. You work here. Of course you do."

I placed the small box containing the deflated yoga ball on the little counter. Then came the bottles of wine and the half-gallon of vodka. Finally, I pulled out the bras and scrunched them into the smallest possible pile.

"Sorry, Professor." Micah grinned. "I gotta see your ID. 'Cause the alcohol."

I pulled out my driver's license and showed it to him, my thumb covering the weight and birth year. He reached for it, and a gentle tug of war ensued.

"Gotta scan 'em, Professor. I give it right back."

I let go, and he slid the license through a slit at the side of the cash register. The machine beeped approval, and Micah examined the license before handing it back to me.

"Looks like you planning one *big* birthday celebration, ah Professor?"

He held up the half-gallon bottle and aimed the scanner gun.

"Oh, no, I—"

"If I had one student pull a *leiomano* on me, I probably be ready for a drink or three myself, guarantee. Eh, this vodka any good, professor?"

"I don't *drink* that," I said. "I put a spray nozzle on it and use it to clean things. You can use it to freshen clothes too."

"You spray vodka on your clothes?"

"It's a theater trick. I learned it from Stephen—from Professor Park. They spray down the costumes after every performance. It saves on dry cleaning."

Micah scanned the wine bottles one by one. Then he picked up the first bra. I fixed my gaze on the cash register's price display so I wouldn't have to make eye contact.

"These ones are real popular," Micah said. "All the *wahine* say how comfortable they are. We just got one batch in and they're almost all gone already. Just the small sizes left. An good price, too."

"Uh huh." I remembered "*wahine*" meant "women." I'd have to take a real Hawaiian language class one of these days. I looked around, but still didn't see Emma anywhere. I did notice that Galimba's had opened another register.

Micah frowned at the bra in his hand, then stared frankly at my chest.

"Eh, Professor," he said, "Hope you don't mind my saying. I think you wearing the wrong size bra."

"I'm sorry?"

"You get too small a cup size an' too big a band size." Micah looked concerned. "'Lotta women make that mistake. Know how you can tell? The part in front, between the cups, gotta sit flat against your breastbone. If you can fit your thumb up in there, you're wearing the wrong size."

I crossed my arms defensively.

"That's very interesting, but I—"

"No worries. I get you the right size. You wait here." Micah scooped up the entire pile of bras and left me standing alone at the cash register.

"Those aren't for me," I protested. But it was too late, even if my lie had been convincing, which it wasn't. I didn't dare look back at the growing line of customers behind me.

"My auntie used to be a fitter at Foxy Lady Lingerie downtown," Micah announced upon his return. He plunked down a pile of bras in an even weirder color assortment than the one I had originally picked out. Teal satin, rust with yellow trim, and chocolate zebra stripes had apparently not sold well at retail. "These'll fit you more better. Give you one good silhouette, and more comfortable too. Guarantee."

Micah untwisted a bra, shook it out and held it aloft as he searched for the price tag.

"Eh, Professor, I signed up for your Business Planning for fall semester. Is it gonna be hard?"

Micah found the price tag and scanned it.

"No, that's not my class." I was grateful for the change of subject. "Rodge Cowper teaches BP."

"Aw, I rather take you than Doctor Rodge," he said. "Coulda swore I saw your name in the fall course listing."

"No, Business Planning is definitely Doctor Rodge's class," I said.

"Aw. I heard you don't learn nothing in Dr. Rodge's class."

"Oh Micah, I wouldn't say that." It was true, but I wouldn't *say* it.

CHAPTER FIFTEEN

Micah held up another bra and aimed the scanner gun. *Beep.*

"Yah, Doctor Rodge? Get some high 'need for affiliation' him. Wants everyone to like him."

"You remember your McClelland." I beamed at him. "I'm impressed."

Micah grinned proudly and continued to scan bras. *Beep. Beep.* How many bras were there, anyway? They seemed to be multiplying right there on the conveyor belt.

"An', Professor, I think you get high achievement need, you."

"Well. That might be true." I was pleased Micah had remembered the lesson, and was flattered by his assessment.

"That's how come I like take your class," he said. "You make sure we all learn, yah? No excuses."

I allowed myself a smile.

"You don't care if anyone likes you," Micah scanned the last of the bras.

Beep.

"Eh, was nice to see you, Professor. See you in class tomorrow." He stuck the wine and vodka bottles into my recycled rice-bag shopping tote, and then stuffed the bras in around them.

"Right," I gave Micah a stiff smile, signed for the purchase, and took my bra- and bottle-packed bag. "Terrific. See you tomorrow."

Emma was already waiting in her car, with the motor running and the air conditioner on.

"Doesn't it defeat the purpose of a hybrid to keep the motor idling like this?" I climbed in, buckled up, and checked the dash clock. "Oh great, I'm late for my hair appointment. I didn't realize this was going to take so long."

"That's exactly how come I can idle my car with a clear conscious," Emma said. "'Cause it hardly uses any gas."

"Conscience," I corrected her. "With an N."

"No, it's *conscious*, cause look, I'm *conscious* and not *unconscious*." Emma tapped her temple. "Geez, I thought you were supposed to be an English major. Okay, I'll take you back to campus so you can get your car. Then I'm gonna go home and set up my new coffee machine."

The outsized box took up most of Emma's back seat.

"You did buy one of those machines. I'm so envious. I wish I could afford one. Wouldn't it be nice to have something like that in my office?"

"If you sold that big blue land yacht and bought a practical car, you might have some money left over for—"

"Oh, stop it. You sound just like my mechanic."

"Oh yah? Maybe you should listen to him then."

"Earl's a competent technician," I said, "but he has no imagination. So how is Jonah doing? Any developments?" I didn't tell Emma about the email from my student, claiming that her brother had to give an emergency guitar lesson.

"Jonah's not doing great."

"What's going on?"

Emma pulled out onto the road, cutting off a lifted pickup. I clutched the door handle.

"That was a little close, Emma." The black truck's grimacing grill and massive chrome bumper filled Emma's back window.

"Serves 'em right for speeding. Eh, tailgating's not gonna make me go any faster, babooz." She slammed the brake for emphasis. I saw the truck's grill plunge. Emma accelerated, leaving the stalled-out truck behind. "Yah, so check it out. There's a police cruiser parked on our street now, about two houses down, in front of the Murakamis' house. A marked car, like fo'real. Not the kine where they jus' stick the little light on top."

A station wagon in front of us slowed to a stop, signaling a left turn into the gas station. Emma swerved into the bike lane and steered around the stopped car, and then back onto the main road. I braced my hands on the dashboard. The black truck had restarted and gained on us, but was now stuck behind the station wagon, too wide to fit into the narrow bike lane.

"I'm not in *that* much of a hurry, Emma. It's okay to drive with all four wheels on the ground."

"I feel sorry for those poor schlemiels that got stuck doing surveillance. Where are they gonna go to the bathroom? Unless they do like the taxi drivers in New York, keep a little jar under the seat."

"So they're just parked on your street?" I interrupted, not particularly keen to hear about the taxi drivers and their little jars.

"That's after they came in an' grilled us."

"Oh. About what?"

"Like, do I know how to give someone kidney failure? What's that, a trick question?"

"Seriously? Who would ever admit—"

"Easy that thing. The guy'd never know what got 'em."

"I hope you didn't tell them that."

"Well not like bragging. I jus' told 'em if I wanted jam up someone's kidneys, I'd sneak some antifreeze into his sports drink."

"Emma. You said that to the *police?*"

Emma slowed in front of the outdoor secondhand furniture store that used to be a gas station, and made a right turn toward campus.

"If I'd of played dumb, they'd of been suspicious," Emma said. "Everyone knows about the antifreeze. That's how you get rid of feral cats."

"People poison *cats* with *antifreeze?* I've never heard of that."

"Diethylene glycol tastes a little bit sweet. There was a thing back in the eighties where some winery put a little of it in their wine to give it the right flavor. Sometimes people try use it on rats, too, but that's a mistake. Rats go die under your house, and it gets all stink."

"So they think Jonah learned this from you, and then poisoned Kent? How do they explain the part about Jonah not even being at the scene?"

"DEG takes a few days to kill someone. Jonah and Kent shared an office. Plenty opportunity. Anyways, hasn't even been twenty-four hours, and Jonah's already getting calls from people cancelling guitar lessons."

"I kind of suspected that was happening."

"Eh Molly, why don't you come over tonight?"

"Tonight? Well it's nice of you to ask, but—"

"Jonah's feeling kinda down. Maybe listening to your English-major jibber jabber would cheer him up. Like a babbling brook."

"Emma, I can't tonight. I have plans with Stephen. He's taking me to dinner."

I checked the time on Emma's dashboard clock. I still had a good chance of making it to Tatsuya's Moderne Beauty in time. Tatsuya is a nice man, but he does not tolerate tardiness.

"I know, it's your birthday. That's how come I said come over. It'll be like a celebration."

"Did you hear the part about Stephen taking me to dinner? What? What's with the eye roll?"

"Okay. Well, when he flakes on you again, we'll be there for you."

"Don't be ridiculous, Emma. Stephen's not going to forget my *birthday*."

CHAPTER SIXTEEN

The Holua Street Shopping Center, home to Tatsuya's Moderne Beauty, has seen better days. Those days appear to have been the early sixties. To the left of Tatsuya's entrance was Peggy-Ann Fashions. To the right was a vacant space where Mahina's only comic book store had folded over a year before.

I locked up my car and pushed through Tatsuya's gold-lettered glass door, setting unseen bells a-jingle. Inside the small salon, a row of pink hairdryer chairs lined one wall. The only other customer was an elderly Japanese lady. She sat in one of the hairdryer chairs, chrome bonnet lowered to eyebrow level, engrossed in a magazine. Tatsuya Masumoto hurried up front to greet me. Tatsuya was trim, with sharp cheekbones and smooth black hair.

"Ah, Miss Molly." He was smiling. I was on time. "Let's do something special for the birthday girl."

He seated me in a worn pink salon chair, pulled out a pink cape and fastened it around my shoulders. The cape had gone through so many washings that the red Tatsuya's dragon logo was faded and worn off in spots. The familiar ammonia smell of permanent-wave chemicals and hair dye was oddly soothing. I settled in to be pampered.

"I was just telling Trudy," Tatusya said. "I do look forward to your visits."

"You do? Why thank you."

"You test the limits of my artistry, Miss Molly. I believe you have the most challenging hair in Mahina. So, did you have anything particular in mind?"

"Just work your magic." I watched Tatsuya in the mirror as he deftly sectioned my hair. "This won't take more than two hours, will it?"

"We'll get you out in plenty of time." Tatsuya started to comb a section of my hair, starting at the ends.

Tatsuya is expensive, but he's worth it. One time, a few months ago, I tried to economize by getting my hair cut at the local beauty school. The stylist-in-training, a young woman with magenta hair and tarantula eyelashes, complained nonstop about my "hair from hell." She cut it while it was wet and used thinning shears, two things I now know you're never supposed to do to curly hair. I walked out of the beauty school looking like the back half of a poodle. That day I swore, Scarlett O'Hara-like, that I would never get a bargain haircut again.

The beauty school is gone now, replaced by a check-cashing store.

"So it looks like you and I are going to be fellow Business Boosters," I said. "I saw the sticker on your door."

"Trudy and I are both Business Boosters. We'll be delighted to have you. Ohhh, have you been using that store-brand conditioner? Bad girl."

Tatsuya was examining the ends of my hair disapprovingly.

"You can *tell*? Of course you can. I didn't do any irreversible damage, did I?"

"No, we'll just trim off these dead ends and everything will be as good as new. You will walk out of here looking absolutely *devastating*. Oh, I heard about what happened at your campus. Poor Kent Lovely. Did you know him?"

"I did know Kent. He was good friends with Rodge Cowper, who has the office next to mine. Did *you* know Kent?"

"Why, Kent and his friend Roger are customers." Tatsuya's voice assumed a confidential tone. "I do Kent's weave. *Did* Kent's weave, I should say. I still can't believe it. Kent was a young man in his prime."

"Rodge Cowper comes here? I sure wouldn't have guessed."

"Roger has such beautifully thick hair." Tatsuya unclipped another section of my hair and started combing it out. "All he needs to do is keep it trimmed. He asked about color, but I told him not to dye it, the grey is so distinguished."

The adjectives "beautiful" and "distinguished" didn't jibe at all with my impression of Rodge Cowper. I supposed Tatsuya Masumoto's job required him to find beauty in unexpected places.

"*Kent* colored his hair, though," I said. "Obviously."

Tatsuya lifted his hands in a don't-blame-me gesture.

"He insisted on doing it himself. I think he was trying to save money. I certainly hope no one thought his dye job was *my* work."

"I know it looked artificial," I said, "but I can't put my finger on why. What would you have done differently? I mean, your hair is black too, but it doesn't look jarring, the way Kent's did."

"True blue-black is *very* hard to wear well," Tatsuya touched his neat coif. "Especially as we age. This shade I have is actually a dark brown, not a true black. It *reads* as black, but it isn't the 01-level black-black. This is a three-A. That's an ash tone, no brass. In any case, Kent was far too fair to wear a dark color. His hair was *so* much darker than his brows and lashes, it looked like a hat."

"You lost me at three-A," I said.

"Oh, it takes years to learn it all." Tatsuya frowned and pulled a piece of my hair taut, then let it spring back into its corkscrew shape. Then he unclipped a piece of hair on the other side of my head and pulled both pieces straight at once.

"Speaking of hair color," I said, "is there any kind of chemical in hair dye that could cause kidney damage?"

"Kidney damage?" Tatsuya stepped back. "Is *that* how Kent Lovely died?"

Whoops. I shouldn't have said anything. The police might have been holding the information back. On the other hand, how much of a secret could it be if they told Emma about it?

"I don't really know." I shrugged under my pink cape. "It's just one of the rumors going around. That's all."

"I've *never* heard of hair color causing kidney failure. Never. Skin irritation, perhaps. Unattractive results, certainly. But never anything as serious as kidney failure."

Tatsuya excused himself to check on his other customer, leaving me to stare at my sallow reflection. There's no better antidote to inflated self-esteem than overhead fluorescent lights.

"Trudy came up with an interesting theory," Tatsuya said when he returned. "She asked if I thought Kent was blackmailing someone."

"Blackmail. That's interesting. Did she have anyone specific in mind?"

I wondered what had gone on between Kent and Vice President Marshall Dixon right before he kissed her manicured hand. Had he threatened to go to her husband? I thought about what Serena had said. *Shame.*

CHAPTER SEVENTEEN

"So Trudy thinks Kent was blackmailing someone?" I asked Tatsuya's reflection. "That's interesting. He did seem like one of those guys who's always looking for an angle."

"He did get some nice goodies for himself." Tatsuya twisted a chunk of my hair and pinned it out of the way. "A top-of-the-line massage chair. I was pricing those, thinking maybe I'd get one for my shop. They're quite expensive."

"You know about the massage chair?"

"I read about it in *Island Confidential*," Tatsuya said.

"I'm all for a healthy, adversarial press," I said. "But this 'whistleblower loses job' piece in *Island Confidential* makes the whole university look bad. What if someone like Emma's grouchy neighbor reads it and writes an angry letter to his state senator? They'll use it as an excuse to cut our budget again. And then we'll ask permission to raise tuition to make up for our reduced budget, and everyone will scream about the rising cost of tuition, and *then* we'll probably get cut *again*, just to punish us for asking."

"You know, Molly, I'm frankly surprised that Jonah Nakamura is a suspect at all. Whistleblower or no. *I'd* be looking for a jealous husband."

"You heard that Jonah Nakamura is a suspect?"

"That's what everyone is saying."

This was all Emma's fault. If she hadn't called in that tip to

Island Confidential, that article wouldn't have been published the day of Kent's death, and no one would even be looking at Jonah. Of course Emma would never blame herself for this. Or anything.

"You don't think Jonah is guilty, though?"

"I don't believe Jonah did it." Tatsuya shook his head. "I know the family, you see. Jonah's always been a nice boy."

"I can't see Jonah as a murderer either. He's too easygoing. And blackmail? If someone ever tried to blackmail Jonah, he'd just say, 'Whatever, dude.'"

"Perhaps Kent was about to blow the whistle on someone himself. Trudy thinks Kent must have had a co-conspirator. Kent was a brash man, and large-scale embezzlement takes careful planning."

"Very true. Especially with our university's byzantine procurement system."

"Trudy is very sensitive to the whole whistleblower situation," Tatsuya said.

"Really? Has she ever had to report something?"

"Oh, yes. She had a situation last year with the Mahina Arts Alliance. She's on the board, you know." Tatsuya snipped, pulled a strand of hair straight, frowned, and snipped a bit more. It looked like he wasn't doing much, but I knew I'd be happy with the result. All I'd have to do was shake my head, and the curls would bounce right into place. "Someone in one of the dance groups received a portion of a grant the Arts Alliance had obtained, and it turned out they were misusing the money. I can't tell you the details, but it was *quite* inappropriate. And it was a children's performance troupe, no less. It put Trudy in an *extremely* awkward position."

"So she reported it?"

"Yes, she did. After much agonizing, I must say. But it was so unpleasant. You'd think they would be grateful, but it was just the opposite. They felt she was making them do a lot of extra work and calling their judgment into question. Nobody appreciated it. At all."

"That sounds exactly like what happened to Jonah when he

tried to report Kent Lovely. The administration was required to follow up on Jonah's complaint, and they did, but it was bare minimum. It seems like Marshall—I mean the administration—wanted to wrap up the investigation as quickly as possible, without actually finding anything."

"Well," Tatsuya said, "enough about *that* depressing subject. What are your birthday plans?"

"Stephen's coming over at six. I left the planning up to him, but I think we're going to Sprezzatura. I'm not sure. It's going to be a surprise."

"Well," Tatsuya looked dubious. "Let's hope it's a *good* surprise."

CHAPTER EIGHTEEN

Surprise!

Stephen Park didn't show. Six o'clock came and went, followed by seven, and then eight.

By nine o'clock, I decided I had waited long enough for Stephen. I found my rice-bag tote and filled it with the wine bottles from Galimba's Bargain Boyz. Then I hopped into the Thunderbird and started up the hill to Emma's house.

Emma opened the door and stared at me. Then she stepped back to get a better look.

"Nah. You got a *beehive*? I haven't seen one of those since I was a kid, when Mrs. Saito used to come over and babysit us. People still know how to do beehives?"

"Tatsuya did it. Emma, this bag is heavy."

"Oh yah, come in. What'd you get?"

"The wine I bought today at Galimba's Bargain Boyz. All of it."

I slipped off my platform shoes and followed Emma into her darkened house.

"So Stephen flake out on you again?"

"I assume that's a rhetorical question. Why are all your lights out?"

"Termite night, that's why."

"What night?"

"Termites are swarming. They're attracted to the light. Just give 'em another few minutes. They're gonna be gone soon."

The glow from the digital clocks on the microwave, coffee

maker and stove let me see where I was going, sort of. I set my bag on the kitchen table and pulled out a bottle. Emma disappeared into the darkness.

"Just a minute." I heard Emma's disembodied voice. "Gonna round up some wine glasses and a corkscrew."

"This one's a screw top." I twisted it open with a pop. "So why do you go through all this turning off the lights for termites? Can't you just get an exterminator?"

"Termites don't call ahead when they decide to swarm." Emma's voice floated in the dark. "They just do it on warm nights like this one. There's probably some down at your house too right now."

"I didn't notice anything swarming at my house. But I was a little preoccupied."

"Cannot let 'em start a new colony near your house. They'll start eating it from the inside out, an' you won't even know it until your cabinets start falling off the wall."

Emma returned to the kitchen table with two coffee mugs. I was able to see well enough to pour wine into them. We sat and drank quietly in the dark. I didn't want to talk about it, and Emma wisely refrained from I-told-you-so's.

"Where's Yoshi?" I asked, finally.

"I dunno. Maybe taking a nap. He just got back from Honolulu a couple hours ago."

"Oh, the MBA networking thing? Why didn't you go? Cornell's your alma mater, too."

"I got a PhD," Emma said. "Not an MBA. Different worlds. PhDs think, MBAs drink."

"Some of us can do both."

Emma lifted her mug and tapped it against mine.

"I can't stand how Yoshi gets around those guys. Bad enough when he complains to *me* about living here. But when he's with his MBA buddies, he goes on and on as if he's stuck living in a third-world country. Like it's the worst tragedy in the world that he can't wear his nice wool suits 'cause it's too hot and humid."

"He didn't grow up in Hawaii?"

"Him? Nah. Yoshi is the biggest *katonk* that ever katonked. Oh good. I think the termites are gone now."

Emma got up and switched on the lights.

"The biggest what that ever what? What was that word?"

"*Katonk.* Mainland Japanese. Cause they're so 'square,' when they roll along they make a sound like katonk, katonk."

Emma took the next bottle of wine out of my shopping bag. We'd already emptied the first one.

"Well that's it," I said. "I'm done."

"Really?" Emma applied the corkscrew and yanked the cork out with a loud pop. "What a lightweight. I'm just getting started."

"I mean with Stephen. I'm done with Stephen."

"Yeah, I heard that one before. You're gonna be all strong until Stephen calls with some story about how he was *so* busy and he lost track of time, and you're gonna drop everything to go be with him."

Emma tipped the wine bottle into my mug. It was bright yellow, decorated with some kind of green cartoon microbe. It looked like something she got for free at one of her conferences.

"Then he's going to say oh, he's so sorry and can he please make it up to you, and before you know it, you'll be making excuses for him."

"That's horrible, Emma." I blinked back tears. "You make me sound so *pathetic.*"

"Well, sorry about that." She was as pitiless as a nurse who had just administered a painful, but necessary, injection.

"And the worst part is, you're right."

"Listen, Molly, I know what I'm talking about—Wait, did you just say I'm right?"

"Yes. You're right. Stephen will call, and he'll be all, you don't understand, Molly, there are so many people who want things from me. The creative mind doesn't work on a schedule. Ordinary peoples' rules shouldn't apply to me, because Art. Like *I'm* not creative, and no one ever wants anything from *me*. Urghh. Why do I tolerate it? I am so, what's the word?"

"Your glass is almost empty." Emma filled it right back up.

"Listen, Molly. You didn't do anything wrong. This is Stephen's fault, not yours."

"Naïve. That's the word I was looking for. I'm so *naïve*."

"You do give people the benefit of the doubt."

"You really think so? I mean, I do try to—"

"Yeah, that's your big mistake."

CHAPTER NINETEEN

"Alone on my birthday." I sighed. "For someone who's supposedly smart, I'm feeling pretty dumb right now."

"Alone? Thanks a lot. So what am I, chopped liver?"

"Sorry, that's not what I meant. Boyfriend-less. I'm boyfriend-less on my birthday. That's what I was trying to say."

"Anyway, you are smart. In some ways. Look at what happened with the job candidate. You tried to convince the committee to do the background check before we made the offer."

"But no one on the search committee believed me until it actually happened."

"Betty and me believed you." Emma said. "But HR wouldn't let us do it. And now we gotta reconvene the committee and meet over the summer. 'Cause it's soooo important to have another associate vice-dean of student enabling and appeasement."

"Well, thanks for trying to make me feel better."

"Oh, and what about the cheaters you busted?"

"The cheaters?"

I ran my finger over the top of the row of wine bottles in front of me, left to right. Empty, empty, on its way to being empty, still sealed. I was starting to forget why I'd been upset in the first place. Which I suppose was the point.

"Remember, Molly? The exit exam in your college? You were the one who figured out who was cheating, and how they were doing it."

"Oh, yeah. I do remember."

"See?" Emma gave me an encouraging shove. "Smart, you."

"But no one appreciated it." I watched Emma refill my mug, again. How many glasses was this? "We had to go back and fail all the cheaters. Destroyed our pass rates for the semester."

"Oh yah. Remember how fast Linda hopped on her broom and flew down from the Student Retention Office to complain to your dean? Anyway, who cares about them? They're all idiots. Especially Stephen Park. Eh, Happy Birthday Molly."

"Happy birthday to me," I repeated, and reached for my glass. A bell tone sounded from inside my purse. I pulled out my phone.

"Stephen sent a text. Rehearsal running late. Call later. See? I knew there was a perfectly good explanation. I'll just text him back—"

Emma snatched the phone out of my hand.

"Do *not* text him back right away like you've been waiting by the phone for the last three hours. You gotta stop being such a schnook."

I attempted to grab the phone back, but my heart wasn't in it. Neither, by that point, was my hand-eye coordination.

"Nah, nah, nah. Don't even. We need reinforcements. Gotta keep you distracted. *Yoshi,*" Emma bellowed. "Jonah. Wanna come say hi to Molly?"

As the echoes died away, I heard a door open, and Jonah came into the kitchen. Emma's baby brother is tall, skinny, and quiet. In other words, pretty much the opposite of Emma.

"Hi Jonah," I chirped, not wanting to inflict my grouchiness on an innocent bystander. He nodded greeting, opened the fridge, got himself a bottle of beer, and sat down at the table with us.

I wondered what to say next. What's the tactful way to open a conversation with someone who's suspected of murder? The best I could come up with was, "So. How are guitar lessons going?"

Jonah quietly considered my question for what seemed like a long time.

"Okay," he finally said to his beer.

I used to hear people described as "painfully shy," and had always assumed the pain was experienced by the shy person. Not necessarily so, I realize every time I try to make conversation with Jonah.

"Molly brought some wine," Emma said. "You should try some."

She turned the bottle to show Jonah the label.

"Aw man, nah." Jonah scooted his chair back, his eyes wide with fear." Those half man-half horse things creep me out. Good thing they're extinct."

"What's the big deal?" Emma chided him. "This? It's just a little picture of a scimitar."

"That's a *centaur*," I said. "Not a scimitar. A scimitar is a curved sword."

"No it's not." Emma lifted the bottle to show me. "Does this look like a curved sword to you?"

"You're right. That looks nothing like a curved sword. Is there any more left in that bottle?"

"Just a little. Hey, Molly, speaking of guitar lessons, didn't you used to play guitar?"

"A long time ago. In grad school."

"What was the name of your band again? It was something kinda dirty, yah?"

"I forget. Hey, I'll take the last of that 'scimitar' wine." I pushed my cup in Emma's direction.

"Molly, you should take guitar lessons from Jonah. He's got extra space in his schedule now after the murder, and *your* social life isn't gonna be taking up too much time now, right? Not after tonight."

"Thanks for pointing that out." Emma hadn't done anything about my empty glass, so I reached over, picked up the wine bottle and tipped the last few drops into my cup.

"If you wanna start lessons, it's cool," Jonah said to his beer. "I got some times available."

"Oh, I don't know. Maybe someday. I'm sure you're a really good teacher, Jonah, but it would be a lot for me to take on right now."

"No worries," Jonah said, clearly not going for the hard sell.

Emma opened the next bottle. Jonah helped himself to another beer. *I should take up guitar again,* I thought. *Someday.*

CHAPTER TWENTY

I did manage to get myself to campus on time the next morning, although I wasn't exactly feeling in A-plus condition. At first, I wondered where my chair was. Then I remembered buying the yoga ball.

I pulled the uninflated ball out of its box, along with the cheap plastic foot pump. It took a while to pump the ball up, and I got a pretty good quadricep workout while I was at it. When I thought I had done enough inflating, I positioned myself over the ball and then carefully lowered myself onto it. The ball was still too soft. By the time I stopped sinking into it, I was completely hidden behind the pile of textbooks on my desk.

I hooked up the foot pump again, stomped air into the ball until it seemed on the verge of popping, then sat down again. Better. I bounced on it a few times, which was kind of fun until I started to feel seasick. Sitting on a yoga ball wasn't so bad. And I'd be getting a workout just by sitting at my desk.

I still had a few minutes before class started. I decided to skip my usual walk up to the cafeteria. My stomach was not up to confronting our cafeteria coffee.

Stephen hadn't made any attempt to contact me after last night's text. I wondered if he was okay. I had just enough time to give him a quick call, to make sure he was safe and not lying in a hospital bed or something. I picked up my office phone and dialed his number, but just as it started to ring, I heard a knock on my door. I replaced the receiver quickly.

"Come in."

The twins pushed into my office. He wore jeans and a black t-shirt. She sported a black tank top under denim overalls. They made me think of human salt-and-pepper shakers.

"Eh, Miss," the girl said, "we was wondering if we get class today?"

"Of course. Are you asking because of Monday's incident? I can make a request for counselors to come in—"

"Nah, nah, nah, not that," the boy shook his head. "'Cause you and Park."

I glanced guiltily at my office phone.

"I'm sorry. Who?"

"Stephen Park," the girl explained. "Professor Park from the Theater Department. Stood you up last night. Terrible, that thing."

"How on earth did you—"

"If you gotta take some personal time off from teaching, it's okay," the boy assured me. "We understand."

The girl nodded solemnly. "Rejection literally hurts, that's how come they call it heartbreak. We learned that in our Psych class."

"I appreciate your concern, but class is not cancelled."

"You get our papers graded yet?" the girl asked.

"They're not quite finished." This was technically true. Also true: I hadn't even started. Most people don't realize how mentally taxing grading is. Not only do you have to be painstakingly consistent, but going through student papers can be a dispiriting reality check on how effective you've been as a teacher.

"That classroom's kinda stink, you know," said the boy. "Probably get some kinda bad stuff in the air or something. Maybe we should cancel class for health reasons."

"Well, that's the room they gave us. Maybe we can try leaving the windows open today. If it starts raining we'll just move away from the windows. Oh, and if you haven't finished today's assignment, now might be a good time to put the finishing touches on it. We still have a few minutes before class starts."

I watched the twins hurry out of my office, then bounced

up from the yoga ball to a standing position. Unfortunately I miscalculated, launched up too fast, and banged my kneecaps on the underside of the desk. I kicked the ball and it rebounded, hitting me in the knees and nearly bowling me over.

I didn't hear the knock on my door frame. Another one of my students, the round young man with the red baseball cap, poked his head in and found me punching the ball angrily.

"Eh, Professor," he said, "I heard class was cancelled."

I pummeled the ball into submission and plumped down on it before it could attack me again.

"Yes. *No.* Class is not cancelled. We are having class. As usual. This is a normal day, and we will have a normal class session."

"You wanna blow off steam you should beat on one heavy bag. They get 'em up at the gym. I can show you how if you like try."

"That's very kind of you to offer. I think I'm okay for now."

"Eh, you wearing your new bra? Looks good, Professor."

My phone rang.

"I have to get this," I said. "I'll see you in class, uh…"

"My name's Micah, Miss."

"Micah. Of course. I'll see you in class, Micah."

He tipped his brim and left.

I didn't answer the phone right away. I didn't want to seem too eager. Two rings, three rings, okay, *now.*

It wasn't Stephen calling. It was Emma.

"You doing the two-rings thing in case Stephen calls?"

"What are you talking about? I've been *way* too busy to think about Stephen. I've had students in and out of here all morning."

"That's my girl. How are you feeling?"

"Fine," I said.

"That's a relief. I was worried about you. Yoshi said he practically had to pour you into the car."

"It was very nice of him to drive me home. Wait a minute. Yoshi drove me home. Why was my car in my carport this morning?"

"I followed him over in your car, and we drove back together. Eh, I never drove your Thunderbird before. Felt like trying to steer a sofa."

"That was considered the height of luxury in 1959."

"You made it through Mount Textbook yet?"

"I'm making progress." That was optimistic of me. The pile looked taller than ever.

"When's your Biz Com class?"

"It's starting in a few minutes."

"Let's go to lunch after," Emma said. "We got some time before the search committee meeting this afternoon."

My right eye started to throb.

"That meeting's today? I was hoping to go home and rest a little after class."

"Eh, isn't your class all the way out at the old Health building? You better get a move on if you don't wanna be late."

Emma was waiting at my office door when I returned from class.

"Man, you look terrible." She put her hand on my forehead. "All clammy too."

"I don't feel great." I groped in my bag for my office key. "At least I managed to hold it together in class. When they asked why I was keeping the lights off I told them natural daylight helps you learn faster."

"You gotta learn to handle your liquor, Molly. So what about lolo boy? He come back?"

"No. Bret wasn't there today. But you know that kid Micah? He was working the cash register yesterday at Galimba's Bargain Boyz? When I walked in he whispered something to the girl next to him. Then they both smiled at me and she gave me a thumbs-up."

"What was that about?"

"I'm not sure. But it made me kind of self-conscious."

I let us into the office and set down my pile of books and papers.

"Hope you brought lunch," Emma said. "Cafeteria's closed today."

I ducked under my desk and retrieved my lunch from my little office fridge.

"Fortunately I have food. Let's not eat in my office, though.

Too hot."

"Yeah, feels like the A/C's out in your building again. You should buy one of those little air conditioners."

"Sure. It's on my list, right after the fancy coffee machine. I think I need to win the lottery."

"You wish. No lottery in Hawaii, you know. That's how come we all go Vegas. Lunch in the theater then?"

The theater was one of our favorite lunch spots. Whatever the weather, the theater was always comfortably cool. There was only one problem with the theater.

"What if Stephen's there?" I asked.

"Stephen already ruined your birthday," Emma said. "You gonna let him ruin your lunch break, too?"

CHAPTER TWENTY-ONE

Emma and I hurried along the uncovered walkway, hoping to reach the shelter of the theater before the drizzle turned to a downpour.

"The last I heard from Stephen was when he texted me last night," I said. "What if he was in an accident, and he's in the emergency room right now?"

"Then you can bring him flowers. Hey, you look like you spilled wine all over yourself."

I looked down and saw that my red silk dry-clean-only blouse was stained dark with streaks of rain.

"Oh, great." (I might have said something less polite, but let's go with "great.")

Unfortunately, there's no way to get from one side of campus to the other without getting rained on. You'd think in a town that gets four times as much rain as Seattle, they would have put in covered walkways.

I'm told that the reason our campus's architecture is so poorly suited to our climate is because of a quirk in our procurement process. Namely, that the architect hired to oversee Mahina State's building boom back in the 1970s hailed from sunny Honolulu and had no idea how to build for wet weather. And also happened to be the brother-in-law of one of the trustees.

"Weren't they going to get this walkway covered, finally?" I asked. "I thought I saw an announcement."

"That was before the latest budget cuts. You coulda brung an umbrella, you know."

"Then I'd have to carry around a wet umbrella all day."

We pulled up to the sheltered theater entrance.

"Well, we're out of the rain now. Come on, let's go inside."

Emma pushed through the glass double door, and I followed.

"So what are you gonna say to Stephen if he's here?"

"Why do I have to say anything?"

We made our way across the empty lobby, our wet shoes squelching on the carpet. Emma pushed open the door to the dark auditorium. Down in front, a red spotlight shone on a bare stage. Emma and I slipped in, and I eased the door shut. We felt our way down the row of nubby chairs in the dark.

"Yeah, covering the walkways," she whispered. "It was part of the deferred maintenance bill. They were gonna upgrade the chemical storage in my building, too."

"So what happened?"

"Oh, the usual," Emma said. "Honolulu legislators don't think it's worth spending any money on our crappy little island, so they blocked it. Someone should store leaky old chemical containers next to *their* offices. That'd get 'em moving. How about here? Right in the middle?"

The red spot on stage faded, and then bloomed again in a shade of blue-green. We heard shuffling and clunking as set pieces were moved around, and then a woman's voice called out something about a "hot spot."

Emma pulled out her lunch and started to eat. I smelled starchy, meaty, and fishy smells intermingled.

"What are you eating?" I asked.

"Spam *musubi*. What'd you bring?" She leaned over and squinted at my lap. "Cheese sticks and apple slices? What is that, the preschool diet?"

"It's easy to pack," I said. "And cheap."

"Nice and cool in here, yah?"

"It's cool all right. I think I can feel an ice crust forming on my blouse. Why is it so—"

Emma elbowed me, hard.

"There he is. That's him, right?"

I felt my stomach clench as I recognized Stephen's familiar silhouette. The fight-or-flight anxiety didn't make any sense, but it was unmistakable.

"If he was in the emergency room last night, he sure made a miraculous recovery," Emma whispered. "You gonna call him out?"

"No. He's right in the middle of working. Anyway, I don't want to deal with this right now. Let's just eat our lunch and then we can go to our stupid meeting."

My eyes had adjusted to the dark, and I could make out the back of Stephen's head, down in the front row. His glossy black ponytail hung down over the back of the seat, and a curl of cigarette smoke rose and dissipated in front of him. A blonde girl walked out from the wings holding what looked like a script. She sat down next to Stephen and they bent their heads together in quiet conversation.

"Who's Blondie?" Emma whispered.

"I'm sure it's just his stage manager or something. Anyway, who cares? I don't care."

"That's the spirit, Molly. Moving on. Finally."

"Yeah, I guess. I wonder how they're going to handle the water this year."

"The what?"

"For Stephen's play. The part where they do The Deluge and everyone sitting in the front gets splashed."

"Oh. We're talking about Stephen again. Okay. Hope he remembers to get the permits this time."

"I'm sure some conscientious woman will do it for him."

Blondie stood up and made her way to the control console in the center of the auditorium. She spotted us, acknowledged our presence with a nod, and then turned her attention to the vast panel of knobs and sliders. The blue spotlight faded, replaced by two discs of white light on the stage.

"Did you see how close she was sitting to Stephen?" Emma whispered. "I think they have a thing. Know what I'm talking about?"

"Yeah. I don't know. She looks really young. I don't think Stephen would get involved with an undergrad."

"Aw, 'cause he's so upstanding and moral? I thought you said he thinks the rules don't apply to him."

"No, not because he's so moral. Because messing around with an undergraduate would be so *cliché*."

"I bet *she* knows where Stephen was last night."

"Shut up," I suggested.

The young woman got up and returned to the front row, sat down next to Stephen, and whispered something to him. I saw her lips brush his ear. Stephen glanced in our direction and quickly turned his attention back to the stage.

"I mean look at them down there."

"I'd rather not."

Emma peered at her watch. "Ready to go?"

"Already?"

"We got five minutes till the meeting starts."

I stuffed the last piece of string cheese into my mouth, although I wasn't hungry. We rose from our seats and slipped out. Emma exited the auditorium first. I may have forgotten to ease the door closed behind us. It slammed shut with a bang.

CHAPTER TWENTY-TWO

"There's Pat Flanagan," Emma exclaimed, as if the lone occupant of the otherwise empty classroom might have somehow escaped my notice.

He was better looking than I remembered, lean and broad-shouldered, with pale blue eyes set in dark lashes. He was sitting in a middle row, working on a stack of papers.

"Thank you, Emma. I can see him too. Why does his name sound so familiar, though? It seems like I've heard it somewhere before."

"In your *dreams*."

"Stop it."

I climbed up the side aisle, edged into the row, and sat down next to Pat. Emma followed me in and pushed past both me and Pat to sit on his other side. I thought he seemed glad to see us, but he was probably just grateful for the interruption.

"Are those the same papers you were grading the other day at the retreat?" I asked.

"Yep. Guilty. This summer class is turning out to be a lot more work than I expected. I thought I was gonna get a grader or a TA or something to help out."

"I never had anything like that. I do all of it. Emma, do you have teaching assistants?"

"Sure," Emma said. "Johnnie Walker, Jim Beam, and Old Grand-Dad."

"Hey Emma," Pat said. "Sorry about all that mess with your brother."

"Who told you about my brother?"

"Emma," I said, "even my hairdresser knows about it."

Emma folded her arms and slouched in her seat.

"This sucks. If *Island Confidential* hadn't of run that story on the exact day Kent got himself killed, Jonah would never be in trouble now."

"Emma, whose fault is that? *You're* the one who sent the story in."

"You send a tip like that to a newspaper, they'll publish it," Pat added.

"Wait, newspaper. Now I know why your name sounded familiar. You're Patrick Flanagan."

"Patrick Flanagan." Emma punched Pat's shoulder. "*County Courier.* I seen your byline!"

"I *was* a reporter at the *County Courier.* Before the layoffs. You guys subscribe?"

"My parents used to," Emma said. "They'd go for the obituaries first, the garage sales, and the Tuesday food ads. But now all that stuff's online for free."

"I don't subscribe anymore either," I said. "I did for a while when I moved here, but the copies kept piling up. And driving the papers down to the recycling station didn't seem like a net positive for the environment."

"Yeah, not in your big blue boat," Emma added.

"The online classifieds killed us," Pat said. "That's my theory."

The classroom door opened. Betty Jackson stepped into the classroom, looked around, and then came up and sat down next to us. She wore her hair natural and ultra-short, which can look really elegant if you're tall and slim like Betty.

"The candidate isn't here yet? I thought *I* was late. Hey, Pat."

"Pat was just telling us how much he loves teaching intro comp," Emma said.

Betty laughed. "I'll bet it's almost as fun as teaching stats to psychology majors. Hey Pat, what's with all the mud on your shoes? You hike down here from the mountain?"

"Just working on my car." He lifted a huge, muddy boot for

Betty's benefit. "My driveway's just dirt, and it rained again, so…"

"Betty," I asked, "how do you and Pat know each other?" Before she could answer, the classroom door opened again, and Linda from the Student Retention Office glided in. Two of her young sidekicks trailed into the room after her.

"We're just waiting for Bob Wilson." Linda went to the front of the room and started twiddling knobs on the A/V panel. "When he gets here, we can begin."

She turned and said something to one of her assistants, who shook his head. He in turn said something to the other assistant. The young woman shrugged.

"Is anyone familiar with the AV equipment in this room?" Linda called out.

"I'll go," I muttered. "I need to do some impression management."

"Is that b-school for sucking up?" Pat asked.

"Yes."

I slung my bag over my shoulder and went down to help. Linda stood aside to supervise me as I punched buttons and twisted dials on the A/V control panel.

"Can you manage, Professor?" the young woman asked.

"There's a setup like this in my classroom." I tried not to be irritated by what sounded like her presumption of either frailty or incompetence. "But I think this whole panel might not be connected. Let me check." I kneeled down and peered under the table. Sure enough, hanging from the underside of the panel were bundles of wire looped and fastened with twist ties. The setup looked like it had just come out of the box.

"It's not hooked up," I said.

"Put in a work order," Linda commanded. "Expedite charge goes on the Student Success Account 6609." The young man immediately pulled out a phone and rushed out of the room.

I stood up and smoothed my skirt. "Oh, so Linda, I was wondering if there was any news on the Student of Concern report I filed?"

"It doesn't ring a bell. Of course I can't remember every piece of paperwork that comes across my desk."

"It was Bret Lampson," I said. "Remember? The student who pulled out a weapon in class? It was on Monday."

How often does that kind of thing happen at Mahina State anyway, I wondered?

"You have to allow the process to proceed, Molly. Our office is very busy. You need to be patient."

"I'm a little concerned because he didn't show up to class today. I hope he's not planning some kind of—"

Bob Wilson came rushing in, his bald head shiny with sweat.

"Ah, Bob is here," Linda said. "Good. We can begin. Molly, let's continue this conversation after we adjourn."

We arranged ourselves into something like a circle, which was awkward with the classroom's stadium seating. Bob Wilson welcomed the members of the Associate Dean of Learning Process Improvement Search Committee to our first meeting of the summer. He pulled a stack of papers from a battered brown briefcase, set it in front of him, and read us the same HR boilerplate we'd heard last semester. Then he updated us on our progress: Unfortunately, our top alternate candidates were no longer available. Even our second-tier candidates had already found other positions or withdrawn. Because of the delay resulting from the committee's top choice not passing his background check, we were down to a few alternates.

Linda and her two henchpersons cornered me as soon as the short meeting was over. That was too bad since I had hoped to talk some more to Pat Flanagan. I watched him leave with Emma and Betty.

"I talked to Dan about your idea, Molly," Linda said.

"You talked to my department chair? Which idea was this, now?"

"About your initiative for the student-directed curriculum."

"My initiative?" I didn't remember introducing any initiatives. Why would I do that? "Student-directed curriculum? It's not ringing a bell, sorry."

"The idea you brought up at the retreat."

"You don't mean when I said, why not just let the students give themselves whatever grades they want? Are you talking about that?"

"Dan wasn't receptive at this point in time," Linda said. "Unfortunately, we've found that some faculty are skeptical about anything that de-centers the traditional power dynamic of the professor as the person who knows things."

"Could be." *De-centers the traditional power dynamic?* I didn't believe for a second that Linda knew what those words meant. She'd probably memorized the phrase at one of her professional development boondoggles.

"We believe your idea was a little outside-the-box for him."

Now *that* was the Linda I knew. I can't stand that expression, by the way. Every time I hear *outside-the-box* I want to brain someone with an MLA style manual. The hardcover edition. It makes sense as a metaphor, I'll give it that, but it's monstrously overused, and always by people who are themselves so inside-the-box they have visible corners.

"It is *very* outside-the-box," I agreed. "The College of Commerce might not be ready for something so advanced. But I will talk to Dan, I promise." To thank him for fending off yet another insane Student Retention Office initiative.

"Good," Linda gave off some unseen signal, which caused her two flunkies to get into formation and follow her out the door. "Make sure to keep us in the loop."

"Keep you in the loop. Of course."

At least I was done for the day. I cheered up a little at the thought of heading home, pulling a lightweight murder mystery off my bookshelf, pouring myself a big glass of wine, curling up on my couch—

My phone buzzed in my hand, reminding me I had an appointment in ten minutes. One I'd nearly managed to forget.

I trudged down to the parking lot, found my car, slid into the driver's seat, pulled the heavy door shut, and started the engine. With my enthusiasm level now well below the detectable threshold, I headed out toward Hotel Drive for my first Business Boosters meeting.

CHAPTER TWENTY-THREE

Small talk comes easily to some people. I am not one of those people. So great is my horror of unstructured socializing that I routinely arrive fifteen minutes late to Mass on purpose, just to avoid the Passing of the Peace. So when I arrived at the Lehua Inn, found the upstairs dining room, signed into my first Business Boosters meeting, and was told to take a seat "anywhere," my heart sank.

Mercedes Yamashiro waved, smiled, and then went back to conversing with the people at her fully-occupied table. Darn. It would have been nice to sit next to the voluble and perpetually cheerful Mercedes. She owned the Cloudforest Bed and Breakfast, where I stayed during my job interview. Mercedes was my first acquaintance in Mahina, one of those people who could make anyone feel at ease. Or so I assume, because I consider myself the boundary case.

My innards launched into spin cycle when I spied Marshall Dixon sitting near the front. She was next to one of the few empty seats in the room, but there was no way I was going to sit there. It was bad enough to feel judged by a room full of strangers. At least strangers might grow to like you at some point.

Fortunately I spotted Tatsuya Masumoto and his wife Trudy at a small table against the paneled wall. I hurried over and wedged myself into the vacant seat between them. We had about half a second to exchange a brief greeting before the program started. Perfect timing.

Trudy, my hairdresser's sweet and sparrow-like wife, hugged me so closely her blonde hair tickled my nose. Then she pulled back and beamed at me

"Rumor has it you look fabulous in a beehive."

"Speaking of disasters," Tatsuya added mischievously, earning a glare from Trudy.

"Oh. I guess everyone knows what happened on my birthday?"

"Don't you worry about him." Trudy straightened my collar, which had managed to get inverted on one side. "There are plenty of other fish in the sea. And some of them don't even smoke."

"We're starting." Tatsuya stood for the Business Boosters anthem. Trudy and I were already standing, so we turned toward the front of the room. I relaxed and inhaled the reassuring diner smell: old cigarette smoke mingled with decades of pancakes and burned coffee.

On the agenda for today's meeting was a discussion of the New Hanohano Hotel, a universally reviled rebuild of a formerly beloved landmark. The assembled Business Boosters stared resentfully out the window at the mold-streaked monstrosity currently under construction. The Business Boosters chapter president, a stern-faced blonde wearing a pastel suit, enumerated the various offenses of the developer, Jimmy Tanaka.

First, the bulldozing of the original Hanohano Hotel had taken place mere days before the quaint plantation house was due to be added to the Register of Historic Places. And that was just the beginning. As soon as construction was underway, the New Hanohano gained a reputation as an aesthetic and environmental catastrophe. Careless grading combined with Mahina's heavy rainfall washed tons of precious topsoil into the bay. Construction waste was discovered dumped in the forest in unincorporated Kuewa, an apparent attempt to avoid landfill fees. Most tragically, a worker had perished in a construction mishap.

The hotel had reopened before the top floor was finished, and the result had been roundly panned on the travel websites. None of the local business organizations, all of whom were generally in favor of expansion and development, had anything good to say about the New Hanohano Hotel. Or Jimmy Tanaka.

Trudy nudged me.

"You know who's single?" she whispered.

"Jimmy Tanaka?"

"No, Silly, see the man over there, dark hair, blue aloha shirt?" She pointed in the general direction of Mercedes Yamashiro's table.

"I guess." In fact there were three or four men at the table who fit Trudy's description.

"His name is Donnie Gonsalves. I'll introduce you after the meeting. He owns Donnie's Drive-Inn. Plate lunches, *loco mocos*, local favorites."

"He sounds interesting." I looked in the direction of their table again.

"He's been on his own since his wife left, and I hear the son is a handful. Anyway, I think you two would get along."

"I'm not ready to meet anyone new yet." I wondered what on earth Trudy imagined I'd have in common with some divorced small-town businessman and his delinquent son. "Thank you so much for looking out for me, though. I appreciate it."

"Well, I never wanted to say anything when you were dating him, but I always felt you were stifling your creativity to spare Stephen's ego. He's the kind of person who always has to take center stage, and I think he's been holding you back."

"Probably," I agreed.

"What have you been doing to nourish your soul?"

"I haven't had time for soul-nourishing. Summer's been awfully busy."

"I thought professors didn't work during the summer."

"We don't get *paid* during the summer," I corrected her. "There's still a surprising amount of work to get done. And I'm teaching a summer class. You know, I noticed the shop seemed pretty quiet too, speaking of summer."

"It has been. But it's not because of the time of year. Someone's been leaving negative reviews online for Tatsuya's Moderne Beauty."

"Really? That's terrible."

"We think we know who it is."

"I left a positive review for you," I said. "But I'll go leave another one. You should put in some good reviews for yourselves too, to counteract the bad ones."

"Oh, we couldn't do that. It would be dishonest. You know, it was bad enough before the internet, when you'd get an unhappy customer complaining to all their friends. Especially after they insist on an unsuitable cut or color, and then they're dissatisfied afterward."

"Did you ever see Kent Lovely's unsuitable color?"

"Oh, that poor, deluded man. I hate to speak ill of the dead, but I think he thought he was Elvis or something."

"At least that wasn't Tatsuya's fault," I said. "He told me he refused to do that color for Kent."

"What do you mean?" Trudy looked surprised. "Tatsuya *did* do Kent's color."

CHAPTER TWENTY-FOUR

"*Tatsuya* did Kent Lovely's hair color?" Tatsuya didn't seem to hear me. He was paying attention to the presentation. "Trudy, are you sure?"

"Oh, yes. I remember when it happened, because Tatsuya was so upset."

"Upset at Kent?"

"At himself, mostly. Kent insisted on that black color, entirely wrong for him of course. My poor husband went along with it because Kent had always been such a good customer. Well. Tatsuya regretted it, let me tell you. And when he offered to fix it for free, Kent not only refused, he started dying it himself with—*boxed hair dye from the drugstore.* Oh, look at us, chatting away." Trudy fanned herself with her hand as if to dissipate the steam from our sizzling-hot gossip. "We should be listening to the discussion."

The Business Boosters were still on the topic of developer Jimmy Tanaka's various crimes against Mahina's economy. I put on an interested expression, and pointed my face at the speaker, just as my students did in my classes. I barely heard the discussion. I was thinking about Kent Lovely.

The last time I had really spoken to Kent—apart from those few words at Monday's retreat—was during the incident I had related to Marshall Dixon.

Under the table, I slipped my phone out of my bag, muted the sound, and pulled up the browser, all the while pretending to pay attention to the meeting.

It didn't take long to find the video online. It was the *kata* section of last year's island-wide karate tournament, featuring Kent Lovely. His coal-black hair was flying around in slow motion for all the internet to see. Watching the video again brought that afternoon's events back vividly.

When I had gone over to Rodge's office to investigate the wall-shaking music, I'd seen Rodge and Kent sitting side-by-side, staring at a laptop computer. On screen, Kent Lovely, clad in a white *gi*, executed a slow motion roundhouse kick. Droplets of sweat flew out in a perfect centripetal pattern. I rapped on the door frame, but the music was so loud that they didn't hear me. I finally just walked into Rodge's office.

"Ah, *la bella professoressa*." Kent wheeled around and grinned.

"Molly-Dolly," Rodge had added, halfheartedly. As glad as Kent was to see me, Rodge was obviously disappointed that Emma wasn't there.

"Listen, Rodge, Kent, I don't want to be a bother, but could you turn down the—"

Kent interrupted me with what sounded like a string of nonsense syllables.

"I'm sorry, Kent, I have no idea what you just said."

"Oh, *signorina* Molly, you don't understand your mother tongue, the language of love? *Peccato.*"

"Ah. Italian?" I guessed.

"*Si, Bellissima.*"

"I wish I did speak it. I had to read *The Divine Comedy* in translation. But no, I'm not Italian. My ancestry is Albanian, actually."

"Im-po-see-bee-lay!" Kent exclaimed.

"What do you mean, 'im-po-see-bee-lay?' Why is it 'im-po-see-bee-lay' that I'm Albanian?"

Emma had recently referred to me as an "off-brand European," and I was feeling a little sensitive about the issue of my ancestry.

Kent moved the computer screen so I had a good view of it. "You need to see this, Molly. This is me, executing a series of *katas,* or karate figures."

"Thank you, I know what *katas* are. I don't want to take up your time, I just wanted—"

"The music is my original composition," Kent interrupted. "Come on, have a seat."

"But there aren't any chai—" Kent patted his scrawny thigh.

"Okay. I think we're done here."

I was so eager to get out of Rodge's office, I bumped into his curio cabinet, knocking over a few of his little statues and tchotchkes. One of the toppled items was a white plastic bottle with a black label, featuring a smiling dark haired woman wearing a cheongsam.

"One of Rodge's students asked him if those were fertility pills," Kent said as I righted the bottle. "Know what Rodge told 'em? *I sure hope not.*"

As Rodge and Kent high-fived each other, I slipped out of Rodge's office and back to the quiet safety of my own.

How many people knew Tatsuya had been Kent Lovely's hairstylist? Silly question. This was Mahina, where everyone knows everything, including your bra size. I glanced over at Tatsuya. He took pride in his work, no question, but I couldn't imagine him going so far as to deliberately poison an embarrassing customer.

Trudy nudged me. "Think about what I said," she whispered. "Nourish your soul."

I nodded and slipped my phone back into my bag. Trudy was right. If the talentless Kent Lovely could express himself creatively, why couldn't I? Kent's "original composition" had been awful, with a canned string section and a dissonant bass line that didn't quite sit in the mix. Why had I let Stephen convince me he was the creative one, while I was just a business-school sellout?

When Business Boosters wrapped up, I hurried out of the dining room, foiling Trudy's plan to set me up with Mahina's Plate Lunch King. I drove straight home and got ready for bed. I pulled the comforter up around my shoulders and drifted into delicious slumber.

I forgot to turn off my ringer. The booming chorus of Carl Orff's "O Fortuna" blasted me out of dreamland. I planted my hand in random places on the nightstand until I found the phone.

"Hello," I gasped. My heart was banging in my chest. Phone calls in the middle of the night are never good news.

Tonight was no exception. It was Stephen Park calling.

I pushed up my sleep mask and squinted at my alarm clock.

"Oh Molly," Stephen's tone was as casual as could be. As if everything were fine. "You weren't asleep, were you?"

"Stephen, it's four in the morning. What do you think?"

"I saw you and Emma in the theater today."

"We just wanted somewhere comfortable to eat lunch. The cafeteria was closed. We didn't mean to bother you. I thought we were being nice and quiet."

"We—I was testing the lighting. I didn't have time to talk."

He wasn't going to bring it up. I'd have to do it.

"Stephen, what happened? I waited for you, and you never showed up."

Pause.

"You, know, on my birthday?"

"Things got kind of hectic."

"It was my birthday, Stephen. You stood me up on my birthday."

"I texted you, didn't I?"

"It would have been nice if you'd told me in advance you couldn't make it. Instead of letting me wait and wonder if you were bleeding to death in an emergency room somewhere."

"I'll come over now," he said, as if he were doing me a huge favor.

"Now? At four in the morning on Wednesday? No, I guess it's Thursday now. Are you *insane?*"

And had my birthday only been the night before last? So much had happened in that short time.

"Why not? We're both awake, and I—"

"Stephen, I'm only awake because *you called me on the phone and woke me up.* I should be asleep now. You should, too."

"You know I don't work that way, Molly. The Muse doesn't

106

punch a clock."

"Ah, yes. Art absolves you of everything. *Unlike* un-creative, clock-punching me. Is that what you're saying?"

"No, that's not what I—"

"No? Did you not just imply I have nothing more important to do than hang around until you randomly and unpredictably see fit to contact me at your convenience?"

"No, I was saying my schedule—"

"Oh, you mean what could I possibly have on *my* schedule more important than waiting until *you* have a spare moment?"

"Molly, you know that's not—"

"Know what? I have a very busy schedule. Me."

"I'm sure you do. I know you're teaching a summer class."

"Not just summer school. I have a big steaming pile of committee work and other uncompensated service. Oh, and you know what else? I'm, I'm, getting serious about my *music*."

Silence.

"That's right. My music. I'm not kidding."

"You're getting your little grad school band back together?"

I closed my eyes and massaged my throbbing temple. "My *little* grad school band. Yes, by all means, be as condescending as possible. That always gets good results. Good bye, Stephen."

CHAPTER TWENTY-FIVE

I woke up for good three hours later. Despite the early-morning call, I felt so energetic I only needed two cups of coffee instead of my usual four or five.

I made a phone call, showered, dressed, hopped into the Thunderbird, and started up the hill before I had time to lose my nerve.

Emma answered her door wearing snug black shorts and a bright yellow jersey.

"Why are you dressed like that?" I asked.

"I'm going paddling. One of these days we're gonna get you to come out with us."

"Sure," I said, insincerely.

"You're lucky Jonah could take you on such short notice."

"Oh, I realize that." I slipped off my shoes and stepped inside. "I'm glad he could fit me in at the last minute."

"Sounds like you're looking forward to your lesson."

"I really am. It's been so long since I've played, so I'm a little apprehensive, of course. I'm afraid I won't be able to remember anything."

"You sure everything's okay Molly? You seem suspiciously cheerful. You been drinking?"

"Of course not. Just coffee."

I didn't feel like telling Emma about Stephen's early morning phone call. I was glad I'd stood up for myself, but I shouldn't have even engaged him. Emma would have simply hung up on him.

"You see the police car out there when you parked?"

"I did."

"It's harassment, is what. I should call the ACLU. So what's new?"

I followed Emma into the kitchen, which smelled pleasantly of coffee.

"I went to my first Business Boosters yesterday." I pulled out a chair and sat down. "I sat with Tatsuya Masumoto and his wife Trudy. Coffee smells good."

"You want some coffee? Was that a hint?"

"Yes, please."

Emma pulled out a green mug emblazoned with the logo of a large and infamous chemical company, and poured me a cup.

"And then?" Emma set the coffee in front of me, along with a carton of cream.

"I escaped before Trudy could try to set me up with some guy who runs a lunch shop. Then I went home. Went to bed early."

"And what else?" Emma sat down across from me and narrowed her eyes. "Something's up, Molly. I can tell. Eh, careful, you're gonna use up all my cream."

"I'll buy you another carton. Um, there was one thing. Stephen called."

"Oh naw. I knew it. You took him back."

"No, I did not. I told him we were through. I tried to get back to sleep afterward, but I couldn't. It was already early morning. So I got up and started going through my boxes."

"The ones in your spare room that you never unpacked yet?"

"Yes. I found a copy of an old weekly newspaper. It was the one where our band was on the cover."

"Oh yeah. Back when you were a mad punk rocker. You told me about it."

"You know, it's mostly because of Stephen that I never kept up with my guitar. I mean, yes, I was busy with the new job and everything, but he'd always sneer at the idea of my playing music. As far as he was concerned, I had no business doing anything creative, because I was the big sellout who'd taken a job in the business school."

"Whatta *putz*. So it's really over with him?"

"Yes. Stephen and I are definitely through."

"Well that's the best news I've heard all year. Okay, you get to your guitar lesson, and I gotta get down to paddling practice. But we still gotta fix this."

Emma jerked her thumb at the living room window. The parked police cruiser was clearly visible.

"Do you want to have lunch tomorrow?" I asked. "A Council of War, as Amelia Peabody might say?"

"Who?"

"Crimefighting Egyptologist."

"You know some of the weirdest people. Invite Iker Legazpi to lunch too, okay? He must have all the latest on Kent Lovely's da kine. Embezzling, yah? If we could find out what Kent was up to, and who was working with him, maybe we could figure out who killed him."

"Bearing in mind we're keeping this all extremely low-profile, because we don't want to alert the murderer. Right?"

"Look, babooz, I'm not gonna send in any more tips to *Island Confidential*, okay?"

"Good. I'll stop by the Accounting Department tomorrow morning and invite Iker to have lunch with us. So where is Jonah?"

"Vedging in his room I bet. JONAHHH."

I winced and rubbed my ears.

"What's wrong with you?" Emma demanded. "You hung over?"

"No, you were just kind of loud."

"Where's your guitar?"

"I assumed Jonah would have one I could use. Should I just…" I pointed at the guest room.

"Yeah, try knock." She headed for the front door.

"The lessons are in Jonah's room?" I called after her. "Isn't it a little, you know?"

"Nah. Lessons are in the laundry room. And you guys gotta keep the door closed. The noise bothers Yoshi. If there's a load

110

washing, just pause it. Make sure you start it again before you leave. Have fun."

The drying clothes hanging from the ceiling filled the laundry room with detergent perfume. A Yngwie Malmsteen poster was taped to the wall above the electrical panel, corners curled from the damp. Jonah brought in two folding chairs and set them up, and then went to fetch two guitars. He handed me one, and I set it on my lap and tried tuning it.

"How long since you played?" he asked.

"Years." The guitar strings felt like cheese-cutter wire on my finger pads. Jonah pondered this for a moment.

"Okay," he said, "I know what we'll start with."

He left me alone in the laundry room. I got as comfortable as I could on the metal folding chair and tried to remember how to play something.

CHAPTER TWENTY-SIX

Jonah walked back in carrying his own guitar and a stack of lesson books. He placed the books on the washing machine and sat down on his folding chair, facing me.

"How's it feel?" he asked.

I examined my left hand and flexed it.

"It's already kind of sore. And I've only been playing for a few seconds."

He took my hand and rubbed his thumb over my fingertips.

"It'll take time. Your finger pads are soft. Emma said you used to play in a band?"

"It was back in grad school. Before I moved to Mahina. I was working on my dissertation, *Reproducing and Resisting: Hegemonic Masculinities and Transgressive—*"

I noticed Jonah starting to glaze over.

"Sorry, you don't need to hear the whole title of my dissertation. It had to do with punk rock, basically, and competing narratives of masculinity, how the privileging and/or marginalization of— *anyway.* When I got to my fieldwork, I was interviewing all of these kids who were playing in their own bands, and I thought, well this looks like fun, and how hard could it be? So a few of us from my cohort got together, and there we were."

"Your band have a name?"

I shrugged dismissively. "It was some postmodern in-joke. I can't really remember it now."

Calling ourselves "Phallus in Wonderland" hadn't been my first choice. But Melanie Polewski, our lead singer, was really into Lacan at the time, and had lobbied hard for her idea of an all-female band with "phallus" in the name. As usual, Melanie got her way.

"Okay, before we start." Jonah handed me a sheet of paper. "Here's the price list for the lessons."

"Is that the price per month? I *guess* that seems fair." It seemed high to me, but I supposed it was worth it to support Emma and get my guitar practice back on track. You can't put a price on nourishing your soul, right?

"Oh. No, sorry," he said. "It's per lesson."

I tried not to look shocked.

"So how many students do you have?"

"Less than before. I'm not really keeping track. Still teaching a few lessons every day. Four or five, I guess."

Let's say four students, five days a week, an hour each. That would be.... not a bad living at all. And certainly enough for Jonah to afford his own place.

Jonah tuned his guitar, then handed it to me and took the one I was holding. Somehow, he intuited what I was thinking.

"It's enough to help Emma with the mortgage." He plucked strings and twisted keys, making nearly imperceptible changes to the pitch.

"Emma charges you *rent*?" The way Emma talked about her brother had always made him sound like a world-class freeloader.

"Sure, I pay rent. I'm not some freeloader. They need the money. Yoshi doesn't have a job."

"What? I thought with his fancy MBA, Yoshi could get a job anywhere."

Jonah shrugged.

"Yoshi? Mister Failure-Isn't-An-Option? He's unemployed?"

"I don't think he's trying that hard. He doesn't like Mahina. No job here's good enough for him. He says he can't live in a place where no one can tell he's wearing a five thousand dollar watch."

"If it's so important to him, he should just leave the price tag on."

"That's what Emma said. He misses the big city, though. Eh, gotta do what makes you happy, yeah?"

Jonah played some difficult, twiddly riffs on his guitar, the kind only other serious guitar players enjoy listening to.

"Let's start with a D chord," he said.

"Major, or minor?"

"D-major. Let's get an idea of your comfort level."

I strummed awkwardly at first, and then with a little more confidence. As I repeated the chord, Jonah picked out a rambling melody that harmonized nicely. When he played, he seemed transported. That's the point I wanted to get to. Where everything was in muscle memory, and I could enjoy the music flowing through me.

Of course I wasn't going to be achieving that blissful flow state if my guitar teacher got hauled off to prison for murder. Emma wanted me to investigate. I might as well start here.

"Jonah, I hope you don't mind my asking. What do you think really happened to Kent?"

Jonah kept playing, eyes down. His melody became more agitated, and then veered off into the atonal.

"Sorry, you don't have to talk about it if you don't want to. But Emma keeps pestering me to help her get to the bottom of it. She's worried about you, and she says you both want your lives back. Do you know anything about it?"

Jonah herded the disjointed notes into an unexpected but satisfying conclusion.

"No." He rested his hands on the guitar and looked up at me. "Wasn't me, is alls I know. *Emma* was the one who was upset about my classes getting cancelled. She's the one who sent the story in to *Island Confidential*. I shoulda just kept my mouth shut and not made the report. And I should never've told Emma about it."

"Jonah, you did the right thing, reporting it. Someone had to."

"Yeah, too bad it was me. I regret it every day, believe me. Here, see if you can follow this one. On your own this time."

He set a sheet of guitar tablature in front of me. It was a simple three-chord progression. I could do this. I arranged my fingers into A-major, which required a little more stretch than the D.

"At least Fujioka's made out," Jonah said.

"Fujioka's Music and Party Supply?"

"It's where Kent was spending all the department's money."

"How infuriating." I tried to strum evenly as I talked. "In my office? I'm sitting on a yoga ball because there's no budget for office furniture. How did Kent manage it anyway? Doesn't someone have to approve university purchases?"

"I dunno. Someone put him in charge of the department budget. Okay, you sound like you know what you're doing. Let's try something a little more challenging." He pulled one of the lesson books from the stack on the washing machine and opened it to the first page.

CHAPTER TWENTY-SEVEN

"Jonah said your lesson went good yesterday." Emma picked over the cafeteria's sparse display of plastic bento boxes, apparently not finding much to her liking. The wet drywall smell from the recent construction lingered unappetizingly.

"My fingers feel like horses have been walking on them." I rubbed the fingertips of my left hand together. "I really need to toughen up. All my callous is gone."

Emma picked up a bento box and examined the contents through the clear plastic top. A fried chicken *katsu* fillet, a chunk of fried fish, and wrinkly beef strips lay across a bed of white rice.

"Please decide on something, Emma. Iker's waiting for us."

Iker Legazpi had brought in his own lunch from home. He had volunteered to sit at one of the cafeteria tables and save seats for us while Emma and I went to buy our food.

"How long we got, like forty five minutes to pick Iker's brain before we gotta go to that search committee meeting?"

"Could you please not use that horrible expression when we're about to eat lunch? This cafeteria is enough of an appetite obstacle course."

"Yah, tell me about it." Emma put the bento box back down.

"This is such a waste of our summer. I can't believe we have to start the whole search again from scratch. You know, I hate to say I told you so—"

"You *love* to say I told you so," Emma interrupted. "Eh,

how did you know that what's his name wasn't gonna pass the background check? Seriously. Tell me."

I picked up the paper napkin from my tray and dabbed my forehead. The cafeteria's aging air conditioning was no match for summer in Mahina.

"Let me think. What was it? I know. It was because he reminded me of Voltore."

"Who's that?" Emma asked. "One of your relatives?"

"A character from a Ben Jonson play. The Vulture. A greedy, immoral, dissembling liar. Why would you think it was one of my relatives?"

"You don't need to get all defensive. So whatever that superpower is of yours, Molly, try put it to good use. Fix this thing with Jonah. I'm sick of that police cruiser parked outside my house."

"Maybe they don't know what else to do. No one else seems to have a motive. Hey, where's the milk for the coffee?"

"Over here." Emma indicated a bowl full of white packets labeled *For Your Coffee*. "I don't think they put milk out in the summer when it's so warm like this. What about Kent's ex-wives? Any one of them coulda killed him."

I picked up a packet and saw a long ingredient list in typeface so small I had to squint and hold it at arm's length. I decided to take my coffee black. Meanwhile, Emma had opened up the drinks cooler and was perusing the selection.

"Emma, are you going to stand in front of that open cooler all day? Poor Iker, his lunch is going to get cold."

"Nothing's getting cold in *this* place. Wish I *could* stand here all day." She chose a poisonous-looking pink can and closed the frosty glass door.

"An *energy drink*? Emma, really?"

"Energy drinks aren't what killed Kent. Too many of these would overload you with caffeine and other stimulants, and would make your heart give out. Kent Lovely died of kidney failure. It's a totally different thing."

"I'm ready to go," I said. "Should I go pay and meet you at the table?"

"Maybe I'll just get the veggie plate. What, one bag of almonds? That's your whole lunch, Molly?"

"Nothing else looked good. Especially compared to what Iker brought. Grilled lamb and poached asparagus."

Emma raised her eyebrows in approval. Not much at our cafeteria is poached or grilled, the preferred cooking methods being either microwaving until chewy, or deep-frying in some kind of industrial lubricant.

We got in line at the single open cash register, right behind Rodge Cowper. He turned around and lit up when he saw Emma.

He grinned at Emma's raw veggie plate. "Hey Emma-Lou, you on a diet now?"

"Rodge," I said, "I wouldn't—"

Rodge archly shook a finger at Emma's veggie plate. "Don't lose too much weight now, Emma-Lou, or you'll be way too pretty to be a college professor."

Rodge paid for his *loco moco* and turned back to wink at Emma. "Catch you later, beautiful."

"Eh babooz," she called after him. "I'm married, ah?"

"That's not your ring finger, Emma." I eased her arm down.

Emma, Iker, and I had the table to ourselves. As a rule, students will only sit next to faculty if there are absolutely no other available seats.

I tore open my bag of almonds and was already eating when I noticed Iker saying grace. I put the bag down and waited until Iker had crossed himself and started eating. Iker doesn't mean to, but he always makes me feel like an inadequate Catholic.

"So." Emma popped open her energy drink. "We all agree Jonah didn't do it, right?"

"I'm sure Jonah is innocent," I agreed. I couldn't imagine the diffident Jonah Nakamura as a murderer. A fatal poisoning would be have to have been motivated by hatred. Or greed. Or at the very least, some kind of strongly held opinion.

"I mean, first degree murder takes some planning and initiative," Emma said. "That should clear my brother right away. Eh, wanna know who really had a motive? That schmuck Rodge.

Mister *Don't lose too much weight, Emma-Lou.* Right, Iker?"

"I do not know." Iker resumed nibbling on an asparagus stalk.

"Rodge Cowper?" I said. "Why would *he* want to get rid of Kent? They were best friends!"

Emma leaned forward, recklessly planting her bare forearms on the hibiscus-print oilcloth. Rings of sticky liquid glinted under the fluorescent lighting.

"Rodge wanted the teaching award. And Kent, who was just a part timer remember, beat 'im out. That hadda hurt."

"Oh, good point. Part-timers aren't usually eligible for these things."

"Yeah, not unless they're shtup—friendly with the Vice President."

Emma stole a quick glance at Iker, but he was occupied with his grilled lamb. He had packed real silverware, and was dining in the European style, keeping his fork in his left hand as he ate. Instead of trimming the fat off and just eating the meat, Iker sliced off a cross-section and popped the whole thing into his mouth, jiggly fat and all.

"I don't know about Rodge," I said. "I mean, *you* just said first degree murder requires some action and initiative. Rodge's whole purpose in life is to expend as little effort as possible. You know he barely gets assigned to committees anymore? Whenever he gets put on a committee, all he has to do is show up and tell one of his jokes, and they immediately yank him out and send him to sensitivity training."

Iker set his utensils down on his plate and gently cleared his throat.

"It is true," he said. "Since Roger Cowper received tenure, he has published not one word. And he gives only the A grades to students. In this way, he avoids the burden of marking papers, and guarantees there will be no contesting of grades. I do not wish to complain about a colleague. But when one man abuses his freedom, we are all in danger the freedom will be taken away."

"But Iker," I asked, "do you think Rodge is capable of murder?"

Iker looked up at Emma, then at me, and then returned to his meal.

"I cannot speculate on this matter of the murder. I have no knowledge of it."

"Oh, come on Iker." Emma waved a celery stalk in my direction. "That never stops Molly."

"It is not our job to chase a wild goose about this tragedy. Molly, to pursue this is...it is against the wishes of Marshall Dixon. And too, to stick our necks into a murder, it may be dangerous."

CHAPTER TWENTY-EIGHT

Emma narrowed her eyes at Iker. Iker continued to eat, avoiding her glare.

"My brother is a *murder* suspect, Iker. Molly and me were hoping you could help us figure out how to clear him. Are you saying you don't wanna get involved?"

Iker's round cheeks flushed. He set down his fork and knife and fixed his gaze on the remaining portion of lamb and asparagus.

"Marshall Dixon told us we must cease to investigate," he said quietly. "She did not wish us to look further."

"Dixon didn't say she was actively *against* our looking into it," I said, with more certainty than I felt. "She just seemed to think there wasn't enough time. Iker, this isn't just an accounting problem anymore."

Seeing his hurt expression I quickly reached over to pat his plump hand. "Sorry, I didn't mean to say 'just' an accounting problem. What I'm trying to say is, the stakes are higher now. Someone *died.* And Emma's brother is in the middle of it."

"Then this is for the policemen," Iker said. "It is their job, not ours. I think we should gracefully bow off. Yes. We should leave this alone. I am very decided on this. Marshall Dixon told me she was satisfied with the draft report. Even though..." Iker's brow crinkled. He was wavering. "The report of the finances, it is still very incomplete."

"You're right, Iker," I said gently. "It *is* incomplete. I'm not sure we did the best job we could. Are you?"

"She has a point, Iker."

Iker continued to eat quietly, not taking the bait.

Emma blew out a weary sigh.

"So Molly, what do you have? Gimme some possibilities."

"Let's see. Kent's involved in some financial shenanigans, Jonah reports him, Kent is bumped off. Obviously not coincidence. What if Kent had a co-conspirator who killed him to keep him quiet? That would put Jonah in the clear, wouldn't it? Jonah wouldn't blow the whistle if he were involved himself."

"*Jonah* wouldn't," Emma said, "but a *clever* person might."

"Ah, to deflect suspicion. Good point. Okay, but if you're going to get back at someone by reporting them to administration, why murder them, too? It seems like overkill, pardon the expression."

"Because maybe Kent could've said, 'Oh, you're gonna report me? I'm gonna report you right back.' And *then* Jonah had to kill him to keep him quiet."

"Emma, you're making a really persuasive case for Jonah's guilt."

"I been thinking about it from the prosecutor's point of view," Emma said. "I mean, you and me know Jonah personally. But if you just look at the cold facts, it looks bad for Jonah."

We both looked at Iker. Iker continued to eat quietly, eyes lowered to his plate.

"So what do we do now?" Emma asked.

"Iker is right," I said carefully. "I don't think it's a good idea to get mixed up in a *murder* investigation and get in the way of the police. But perhaps if we were to finish up our *financial* investigation, the one Iker and I were supposed to be working on, we might find something helpful in the course of our inquiry. Iker, what do you think? Shouldn't we finish the report that we started?"

Iker opened his mouth to speak, and then closed it. Two competing versions of the Right and Proper Thing were battling in his mind.

"Are you okay with continuing the investigation into purchases on campus?" I asked Emma.

"Course. Why wouldn't I be?"

"No reason."

Iker had mentioned some irregularities in the Biology Department. Of course, it didn't necessarily mean Emma was involved. Biology is a big department.

"I'm sick of sitting around being spied on," Emma said. "Someone needs to give this thing a kick in the *'okole* an' get it moving in the right direction."

Finally Iker said, "Yes. You are right. We must not do a halfway job."

I felt like jumping up and high-fiving Emma on the spot, but I didn't want to startle Iker into reconsidering.

"Good," I said. "Now. Something's been bothering me. When Marshall Dixon got that report from Jonah, his account pointed right to Kent and the Music Department, but when she turned the investigation over to you, Iker, she didn't show you the original report. And she didn't even mention the music department. It was like she wanted you to waste your time chasing this thing across the entire College of Arts and Sciences."

"Dr. Dixon was not necessarily concealing something," Iker said. "Perhaps she did not wish to prejudice us. She wished for us to find our own results."

"Dixon was sure hiding *something*," Emma said.

"Emma, why do you say this?"

"Where are we on getting copies of the purchase orders?" I interrupted. I didn't want the conversation to go to that furtive kiss that Emma and I had witnessed. Maybe I wanted to protect Iker's innocence. Or Dixon's honor. Or my lunch. "Iker, you didn't cancel the document requests already, did you?"

"Yes," Iker said. "I did as Marshall Dixon asked, and cancelled the request for copies of the purchase orders."

Emma and I both groaned.

"I know that our business office is very busy," Iker continued, "so I marked the cancellation request as the lowest priority."

"That was thoughtful of you," I said, trying to hide my disappointment.

"The result is this. By that time the cancellation is processed, the original request will be already completed."

Emma lit up. "Really?"

I thought she was going to hug him.

"Yes. The original request was highest priority. I did not wish to follow with still another high priority request when it was not needed."

"Iker," I exclaimed, "You're a genius!"

A group of students at a nearby table stopped their conversation and looked over at us.

"So," I continued quietly, "we should be—I mean *you* should be—getting copies of the purchase orders before your cancellation goes through. Is there anything else we can do while we're waiting?"

"We should probably look around Jonah and Kent's office," Emma said.

"Are we allowed to go in there? Jonah's not officially an employee now that his classes were cancelled."

"But I bet he never got around to returning the key."

Emma pulled out her phone and dialed.

"Eh, Dummy," she said. "You still get the key to your office on campus?"

She waited, drumming her fingers.

"Thought so. Okay. You gonna be home in later on? Yah. See ya then."

She disconnected. "We'll go back to my house right after our meeting."

"Sounds perfect," I said.

Iker looked worried, but didn't object.

Chapter Twenty-Nine

Emma and I were passing the old Humanities building when Pat Flanagan fell into step behind us.

"Pat, where did *you* come from?" I wondered if that sounded too hostile. "I mean, what a nice surprise to see you." Now that sounded overly friendly. Why do I even bother talking to people? I should just clam up and let everyone assume I'm enigmatic and wise.

"My comp class just got out." He inclined his head toward the dilapidated Humanities building.

"They are not having a class in that building." Emma exclaimed. "Are they for real? Didn't they have to move everyone out to fix the damage?"

"It's even worse than the old Health building," I agreed. "At least the Health building didn't almost crack in half during the earthquake."

The two-story Humanities building had not been renovated since the 1950s. Rust had recolored most of the formerly-green metal roof. Arched, mullioned windows with mold-speckled white jambs stood out against solid gray siding. Much of the glass had been replaced by plywood, and the front entrance was boarded up.

Pat shrugged. "They told us it was structurally sound and not to worry about it."

"It's too bad," I said. "It could be beautiful if they renovated it. I'll take this any day over those brutalist 1970s concrete cellblocks."

"No way is that structurally sound," Emma said. "That thing's full of termites. It needs to be tented yesterday."

"After today's class, getting crushed in a building collapse would be a relief."

"I'm sorry to hear that," I said. "Care to share?"

"These kids somehow got the idea that they're perfect writers," Pat said. "I can't tell them anything. Why do they think they placed into Bonehead Writing to begin with?"

"I don't think you're supposed to call it 'bonehead' writing," I said.

"Sorry, remedial."

"Developmental," Emma said. "We're not allowed to say remedial."

"I don't think we can say 'developmental' anymore either," I said. "I think it's 'tutorial' now."

"Eh, speaking of teaching headaches," Emma said. "Molly, what's going on with your crazy student?"

"You can't say 'developmental'," Pat said, "but you can say 'crazy'?"

"No, we are not supposed to say 'crazy.' Emma. Anyway, no, Bret hasn't been back to class. I'm relieved for myself and my other students, but a little worried about him."

"What was this about?" Pat asked.

"Molly got this ticking time bomb who sits in the back row, and he pulled out a shark tooth club in class. We gotta fill you in on that whole *mishegas*. Over drinks sometime."

"Here we are." Pat held the classroom door open for Emma and me. "Did you say *mishegas*?"

"She got her PhD at Cornell," I said.

Linda was busy down in the front of the classroom, setting up the projector. Betty Jackson was sitting near the back. Betty waved us over and we made our way up to join her. She stood and embraced Pat.

"So the Humanities building made it through another day?" she asked.

Before Pat could answer, Linda cleared her throat to start the meeting and we took our seats. Emma raised her hand.

"Don't we have to wait for Bob Wilson?"

"Bob has decided to apply for the position. So he's stepped down from this search committee."

"Wish *I'd* thought of that," Emma muttered.

"Today we'll be meeting the first of our candidates in person," Linda said. "While we're waiting for him to arrive, I'd like to review our procedural guidelines."

Linda distributed several trees' worth of printouts, and then reiterated our HR procedures. The room was dim, and the temperature and humidity were both well into the 80s. It's hard for me to stay awake after lunch in any case, and with the ambient conditions approximating a womb, I didn't stand a chance.

"...see our student *evals*?"

Emma's loud voice knocked me out of dreamland.

"What? What about student evals?" I blinked and looked around. Fortunately the candidate hadn't arrived yet, so at least I hadn't been asleep long, nor had I dozed off in front of a stranger.

"Several of us in the Psychology Department have significant concerns about our current evaluation methods," Betty Jackson said. "The instrument we are using is neither valid nor reliable. The way it's administered is inconsistent. We have two excellent psychometricians in our department, but their efforts have never—"

"Then you'll be happy to know we're phasing out our student evaluations of teaching," Linda interrupted.

"We are?" Emma said.

"We are?" Betty echoed.

"We're going to transition to using the online review sites instead."

Emma placed her elbows on the desk, her hands clutching her face.

"We're gonna decide peoples' promotion and tenure cases based off a stupid website?"

"No, this is very scientific," Linda said. "This method takes advantage of the wisdom of crowds. It's called crowdsurfing."

"Do you mean crowd*sourcing*?" I asked.

Pat raised his hand. "If this is the online review site I'm thinking of, what's to stop any of us from going online and leaving good reviews for our friends, and bad ones for our enemies?"

"We are confident this is a very forward-thinking modality. This new generation is digitally native." Her answer made so little sense to me I wondered whether Pat's question had tripped a flaw in Linda's programming. I imagined her repeating "Does not compute," as smoke curled out of her ears.

"Our chancellor is one hundred and ten percent behind this innovation," Linda continued. "And here's our candidate now."

Linda's young sidekick from the faculty retreat had entered the classroom through the lower door in the company of a thin, sour-looking man.

"Doctor Kobelt, we have your presentation set up. Thank you, Javier. Please come back in forty five minutes to escort the candidate to the student forum."

"They're having a student forum in the summer?" Emma whispered to me. "They think students are gonna show up in the summer to listen to some candidate for associate vice-deanlet of handholding and nose wiping?"

"Don't criticize," I whispered back. "Or they'll put you in charge of some committee to investigate it."

"Good point." Emma and I both put on our Paying Attention faces. I heard Pat clacking away on his laptop.

"What's your Spidey Sense say about this one?" Emma whispered.

"He hasn't said anything yet."

"He looks like an insect," Emma persisted.

"Let's hear what he has to say."

Dr. Gunnar Kobelt began his talk by describing some promising campus sustainability projects in which he'd been involved. He then digressed into general observations about universities and leadership and society, and I started to drift off again. I wished I'd brought a laptop to take notes, as Pat Flanagan was doing. At least the effort of typing might help me to stay awake.

Betty Jackson raised her hand.

"How would you describe your management style?" she asked.

"Ah, young lady. You have heard of the Myers Briggs personality types?"

"Yes I have." Betty Jackson is a professor of social psychology.

"I have the INTJ personality type," said Dr. Kobelt. "That is the rarest of the sixteen types. It means that I am very logical. This is extremely annoying to my wife, because it means I win every argument. You can imagine she does not like it."

The candidate went on to describe his "open door" management style and his appreciation for diverse perspectives. This was presumably to distinguish himself from all those other job candidates out there who are trying to impress search committees with their autocratic management style and their hatred of diversity.

Pat Flanagan kept typing.

Emma raised her hand.

"How come you applied for this job?" she asked. "Why do you want to leave your current position and come to Mahina State?"

"I like to work with people who are smarter than I am. Unfortunately, in my current position I don't get the opportunity very often." He chuckled, although no one else did. "That's a complement to *you* fine folks."

The classroom door cracked open, and I could see Linda's sidekick, Javier, peeking through. Up in the front row, Linda checked her wrist.

"Well, it looks like we're already a little over time on Dr. Kobelt's talk, so that's all the questions we have time for. We need to get to our next meeting."

As we were packing up to leave, Emma said, "Hey Betty, you ever heard of the Myers Briggs? Geez, even *I've* heard of it. What a pompous jackass."

"As long as he's sharing the results of his personality tests," Betty said, "I'd love to see how he scores on narcissism. Oh, Emma, how is Jonah? How are *you*?"

"Police car's still parked outside my house," Emma said. "I

don't know what they think they're gonna see."

"Yeah, Emma's been doing a *great* job deflecting suspicion," I said. "She told the police if she wanted to kill someone she'd slip antifreeze into their energy drink."

"Emma, are you *trying* to get arrested?" Pat asked.

Betty laughed. "Well, you're sure not acting like someone who has a guilty conscience. Listen kids, I have to go. My class starts in seven minutes."

"What're you teaching?" Emma asked.

"Stats."

"Aw, shoot," Emma sympathized.

"Yeah. Summer stats class is not a happy place. I have a lot of repeat customers."

"Don't you get in trouble when you fail students?" I asked.

"Sure, every time I record a D or an F, Linda comes by to harass me about it," Betty said. "But I have tenure. So let the Student Retention Office huff and puff and try to blow my house down. I do my job, and I have a clear conscience."

"That can't be what the Foundation was hoping for when they gave us the grant," I said. "Don't they realize the Student Retention Office is just arm-twisting the faculty to pass everyone?"

"Yeah. I told Molly, she should report them to the Foundation."

"Easy for you to say, Emma," Pat said. "You know what happens to whistleblowers. Molly, if you do report the SRO, don't do it from your own computer, and don't log on to any of your accounts."

"Pat's right," Betty called back as she and Pat exited the classroom. "Look out for yourself, Molly. It's a lot harder to do the right thing when you're unemployed."

"Betty's the one who should've gotten the teaching award," I said to Emma, when Betty and Pat had gone.

"She said it was nice to be nominated but she was actually relieved she didn't get it. She already gets put on so many different committees and panels, she said if she got this teaching award, she'd end up as a full-time role model, and she'd never be able to get any work done."

"Do you think they're serious about using the website to evaluate us?" I asked.

"I heard it on *Campus Spotlight* this morning when I was driving to work," Emma said. "But I thought it was one of their jokes!"

"What's *Campus Spotlight?*"

"*Campus Spotlight* is the daily feature on the local radio—oh, I forgot, you only ever listen to NPR."

"Not true," I protested. "Sometimes I listen to the classic rock station. When they're playing 80s music."

As Emma gathered her papers together I noticed something that looked like a purchase order.

"Hey Emma, what's that for? Why does it have the biohazard symbol? Is it dangerous?"

Emma knocked my hand away and tucked the paper away quickly.

"It's nothing. Just some stuff for my lab. So, ready?"

"Are we going to your house now?"

"Yeah. Now's a good time. Jonah's gonna be at home. Hey Molly, you know I never butt into your private business, yah?"

"What? Are you kidding me?"

"Unless I have a really good reason. So listen. Now that you're done with Stephen, an' you're free and single, you know who else is single?"

I shrugged. "Priests? Hermits? Guys on death row?"

"Nah. Jonah."

"Emma, you can't be—I mean, Jonah is very nice, but I'm *perfectly* happy just being his guitar student for now. You know how it is. I'm still not over Stephen."

Stephen had nothing to do with it, but I was trying to be tactful. Attempting to make conversation with Jonah Nakamura was hard enough. I couldn't imagine what kind of effort it would take to keep an actual relationship going. Actually, yes I could imagine it. Jonah would probably be fine with having a relationship, as long as I did all the heavy lifting and he was allowed to sit around and play guitar all day. No thank you.

"How could you not be over Stephen?" Emma demanded.

"He's a selfish jerk. He stood you up on your birthday, and never apologized. And was probably two-timing you the whole time with Stage Manager Barbie from the theater."

"You really want Jonah out of your house so badly?"

Emma sighed. "Yoshi's been *kvetching* about it nonstop."

"So if Jonah were out of the house, you're saying Yoshi would be *happy*?"

"Nah, probably not. If Jonah left, Yoshi would just find something else to complain about. Anyway, let's go get Iker, and then we can go back to my house."

"Maybe we should've asked Pat if he wanted to come along. He used to be a reporter. He might know what to look for."

"Don't be stupid," Emma said. "We hardly know him."

She was right. We weren't really supposed to be poking around in Kent Lovely's murder to begin with. It probably wouldn't be the smartest move to start recruiting accomplices.

CHAPTER THIRTY

We arrived at Emma's house to find Jonah on the living room couch, playing his guitar. He had his eyes closed, and was picking out a lightning-fast lead over a recorded rhythm section. It wasn't exactly pleasant to listen to. To me, extended lead guitar solos are like the directors' cuts of music, self-indulgent and interesting to no one except the artist—but I had to admire his skill.

Emma went to the sound system and punched the power button, cutting out the recorded music. Jonah played a few more notes before he realized the music was gone, and opened his eyes.

"So Yoshi's out somewhere?" Emma said. "'Cause if he was here, you wouldn't be making all this racket, ah?"

Jonah shrugged and resumed playing.

"You ready? We gonna go take a look around your office, see what we can find."

"Fine with me," he said, still noodling quietly on the guitar.

"We drove by your building on the way here," I said. "There isn't police tape on the door or anything, so I thought it might be okay for us to go in."

"For the purpose of our financial investigation," Iker added.

"Guess so," Jonah said. "Oh. This just came in the mail."

Jonah set his guitar aside, leaned forward, and pulled a piece of paper from the back pocket of his jeans.

"Check it out."

He started to hand the letter to me, but Emma grabbed it away before I could see it. Her mouth fell open as she read. She sank into a chair.

"Nah. They want *you* to teach Kent Lovely's classes in the fall?"
Jonah shrugged.

"Sure didn't see *that* coming," Emma said.

"So it wasn't retaliation," I said.

"Guess not." Jonah picked his guitar back up and played a
funky bass line.

"Emma was absolutely convinced there was a conspiracy to get
back at you for making that report about Kent," I said. "Emma
was in my office for a good hour, talking about it."

"Not."

"Yes, you were. You made me late for class."

"Not my fault you walk so slow."

"But now it turns out, it wasn't personal after all," I said.

"I never said it was personal," Emma declared. "For it to be
personal, they'd have to think of him as a *person*. Iker, sit down.
You're making me nervous standing there."

Iker obeyed, sinking quietly into a chair.

"What does it say?" I asked. "Can I see?"

Emma handed me the letter.

"Dear Mr./Ms. Nakamura, we are pleased to offer you an
appointment as an adjunct member of the faculty in the College
of Arts and Sciences, Department of Music. Please note this
appointment is for the Fall semester only and is not a guarantee
of future appointments. This offer is contingent upon sufficient
enrollment, satisfactory teaching evaluations, and continued
course offerings. Upon acceptance of the offer, please contact
the Department of Human Resources to schedule drug testing.
This offer is also contingent upon the successful completion of a
criminal background check."

Emma reached down and shoved Jonah's shoulder. "Are you
gonna do it?"

"Nah."

"'Course not. Why take a perfectly good job offer when you can
sit around the house all day instead? Eh dummy, you gotta play
while we're talking?"

Jonah's bouncy baseline squelched into a sour note and died away.

"Nah, I get it," Emma said. "You'd never pass the drug test. Actually with the new testing requirement, I don't know *who* they think they're gonna get to teach guitar."

"It's not 'cause the *drug testing*, Emma." Jonah sat up straighter. "I don't teach computer music, that's why."

Emma and Jonah glared at each other. Iker quietly examined his folded hands.

"Um," I said, "Jonah? Do you still have the key to your office?"

"Yeah, I do," Jonah sighed. "You guys can go look around. Don't get caught."

"Come with us," Emma commanded.

"Aw, man," Jonah groaned, but he complied, and all four of us piled into Emma's car.

Emma pulled into a spot shaded by a silvery-leafed kukui tree. We waited in her car until the rain subsided, then crossed the lower parking lot to the prefab buildings that housed Music and Fine Arts. Water vapor curled up from the hot asphalt and swirled around our ankles as we walked.

The portables had been installed decades earlier as a temporary solution for a rapidly growing campus. Subsequent budget cuts and our legislature's increasing focus on "useful" degrees had put the kibosh on plans for a permanent music building, so the "temporary" structures had become permanent. The neglected Music portables have weathered so hard they now attract a particular type of photographer, the kind who works exclusively in black and white and specializes in images of decay.

I increased my pace and pulled up next to Jonah.

"Did you ever talk to Kent about his behavior?" I asked. "I mean, before you made the report?"

"Yeah. He blew me off."

"Then you made the report?"

"Nah, I followed up with email."

"That was very wise, Jonah." Iker puffed as he struggled to keep up with Emma and Jonah. Jonah has long legs, but Emma doesn't, so I'm not sure why she has to walk so fast. She'd probably claim that walking quickly was a habit she picked up in New York, and then she'd remind everyone once again that she got her PhD at Cornell.

"Then there is a paper trail," Iker said. "It is not literally paper in this case, of course."

"So did Kent respond to your email?" I asked.

"Nah. Just an autoreply. Check this out."

Jonah pulled a cell phone out of his back pocket and tapped on the screen. Emma grabbed the phone from Jonah's hand.

"Thank you for your email," Emma read. "*Sadly, it will be deleted.*"

"To delete a message so thoughtlessly?" Iker said. "That is extremely impolite."

"And completely in character for Kent," I added.

"Wait, there's more. He says, *To regain sanity, I am taking a break from email until August 31. If still relevant, please email me again after that date.*"

"Even from beyond the grave Kent manages to be infuriating," I said. "Quite an accomplishment."

"He's got *chutzpah* for sure." Emma handed Jonah's phone back to him. "Jonah, Kent was an idiot. You should teach his dumb classes and take the money. No way you could do any worse than him."

"Emma, I told you. I don't know anything about computer music. It'd be so much prep just to teach a couple classes, it wouldn't even be worth it. Oh, weird. His car's still here."

Kent's red convertible was parked across two spaces, a can of energy drink still in the cup holder. The car had a single bumper sticker, from a local martial arts studio. A white karate *gi* was crumpled on the back seat, and miniature nunchucks dangled from the rear view mirror.

"Of *course* that would be Kent's car," I said.

"It practically screams Insecure White Guy," Emma added.

"If his automobile is here," Iker asked, "how did he travel to the Lehua Inn for the retreat?"

"Probably carpooled with Rodge," I said quickly.

"Rodge rides a motorcycle," Jonah pointed out. "Ever since his last DUI."

"That's right," Emma exclaimed. "You guys remember when it was in the police blotter? In the *County Courier?* Yah, it was one proud day for Mahina State. "

"So if Rodge Cowper is riding the motorcycle," Iker said, "how did Kent Lovely travel to the retreat?"

"Probably rode with Rodge on his motorcycle," Emma said.

"I agree, Emma." I nodded vigorously. "That sounds like the most likely explanation. Rode in with Rodge."

"Feel the wind in your hair," Emma said. "Right?"

"Plus, it's easier to find parking for a motorcycle, compared to a car."

I thought it was far more likely Kent had gotten a ride over with Marshall Dixon. I was sure that Emma was thinking the same thing.

"But it was raining on that day," Iker said, "It was not a good day to drive a motorcycle."

"So they gonna let Kent's car sit here taking up two spaces until it rots?"

I mentally applauded Emma for changing the subject so deftly. "With parking on campus so scarce," I added.

Jonah gave Emma and me a funny look, then resumed walking with his eyes fixed on the ground, hands in his jeans pockets. He could tell that we were holding something back, but I didn't want to tell Jonah and Iker about Marshall Dixon's indiscretion. And neither did Emma, obviously. It would be an embarrassing distraction, and I didn't see how telling the guys about it would help to solve Kent's murder.

"I believe that such property as this automobile is confiscated as a rule," Iker said, "and then it will appear at the auction of Central Supply."

"Well that car'll be a great deal for someone," I said.

"Sure," Emma agreed. "Someone who wants to drive around looking like a huge *putz.*"

We approached the dilapidated portable building and stood aside to let Jonah unlock the door and let us in. He lingered for a moment, then turned to leave.

"Where are you going?" Emma demanded. Jonah shook his head and walked off.

"You're not coming in?" I called after him.

"Nah," he called back. "You guys have fun."

"How is he going to get home?" I asked Emma.

"Probably hitchhike. Or just walk back."

"Doesn't he want to wait for us?"

"Nah. Look, the main road's right out there."

"Is it safe?" I asked.

"Oh yah. He'll be fine."

CHAPTER THIRTY-ONE

The office Kent and Jonah had shared was even gloomier than mine. As in all the faculty offices, half the light tubes had been removed. The only daylight came from a single, small window, positioned high on the wall, under a light-blocking exterior eave. The walls were dark, covered with faux paneling, split and splintered over the years. The small space was chockablock with computers and cables and keyboards, both the computer and the music kind.

"Kent and Jonah didn't share a single desk, did they?" I asked Emma. "Why is there only one?"

"There is the small one in the corner." Iker pointed out. The tiny desk was buried under piles of sound cards, synths, cables, and several still-sealed boxes. Kent had claimed the entire space.

"I knew Kent was an inconsiderate schmuck," Emma said. "But this... It's like some creepy nature show dominance display. Like he was marking his territory, leaving his junk everywhere."

"I'm so glad I don't have to share an office." I knocked on the wall, and got a flimsy "pock, pock" sound. There was no drywall underneath. The paneling had been installed over bare studs. The shortcut probably violated even the minimal building codes of the time.

"Me, too," Emma agreed. "Sucks to be a part-timer, ah?"

"Wow, nice chairs, though." I ran my hand over the back of one of the ergonomic chairs that faced the main desk. The black mesh looked gossamer light, but felt slick and solid. "Not bad for

139

a university without a *furniture budget*."

Iker sat down in the other chair, the one I wasn't fondling, and pulled a binder out of his briefcase.

"Emma, have you been inside this office before?" I asked.

"Nah." Emma went back behind the big desk and plopped down into what had apparently been Kent's seat, a cushioned leather throne with a high back. "Even Jonah didn't spend a lotta time here. Can't blame 'im."

"If Iker and I had seen this earlier," I said, "we would have known exactly where to find the financial discrepancies. This is even more of a smoking gun than Kent's portable sound system."

"I wonder what they're gonna do with this chair now. Now that Kent's dead." Emma regally surveyed the office, her head so far below the top of the chair she looked like a child emperor.

"It appears Kent did not buy these furnitures with his private funds," Iker examined his binder, which was open on his lap. He ran his finger down a dense row of numbers on the printout. "These two ergonomic chairs have been purchased against the department budget. The large chair behind the desk, however, I cannot find a record."

"It must be in there somewhere," Emma said. "No way that *gonif* paid for this leather chair himself. Aren't there keywords you can search for?"

"That's a paper printout, Emma, you can't search—Did you just say *gonif*? Never mind, I know. Cornell."

"It is not so simple," Iker said. "The merchandise description is often not straightforward. Purchases can be bundled in a special transaction. I purchase four chairs, I receive the table for no additional charge. It is like that."

"I can imagine how frustrating this must have been for Jonah," I said. "No wonder he didn't want to come in with us."

"Right? I mean, how much to you think *this* thing cost, all soft leather—"

Emma caressed the side of the chair and accidentally hit a button. The chair began to undulate around her. She yelped and jumped to a standing position.

"So it's true," I said. "He did have a massage chair,"

"What the—" Emma lowered herself cautiously into the still-churning chair.

"Kent Lovely bought himself a *massage chair*. And I just had to buy myself a yoga ball to sit on because we supposedly don't have a *furniture budget*."

"Molly," Iker said "Such an anger is corrosive to the spirit. Kent Lovely is dead. You cannot kill him again."

"What, me? I'm not angry. How ridiculous."

"You know what Kent would say, Molly. *Winners find a way.* Oooooh. Hey, this isn't bad." Emma sank back into the chair and let it knead her head.

"I think it's not adjusted properly for your height," I said. "Can I try? I'm taller."

"Just a sec," Emma sighed, her eyelids at half-mast. "Settle down, Molly. You'll get your turn."

I stood up and prowled around the office. Iker studied his printouts and Emma luxuriated in the massage chair. A bright red binder on a shelf caught my eye. I pulled it down and examined the spine. On it, someone had written SOS with a black Sharpie.

"SOS." I opened the binder and leafed through it. "Why do they have this here? Is this building in the tsunami zone, or—oh, wait. *Sounds of Seduction?* What the—"

Emma switched the chair off, leaned over the desk and reached her short arms toward me for the binder.

"What?" I said. "Use your words."

"Gimme."

"Fine. Enjoy." I slid the binder over to her. She opened it and started reading. Her expression quickly changed from curiosity to disgust.

"Music scientifically designed to maximize the—Ew! The *female's* accelerating heart rate? Who uses female as a *noun*? It's like he's talking about chimpanzees or prairie voles, not human beings. Ooh, look. Hey, you guys wanna hear Kent's seductive original compositions?"

"No," I said.

Iker continued leafing silently through his paperwork.

"Looks like he has everything on his computer." Emma mashed the keys on the keyboard and then jiggled the mouse to bring the computer to life.

"What do you think his password is?" She squinted at the screen.

I walked around to join her behind Kent's desk.

"May I sit in the chair?"

"Eh, try wait, ah? So impatient, you. How about the name of the energy drink he was always drinking?"

She tried typing it in, with no success.

"Did he have any pets?" I asked.

"How should I know?"

"Oh, wait, I know." I whispered into her ear. Emma typed in "Marshall." It worked.

Emma rooted around until she found the file and selected it. A digital audio workstation started up and filled the screen.

"Shoot," Emma said. "Now what?"

"Let me try." I found the transport controls and pressed "play." Cheesy music blasted from the computer speakers, heavy on the synthesized saxophone.

"What *is* this?" Emma stared at the screen incredulously. "So junk, this music."

"There's only so much a computer can do," I said. "All of the tracks are automatically set to the same beats per minute, but it can still sound wrong if the alignment is off. I think that's what's going on here. In fact, look. See this track? How the peaks aren't lined up with the gridlines? It's going to make it sound a little jarring. And the other reason this sounds so awful is even though everything's in the same key and at the same tempo, he's piled on way too many tracks."

"I get the idea, Molly."

"What are you saying? Have you heard enough?"

"Yes. Make it stop."

I pressed the "pause" button and then closed out the program.

"Well that was horrible," I said.

"Sounds of Seduction?" Emma smacked the side of the chair to shut off the massage action. "He shoulda sold it to the government and called it 'Enhanced Interrogation.' My poor brother."

"May I try the chair now?" I asked.

"I'm not done here." She leaned forward and started yanking open desk drawers.

"What's in there?"

"More cables and computer stuff. Extra cans of energy drink. Oh, look, a book."

Emma reached down and pulled up a thick paperback book with an orange cover.

"Looks like one of those self-help books. *The Twenty Minute Workday*."

"Sounds about right. Because putting in an honest day's work is for suckers."

"But stealing from your job and *schtupping* your way to the teaching award?"

"Exactly," I said, "in Kent's moral universe, *that's* awesome, apparently."

I glanced over at Iker. He was still studying the printouts.

"Anything interesting in there, Iker?"

"I do not yet know," Iker said. "This requires further study."

Emma pulled open a drawer and pulled out a black object, covered with little knobs.

"What's this thing?" she asked.

"No way," I exclaimed. "Can I see it?"

Emma handed it to me. It was black, about the size of a cafeteria tray. I ran my fingers over the knobs. It had the heft of quality.

"Molly, quit making out with that thing. What is it anyways?"

"It's a synthesizer," I said. "This model probably cost Kent two months' salary. I can't believe he left it lying around his office."

Emma grabbed it from me and turned it upside down.

"It doesn't have any piano keys on it or nothing. How do you play it?"

"You connect it to the computer. See all these inputs back here? The computer sends it a signal that tells it which sound

143

to make and what notes to play. Or it can generate or process sounds itself."

"Great. I can't even buy slide covers and that schmuck is up to his neck in expensive *tchotchke*s. Man, *I'd* sure like to have some glistening new equipment in my lab!"

I lifted the synthesizer out of Emma's hands and gently set it back down on the desk.

"Gleaming," I said. "Not glistening."

"Same thing."

"No, it is not the same thing. When you go to the hospital to have an operation? And you walk into the operating room, and see the surgeon's tools lying there, ready for you? You want them to be *gleaming*. Not *glistening*."

"Aw, that's gross."

"Exactly my point."

"So Kent was ripping off the university and buying himself massage chairs and fancy toys. Case closed. QED, ipso facto, expialadocious. Right, Iker?"

"Many of these items match the purchase records, as they should," Iker said. "And even if there is no record, then they may have been the private property of Kent Lovely. The purchases may show poor judgment, but we must be very circumspect with accusations of fraud."

"Shoot," Emma said. "That's disappointing."

"But there may still be fraud," Iker continued. "We cannot rule out the possibility. Some of the purchases appear to have strange amounts and missing information. And there are also many purchases here of items I do not see in this office."

"Could Kent have been selling equipment and keeping the money?" I asked Iker.

"But who was buying it?" Emma interrupted. "If we could find out, maybe we could figure out who the murderer is."

"Emma," Iker said gently, "to solve a murder is not our *kuleana*, as you say. We are here to examine the fraud only."

Emma sighed and pushed herself up from the massage chair.

"So are we done here?" Emma asked. "I'm so ready to get out

of this little spider hole."

I was ready to follow Emma out, resigned to not getting my turn in the massage chair. Then I noticed something.

"Look behind you," I said. "The wall calendar."

CHAPTER THIRTY-TWO

The calendar hung on the paneled wall behind Kent's desk, above Emma's head. It was about two by three feet, emblazoned with the logo of a furniture distributor.

"Something's written in for the day of the retreat," I said. "I can't read it from here."

Emma climbed up onto the seat of Kent's massage chair and leaned in to examine the calendar. Iker stayed seated, holding the binder open on his lap. I saw columns of numbers that I couldn't begin to decipher.

"Someone drew two little hearts here," Emma said. "One has the number twelve written inside, and the other has the number thirteen."

"Adorable. Does that mean anything to anyone?"

Emma shook her head no.

"Thirteen is said to be bad luck," Iker said.

"Sure was for him." Emma said.

Iker winced and eased the binder shut. "Perhaps it is time for us to leave this place."

"I just want to check one more thing." I picked up the receiver on Kent's desk phone and pressed the speaker button. The sound of the dial tone filled the office. Then I pressed the redial button.

"Hi, this is Linda," said Kent's phone, in Linda Wilson's voice. "Leave a message and I'll get right back to you. Have a great day."

"Redial." Emma climbed down from the massage chair. "Good

idea. See, clever you, Molly. I'm surprised it wasn't Vice President da kine."

Iker quietly tucked the binder into his satchel. If he knew what Emma was hinting at, he gave no sign of it.

"So Kent's last call was to the Student Retention Office," I said. "Do you think this was about the teaching award, which we now know was fixed in advance?"

"It wasn't Linda's office message."

"Emma, how do you know?"

"I been in the doghouse with the Student Retention Office enough times. I *know* Linda's office message. And that's not it. Must be her personal phone."

"Iker," I asked, "did we ever get purchase records from the Student Retention Office? Kent Lovely's last phone call was to Linda Wilson's personal number. It's worth looking into, don't you think?"

"I do not have the records of the Student Retention Office," Iker said. "Only Arts and Sciences was included in the investigation."

"Kent must have had an accomplice. The scale of this—"

"Totally," Emma interrupted. "No way was Kent smart enough to figure out how to cheat the system all by himself. Oh man, if the Student Retention Office is in on this, we can take 'em *down*."

"It is not our place to take someone down." Iker looked shocked.

"No, of course not." I shot Emma a stern look. "But we should follow the evidence. Don't you agree, Iker?"

"I do not wish to involve myself in that which is not my business," Iker said.

"No, no, neither do I." This provoked an extravagant eye roll from Emma. "But we can't do a complete investigation without all of the information. I think if *you* asked Marshall Dixon for the Student Retention Office's records, she might consider it."

I knew it was hopeless for me to try asking Dixon directly. For some reason, Marshall Dixon seemed to think I was a loose cannon.

"I do not believe Marshall Dixon would welcome such a request." Iker's round face was gloomy. "As you heard, she prefers us to back away."

"Well, maybe we shouldn't approach her right away. She's busy working on Skip Kojima for that big donation, and she probably doesn't want to be bothered."

"I'm telling you," Emma said. "You guys should interrogate Rodge Cowper."

"You think Rodge knows how to poison someone?" I asked.

"Pfft. Poisoning's not too hard. Now we gotta wipe this place down or what?"

"Of course not. We're not criminals." As I replaced Kent's red binder on the shelf, I discreetly rubbed it with my sleeve. Just in case anyone looked for fingerprints.

CHAPTER THIRTY-THREE

Sprezzatura was Mahina's finest dining establishment, the only restaurant in town with white tablecloths. This was where I had hoped Stephen would take me for my birthday. Scents of fresh basil and crushed garlic wafted from the kitchen. A decent Saturday-night crowd filled the tables and clustered in the small area by the hostess station.

Unfortunately, I wasn't on any kind of romantic date, although to the untrained eye it might have looked like one. I was sitting across the table from Emma's brother Jonah, and both of us were waiting for Emma to show up. Jonah was appropriately dressed, which I assumed was Emma's doing. Instead of a laundry-beaten t-shirt, he wore a pressed aloha shirt in an inoffensive navy and white hibiscus print. His lank hair was combed back and tucked behind his ears, and he (or Emma) had shaved off his wispy goatee.

This dinner had been Emma's idea. Jonah had been close-mouthed on the subject of Kent Lovely, insisting he wanted to forget about the whole thing. Emma thought Jonah might be forthcoming if we plied him with food and drink. At the time she'd suggested it, Emma's plan seemed sound. I'd even suggested inviting Iker Legazpi along, but Emma vetoed the idea. She'd pointed out, correctly, that our gentle colleague would not wish to be present at anything that resembled an interrogation. Plus, Iker was being a bit of a stickler about how we technically weren't supposed to be investigating any murders.

Now, sitting here with Jonah, I wondered how much we'd really be able to pry out of him. Jonah and I had sat down, exchanged a few words about guitar practice, and then run out of conversation.

I sipped my ice water and watched as Jonah wordlessly annihilated the contents of the breadbasket.

We really should have invited Pat Flanagan, I thought. He had been a crime reporter, and would know exactly what questions to ask. But Emma had countered with the fact we didn't know Pat well. Furthermore, Pat had showed up at the retreat when he wasn't even required to, so how did we know he wasn't the murderer?

Jonah had nearly emptied the breadbasket, leaving a single end piece for me. I took it. It was spongy and bland with a cap of hard crust, which made it an ideal carrier for the olive tapenade. In the absence of conversation, I listened to the gentle clinking and murmuring of our fellow diners, and the loud chewing noise inside my head.

I felt a wave of relief when a dark-haired woman in a white blouse and black slacks approached our table. She introduced herself and asked for our drink order.

"Longboard lager for me," Jonah said. "You want something?"

"I'll stick with water until Emma gets here." I wanted to keep a clear head, and I didn't want to get too far ahead of Emma, who can hold her liquor a lot better than I can. Where was Emma, anyway?

My phone hummed in my bag.

"I'll leave the wine list with you, ma'am," the server said to me, with a practiced smile. "Be right back with your Longboard Lager, sir."

"Sorry, Jonah." I pulled out my phone and checked the caller ID. "I need to get this. It's your sister."

"No worries." Jonah pulled out his own phone and started doing something on it, which was apparently much more absorbing than talking with me. I took another look at the wine list.

"Listen, Jonah, I'm going to take this call outside. When she comes back, can you order me a Cabernet? Wait, no." I remembered that red wine stains my lips and teeth purple, imparting that unlovely look Emma calls "vampire mouth."

"I changed my mind. Chardonnay. Can you order me a Chardonnay?"

"You just said that." Jonah didn't look up from his phone.

"No. *Cabernet* is red. *Chardonnay* is white. I'll be right back. *Chardonnay*."

I stepped out onto the sidewalk. With the rain drumming on Sprezzatura's little red awning, and the cars splashing by, I had to mash my phone against my ear to hear anything.

"Emma," I shouted into the phone, "where are you?"

"Where are *you*? Sounds like you're inside a carwash."

"Pretty much. I'm right outside Sprezzatura. It's raining, and this is a pretty busy intersection. You know, this neighborhood's kind of sketchy at night."

"I've seen worse," Emma said.

"I know. I'm sure New York City is much scarier at night than downtown Mahina. So what's going on? When are you going to be here?"

"Sorry, Molly, something's come up. I can't make it."

"What? What do you mean you can't make it? Jonah already ate all the bread and ordered beer. You can't just—"

"Nah, nah, it's okay. You're really good with people, Molly. You can get the information from Jonah yourself."

"I am not good with people. Why would you even say that?"

"No worries. Jonah's gonna pick up the tab."

"Does *he* know that?"

"I gave him my credit card."

"Emma, this is silly. If you can't come, there's no point. It's not too late. We haven't ordered dinner yet. I'll just go inside and we'll apologize and pay for Jonah's beer and cancel—"

"No. Stay there and enjoy your dinner. Come on, you don't have anything better to do tonight, right?"

How could I not have seen this?

"You were never planning to show up."

"Whaaaat?"

"This was a setup, Emma. Wasn't it? Does Jonah know about this little scheme of yours?"

"I don't know what you're talking about. Welp, you better get back to your table. You don't want to keep Jonah waiting by himself. It would be rude."

"Emma, look. Jonah's a great guitar teacher, and you know I'm completely on his side in the sense of not thinking he murdered Kent Lovely, but that's as far as it—"

There was no point in going on. Emma had already hung up.

Chapter Thirty-Four

I came back into Sprezzatura's dining room to find Jonah staring off into space. He was humming to himself and drumming his fingers on the tablecloth as if he were listening to a song playing inside his head. At least he'd put his phone away.

"The server hasn't come back yet?" I seated myself and checked the bread supply. The napkin lining the empty basket was sprinkled with flecks of crust.

"Huh? Nah. Not yet."

I looked around the dining room, but I didn't see our server. That was too bad. I could really use that glass of chardonnay.

"Emma called to say something came up. So, she's not going to be able to join us."

Jonah nodded slightly and stared off into space.

"So if you'd rather do this some other time we can just ask for the...Jonah? Jonah."

"Huh?"

"What did Emma tell you this meeting tonight, this dinner, was about?"

Jonah shrugged.

"She must have told you *something*," I persisted.

Jonah looked uncomfortable.

"She just said we were gonna go to dinner. You and me."

"Right. Here we are. What else did she tell you?"

"She said to let you talk as much as you want."

"Emma said *you* were supposed to let *me* talk?"

Jonah nodded stiffly.

I looked around for the server. Forget the dinky little glass of house chardonnay. I was going to order a bottle of something fancy. And Emma could bloody well pay for it.

"Jonah, did Emma tell you what we saw in your office? All the fancy equipment and furniture?"

"Sorta. I mean, she talks real fast when she's upset. I didn't really understand what she was saying. Something about golf and putts."

"What? We didn't find any golf—Oh. She was probably calling Kent Lovely a *gonif* and a *putz*."

"Huh?"

"*Gonif.* That's a thief or a con man. *Putz* is...more of an all-purpose insult. Listen, Jonah, we found a top-of-the-line synthesizer, just sitting in Kent's desk drawer. It was so new I'm not sure Kent even used it. It still had the peel-off plastic over some of the input jacks. He had nicer office furniture than the stuff my dean has in *his* office. He had a massage chair, for crying out loud."

"Yeah. I know."

"Of course. You were the one who filed the complaint with Marshall Dixon's office. Did you ever happen to look at Kent's calendar?"

Jonah shrugged.

"You know, that big one hanging behind his desk?"

Jonah stared at the table.

"Jonah, listen. On the day of the retreat? The day Kent Lovely died?"

"I thought he died later."

"True. Kent passed away later that night, after they'd airlifted him over to Oahu. But the day of his retreat. There were two numbers written down. Twelve and Thirteen. Are those some kind of codes? Do twelve and thirteen mean anything?"

Jonah blinked.

"Okay. Forget about the numbers themselves. But they were written inside of these heart shapes. Like the suit? In cards?

154

Hearts? Clubs? Spades? Diamonds? Was Kent smuggling diamonds?"

"Dunno."

"Jonah, you have to help me out here. You must have *some* ideas."

The couple at the next table stared at us. I glared at them, and they looked away.

"Twelve plus thirteen is twenty-five. Does the number twenty-five mean something?"

The server came by, deposited a fresh basket of bread and another glass of beer for Jonah. She disappeared before I could ask about my wine.

"Okay, what about *this*? Did Emma tell you the last call from your and Kent's office phone was to Linda's private cell number?"

"Yeah, I think she said something about the office phone. Who'd Kent call?"

"Linda Wilson, from the Student Retention Office. Do you know anything about it? *You* weren't the one who made the call to Linda's phone, by any chance?"

"Wasn't me. Hey, it's Park."

Whoever Jonah was talking about was right behind me, so there was no way for me to twist around for a look without being obvious.

"Who?" I whispered.

"Stephen Park. From theater."

"Stephen *Park* is here? At Sprezzatura? The exact same restaurant he was supposed to—Who's he with?"

"By himself. I think it's him. Looks like him anyway."

Stephen was eating at Sprezzatura by himself? What on earth was he up to? Of course Jonah could be wrong. It might just be some other artsy-looking guy with a ponytail.

"You know what? This would be a good time for me to go wash my hands. If the server comes by, can you order me the calamari appetizer? And please remind her about my chardonnay. Oh, and I'd like a bottle, not just a glass. And it doesn't have to be the house wine. Ask her what she recommends. Thank you."

I stood up and headed to the rear of the restaurant. In the low light, I could see a man sitting at a table by himself. He was wearing a black turtleneck, and his black hair was slicked back into a ponytail. Pale, oval face. Pointed chin. Stunning cheekbones. Unable to smoke inside the restaurant, he was rolling a piece of bread back and forth in his fingers.

Thankfully, Stephen Park was facing away from me, so I was able to scurry past him unseen. The tiny restaurant bathroom had a single stall, currently occupied. The pillow-shaped fluorescent ceiling fixture was clearly intended for a much larger space. The blue-white glare flooded the tiny bathroom and threw my every complexion flaw into harsh relief. The Molly who dolled herself up for dinner earlier this evening had looked smooth and pretty in my bathroom mirror. The Molly who stared back at me now looked like something from a Grand Guignol poster. I swore to myself I would start getting a full eight hours' sleep every night, beginning tonight. I dispensed a puff of foamy soap and turned on the faucet to wash my hands. They looked weathered and veiny in the unforgiving light.

A young blonde emerged from the stall. I had seen her somewhere before. Maybe that trendy jewelry boutique downtown? She had the look: sleek bun fastened with a pair of chopsticks, an outfit of charcoal and black layers, severe purple lipstick against pale skin.

"Oh." She looked startled. "Professor Molly. Hi."

Chapter Thirty-Five

I gave her a tiny smile and a nod of acknowledgement. Was I supposed to know her name? I pulled out a brown paper towel and used it to shut off the faucet without making direct contact with the metal.

"I'm sorry," I said. "I'm not very good with names."

"Oh. My name's Alicia. I'm a student at Mahina State. That's how come I, um, I recognized you."

And in a flash, I recognized her right back. She was the young woman who had been in the theater with Stephen that day Emma and I had sneaked into the back row to eat lunch. Stage-manager Barbie. Stephen hadn't come to Sprezzatura by himself. He was sitting alone at the table because his date had gone to the bathroom.

I felt my heart thumping, and willed myself to stay calm. Stephen's behavior wasn't little Alicia's fault. Stephen was the responsible party. He was the grown-up. Anyway, what was I going to do? Get into a hair-pulling fight with an undergraduate? In fact, why should I even be upset? I was over Stephen. Completely.

"So what's good here?" I asked offhandedly. "Any recommendations? This is my first time at Sprezzatura, and we haven't ordered yet."

"Mine too. I haven't even had a chance to look at the menu. Stephen and me—I mean—um, sorry. I'm here with Stephen."

Great. She knew about my history with Stephen. She must have been spending time with him while our relationship fell apart. Maybe she was the *reason* our relationship fell apart.

"Oh, sure, I saw him out in the dining room just now." As if it were no big deal.

"Oh. Okay. Like I said, we haven't even looked at the menu yet. We've just been talking. He's such an interesting conversation-ist."

I'd have bet money that she had been doing very little of the talking in their "conversation."

"So let me guess. He's telling you all about Korean culture?"

Alicia stared at me wide-eyed. "How did you know?"

I shrugged, as if to say, lucky guess. "What's your interest? Are you a Korean Studies major?"

"No, I'm a theater major, but I'm *really* interested in world cultures."

I'm not completely proud of what I did next. I mean, I was telling the truth, but still.

"You know, Stephen Park is not Korean."

Alicia's lovely young features slacked with surprise.

"What do you mean?"

People assume Stephen Park has Korean ancestry. He doesn't. Not a drop. Rather than set them straight, he encourages the misconception. In his mind, being thought of as part-Asian gives him extra cool points or something.

"Stephen's father is from Scotland," I said. "Park is a Scots name. And his mother is a Schwartz from New Jersey. They live in LA. Have you been to LA?"

"I, uh, yeah?"

"Stephen's parents own and operate Beverly Hills Aesthetic Centre. You might've seen the billboards. It's not *in* Beverly Hills, of course, but as it happens it's perfectly legal to put Beverly Hills in the name."

"I thought Stephen was part Korean."

"But he didn't actually tell you that."

"Well..."

"I'm sure he didn't." I pasted on a pleasant smile. "I mean, Stephen wouldn't *lie*."

Alicia hurried out of the tiny bathroom without washing her hands. I wondered if the lovely young Alicia, so eager to sample the exotic flavors of the East, would continue to find Stephen Park so *fascinating* now that he was just some white guy whose parents ran a plastic surgery center.

I stayed and reapplied my lipstick (Russian Red) smoothing it with my pinky until the edges were blended. I dabbed crumbs of stray mascara from under my eyes. I'd have to get a fixture like this in my bathroom at home. This light was really good.

By the time I went back out to join Jonah, the table where Stephen had been sitting was empty.

Jonah noticed me staring at the table.

"They left," Jonah said. "A girl came over, and said something to him, and then she walked out. Then Park got up and went after her. Dunno what it was about."

I smiled brightly. "Well, it's none of *our* business, anyway."

"Didn't you used to go out with him?" Jonah asked.

"Briefly." I settled into my seat. "Is this mine?"

Thin slices of raw beef were arranged on a large white plate, and drizzled with vinaigrette.

"Wanna try a mozzarella stick?" Jonah proffered his own half-finished plate.

"No, thanks for offering, though," I said.

"That's what you wanted, right? I wasn't sure cause it looks like it's raw."

"I think I asked for calamari. This is carpaccio. But—sure. Why not try something new?"

I prodded the carpaccio with my fork, half expecting it to twitch. I don't even like my meat rare, much less completely uncooked. It was my own fault for leaving Jonah unsupervised to order for me. What was I thinking? This is the guy who got into an argument with Emma about dinosaurs being a hoax because their names are in Latin, and Jonah's reasoning had been, where would dinosaurs have learned Latin?

"Jonah." I stared down the translucent slice of beef dangling from my fork, "what do you know about Kent's red binder?"

"Huh? What red binder?"

The server had left a nice bottle of Napa chardonnay and a chilled glass. First things first. I placed the beef back down, poured half a glass, and took a sip. This was better. Although she probably wondered why I'd ordered white wine with raw beef.

"The binder said SOS on the spine. Sounds of—" I lowered my voice to a whisper. "Seduction?"

"Oh. That." Jonah's nose crinkled with distaste.

"I know. We listened to a little of it. It was horrible. But is it possible someone wanted it for some reason? Would someone have killed for it?"

"It was junk. Kent's whole concept was match tempo to heart rate, but it wasn't even his idea. Lots of people did it before him."

I stuffed the carpaccio into my mouth. It wasn't as bad as I expected. The raw beef slices had been pounded thin and drowned in tangy vinaigrette, so I could trick myself into thinking it was mushrooms or something.

"Anyway," Jonah said, "if that binder was so important, how come you guys found it in the office? Wouldn't the killer have stolen it?"

"Hm. Good point."

For someone who thought centaurs (but not dinosaurs) once roamed the earth, Jonah was making a lot of sense.

"So do you have any ideas about what happened? Any theories? Anything?"

"Nuh-uh. Hey, here's our waitress. You ready to order dinner?"

"With Emma treating? Sure." I picked up the menu and scanned it for something expensive and delicious.

Chapter Thirty-Six

"So Stephen's really moved on, ah?" Emma repositioned her elbows on the table and resumed paging through the coupon section of the Sunday paper.

Emma and I have a Sunday morning routine. I attend Mass at St. Damien's, Emma goes to paddling practice, and afterwards we meet at the Pair-O-Dice Bar and Grill. The establishment's one outstanding feature is a custom neon sign. "Pair-O-Dice" is spelled out in curvy blue script. An animated pink pair of dice rolls underneath. Green and yellow neon palm trees sway jerkily on either side. The bar's interior is nothing special: sticky concrete floors and wobbly wooden tables.

So what's the big draw? The Pair-O-Dice may be a dump, but it affords us a little privacy in a town with none. I've never seen anyone from Mahina State there. It's too down-market for most university employees, and it's not lively enough for students, who prefer the nightlife down on Hotel Drive. It's a perfect refuge.

"It's not that I want Stephen back," I said. "But it's hard to accept I'm so replaceable."

"Oh big deal. You totally moved on, too. Right? You went on a date last night, don't forget. Oh, hope you enjoyed your New Zealand rack of lamb and your bottle of Chateau Cha-Ching. You're welcome."

"It was delicious. Thank you. But it wasn't a date."

"Of course it was a date. You and Jonah, table for two at Sprezzatura, and bonus, Stephen saw you."

"I don't think he saw...Oh. Maybe he did. You think Stephen saw us?"

"Why do you care if Stephen saw you? You just said you were over him and you weren't on a date anyway." Emma turned a page and studied the department store sale coupons. "Eh, you manage to dodge the Passing of the Peace today?"

"I got there just as people were sitting back down. My timing was perfect."

I picked up a leathery fried wonton from its grease-translucent paper.

"These aren't very good,"

"Told you you shoulda got the French fries."

"You know what? I *am* over Stephen. What kind of adult man carries on with an undergraduate? It's such a, a—"

"Breach of trust?" Emma suggested. "Abuse of authority?"

"I was going to say cliché. But what you said works too."

"Shoulda seen it coming," Emma said. "Stephen likes to be the teacher. The expert. He wants a wide-eyed undergrad who's completely impressed with him, not some—well, you know."

"Some what, Emma? I don't know. Please elaborate."

"Alls I'm saying is Stephen liked you 'cause he thought you were a challenge. But once you saw through his act and quit fluffing up his ego, he went looking somewhere else."

"But a *student*, Emma. An undergraduate. Can he do that?"

"I don't think there's an actual rule against professors dating students. Is there?"

"How should I know? It's not exactly the kind of thing you ask during your job interview."

"Hey, can I have this coupon?" Emma asked.

"Sure. Take it. Air freshener makes me sneeze. I wonder how impressed his fresh-faced little ingénue is with him *now*."

Emma looked up from the paper and raised her eyebrows at me.

"Why? What'd you do?"

"Nothing. Let's talk about Jonah."

"Now you're talking sense. Jonah's a much better match for

you."

"I don't mean that. I mean, let's talk about how we're going to keep your brother off death row."

"Right on time. Eh, Dummy," Emma shouted. "Over here."

Jonah paused in the door, silhouetted against the sunlight outside. It wasn't hard for him to find us, once his eyes adjusted. Emma and I were the only customers in the Pair-O-Dice.

"You invited *Jonah*?"

"He couldn't wait to see you again." Emma socked me encouragingly on the shoulder.

"I don't believe that for a second." I rubbed my shoulder, and not just for show. Emma punches hard. "Oh, hi Jonah. Wow, A Mr. Zog's Sex Wax shirt. I haven't seen one of those since high school!"

"You two had a good time at dinner last night, ah?"

Jonah grunted (which presumably meant "yes"), sat down with us, and picked up the "Island Life" section of the newspaper.

"Nothing about *you* today in the paper, anyways," Emma said. "Front page today is all about some fistfight at Laukapu High School."

"A fight at the high school makes the front page?" I asked.

"Yeah, when it's two of the moms."

"Whoa." Jonah frowned at the paper. "The world's oldest man died *again*?"

Emma cleared her throat.

"So, you two, how was Sprezzatura?"

"We didn't really come up with any new insights," I said. "It might have been helpful if you'd been able to join us. But the food was very nice."

"I dunno." Jonah didn't take his eyes off the paper. "I didn't like the house dressing. It was totally different from the house dressing at Spiros, remember Emma, the place you took me when I visited you in Ithaca?"

"'Course it's different, Dummy. You familiar with the concept of *house* dressing?"

"Jonah told me he wasn't the one who called Linda from the

163

office," I said. "So we're back to assuming it was Kent."

"So you think it hadda do with the teaching award?"

"I can't imagine someone committing murder over the teaching award. It's just a paper certificate. There's not even cash involved."

"Jonah." Emma nudged him. "Whadda you think?"

Jonah shrugged. Emma gave me an exasperated look.

"One of us should talk to Rodge Cowper," I said. "He has to know something."

"You can talk to Rodge Cowper," Emma said. "I'm not gonna do it."

"What's the big deal?" Jonah asked.

"Oh Jonah, you have no idea."

While Rodge wasn't necessarily my favorite colleague, my interactions with him had always been tolerable. This was because I wasn't his type. Emma was a different story. Rodge was relentless, trying to work his pickup artist magic on her. He remarked on her "exotic" looks, teased her about her weight, and hinted that when she was ready to trade up from her current husband, he'd consider accommodating her. At first Emma had found him amusing. Then he became annoying. Finally Emma decided she'd exceeded her lifetime exposure limit.

"Even if Rodge Cowper does know something, Molly, how're you gonna get him to talk to you? Anyways, I'm sure the police already talked to 'im, and whatever they got outta him already wasn't any help to Jonah."

We sighed and sat silent for a moment.

"The police car's gone," Jonah said.

"Really?" Emma brightened. "When'd they leave?"

"When I left to come here, I saw the car pull out an' drive away."

"So they followed you," Emma said.

"Oh." Jonah hadn't thought of that.

"Jonah," Emma's voice broke, "When are you ever gonna learn to pay attention—"

A shadow fell across our table.

164

The police officer was about Jonah's age, stocky and clean-cut. He pressed his mouth into a line, an expression that said I don't like this any more than you do.

"Emma Nakamura," said the officer, "you are under arrest for the murder of Jeffrey Kenston Lovely."

"*Emma?*" I said.

"*Emma?*" Jonah repeated.

"*Jeffrey?*" Emma exclaimed.

CHAPTER THIRTY-SEVEN

Emma's husband Yoshi made some calls to his MBA friends and quickly got a referral to a top-notch criminal lawyer. Emma and Yoshi had enough equity in their house to make bail, and Emma's new attorney worked fast. It was close, but they made the five o'clock cutoff, and Emma didn't have to spend the night in jail. While Yoshi was signing the house over to the bail bondsman, I went to pick Emma up from the police station. Neither of us said much until we were both buckled in to the Thunderbird and on our way back up the hill to Emma's house.

"It's great to see the outdoors again," Emma said.

"Oh yeah, you were on the inside for what, two hours?"

Emma settled back in my turquoise and white vinyl bucket seat and gazed out at the drizzle-soaked street. We were rolling through a neighborhood of rusty metal roofs and gone-to-seed lawns decorated with rusty cars in various states of dismemberment.

"So what happened?" I asked. "I guess it was you they were watching this whole time. Not Jonah. What did they think you had against Kent?"

"Some blabbermouth told the police Kent left his can of energy drink on the buffet table, where you and me were getting our food. So supposably I had the opportunity to poison him."

"Who would say that?"

Emma shrugged.

"Nice to know how eagerly your coworkers will throw you under the bus the minute they get a chance. So then did anyone analyze the can? Did they find any poison?"

"I dunno."

I slowed and signaled a right turn, squinting into the dusk. The streetlights weren't on yet. My headlights lit up the raindrops right in front of them but didn't do much to illuminate the road.

"So Kent left the can there, and you somehow inserted poison into it on the spot? Do they think you showed up at our faculty retreat wearing your Cesare Borgia poison ring?"

"Yeah. Prosecutor's an idiot."

"Probably not the kind of thing you should be saying out loud, Emma."

"Hey, I'm just repeating what Feinman told me."

"Did you say Feinman? *Alika Feinman*? He's your lawyer?"

"Yeah, nothing but the best, Ah? Yoshi's pals don't cut corners."

"Even I've heard of him. Wow. So now what? Is there a court date? Do you have to not leave town? Do you need to report to anyone?"

"I gotta stick around. I'm not supposed to leave the island. I'm just gonna let Feinman handle everything. Man. This sucks so bad."

"No one has to know about your arrest, right? It's summer. Most of our students are out of town. And I'm not going to tell anyone."

"You don't know Mahina," Emma said. "The cop that arrested me? Little Matty Ferreira? He's one of Jonah's high school buddies."

"Really?"

"Really. They used to get high together in our dad's smoking shed back of the house."

"Well, what do you expect? If you have something called a *smoking* shed?"

"It's for smoking *meat*, Molly."

I could tell Emma was deeply shaken. She didn't even bother to punch me in the arm.

CHAPTER THIRTY-EIGHT

Iker Legazpi and I were strolling up the narrow walkway toward the College of Commerce building. I had my eyes on the ground, watching for places where the asphalt had buckled. Already, I'd almost broken my heel off in one of the cracks.

"Boy, fate can really surprise you sometimes."

"In what way?" Iker turned to me expectantly. I had been considering Emma's predicament and hadn't realized I had been talking out loud.

"Oh just, you know, life in general, how things can turn out. Like, uh, I never thought I'd end up working in a business school. Or living in a house right next to a graveyard. Stuff like that."

I had promised Emma that I would keep quiet about her legal difficulties. Emma's attorney had arranged for her arrest not to be public. Amazingly, whatever tactics the celebrated Alika Feinman was using were working. The news was absent not only from the papers but from the coconut wireless as well. It didn't hurt that public interest in Kent Lovely's death had died down, overtaken by the usual stories of drowning tourists, toddler-gobbling pit bulls, and the new marijuana bill.

"Life did not turn out as expected for Kent Lovely," Iker said.

"Kent Lovely? Did I say something about Kent Lovely?"

"James four, thirteen. You know this one?"

"Of course. Although off the top of my head, I don't exactly, um, what does it say again?"

"You may make many plans for yourself, but you do not even

168

know what tomorrow may bring."

"Right. Yes. I know that one. But you do have to make *some* plans, right? You can't just float around in life."

I moved to the center of the walkway to avoid snagging my blouse on an aggressive growth of strawberry guava.

"We make our plans to do this or that, yes, the Lord willing. However, we are not the masters of our own destiny. As you say, it was not at first your plan to teach here, at Mahina State University, in the College of Commerce."

"No. I always imagined myself teaching bright English majors, on some stately, leafy campus—"

"And you see." Iker pushed an encroaching monstera leaf out of the way, and held it to make sure it didn't spring back and smack me. "Sometimes our prayers are answered in a way we did not expect."

"Good point," I said. "This is a leafy campus, no question. Speaking of answered prayers, thank you again for coming to talk to Rodge Cowper with me. I appreciate it."

"I do this thing for you, Molly," Iker said. "Although I do not know if it will be a fruitful conversation. And as I have said, I think it is unwise to intrude upon a murder investigation."

"Oh no, I would never intrude. I'm just wondering if Rodge might have some insights. Which we could then pass along to the police."

The strains of a hula chant floated out from a building as we passed, the voices clear and strong. Iker and I walked until the voices faded behind us.

"Why is this sudden urgency?" Iker asked. "This is not your *kuleana*, as they say."

"It's not sudden. This terrible thing happened to someone in our campus community. The person who did it is still out there, and no one knows who's next." *And my best friend was just arrested for this murder,* I didn't add.

The air conditioning in the College of Commerce building was laboring under the load of Mahina's summer humidity. It was eking out the bare minimum of cold air, and at the same time releasing a sour stench, which permeated the building. I waited until Iker wasn't looking, and then pulled my blouse away from my chest and shook the fabric to get air circulating next to my skin.

"Molly," Serena called out as we passed by the main office. "Iker. Spring semester evals, ah? In your mailboxes."

I stopped and laid a hand on Iker's arm.

"Iker, that's it. We can use our student evaluations. They're a perfect conversation starter."

I hurried in to the office and retrieved the manila envelopes from my cubby, leaving the rest of my mail for another time. As Iker calmly collected his own envelopes, I tried to ignore the familiar dread welling up in my stomach. Student evaluation season was nerve-racking for me.

Our students used the anonymous end-of-semester evaluations to comment on their professors' physical appearance, suitability for continued employment, and personal appeal. Thanks to our student evaluation process, I knew some of my students hated my hairstyle, others deemed me a "PILF," and a surprising number seemed to have me confused with someone who teaches in the Chemistry Department. I was never able to work out how this information was supposed to help me improve my teaching.

As we made our way down the hall, Iker worked open one of his envelopes without tearing the flap. He began leafing placidly through his evaluations as we neared Rodge's office.

"How's it look?" I asked him.

"It is a curious thing. This practice of the student evaluation. The student who works hard, this student is satisfied and gives high marks on this form. The one who has not been to class, who has never visited me in my office, this is the one who now has many things to say on this little paper. There is a proverb. I cannot recall it at the moment."

"Oh, I know which one you mean. *The lunatics have taken over the asylum.*"

"No, it is not that one. Ah, yes. I recall it. *Beware of women with beards and men without beards.*"

170

"I think you'll have to explain that one to me later." We had arrived at Rodge's office. The door was propped open, indicating Rodge was present and taking visitors.

"Please explain to me this plan again," Iker whispered. "What are we doing with these evaluations?"

"They're an icebreaker, to get the conversation going. This gives us a plausible excuse to drop in on Rodge, and you can snoop around his office for ill-gotten loot."

Iker stared at me, a horrified expression on his baby face.

"I do not think it is right that I snoop."

"Not snoop," I corrected myself. "That was the wrong word. Forget I said it. We'll just talk to Rodge. Get an idea of what kind of person Kent Lovely was, and what he might have been up to. Of course if you *happen* to see anything out of place in Rodge's office, you can make a mental note of it."

"Will Roger permit this?"

"All you have to do is observe," I said. "Just what you'd normally do. Rodge may not have gotten the teaching award, but he's still a very popular teacher. So it would be perfectly natural for you and me to stop by his office for some helpful advice. I'll ask him for tips on how to improve my performance in the classroom, and that'll give you some time to—"

"But Roger Cowper is *not* a good teacher," Iker exclaimed. I made frantic shushing gestures, and Iker lowered his voice.

"He gives an A to every student," Iker whispered. "Even the very stupid ones."

"We're not supposed to say the S-word, Iker. It's 'kinesthetic learner.' Come on, let's get this over with."

I knocked on Rodge's door frame.

"Come," commanded Rodge's booze-roughened voice. I pushed the door open, and we entered the dark office.

"Hey. Molly Wolly Doodle." Rodge leaned back in his chair. "Iker the Biker. Ya here to count some beans? Come on in."

The name "Iker" rhymes with "beaker," not "biker." Rodge should know better. Also, if there's one thing I know about accountants (and one thing is about all I do know) it's that they hate to be called bean-counters. Iker seemed much less worried about invading Rodge's privacy now. He was looking around the office and mentally cataloging everything.

Rodge's office was so dim it took a moment for my eyes to adjust. Like everyone else in our building, Rodge had had two of the four fluorescent tubes removed from his light fixture. Then, to provide "atmosphere," Rodge had tacked a red and orange paisley cloth over the whole thing.

Rodge already had his student evaluations out of their envelopes and spread all over his desk. Now with Kent gone, I wondered whether these little paper affirmations were Rodge's only friends. *Wow, how maudlin. And probably not even true.* No doubt Rodge had plenty of friends. *Focus, Molly.*

"I see you got your evals," I said. "I just got mine too."

"And I as well," Iker added.

"It's the best part of the semester." Rodge said. "This is when you know it's all worthwhile."

"Sure," I said. "That's exactly what I was thinking, too."

"Come on, guys. Siddown. Enjoy the weather."

CHAPTER THIRTY-NINE

Rodge's futon couch was a bottom-of-the-line model, a faded red mattress folded over a black powder-coated frame. As soon as I sat down, I could feel the metal rail through the thin cushion. Iker, wisely, remained standing.

"You have a paper shredder in your office?" I asked.

"It's a portable air conditioner. Came in last week, just in time for the heat wave."

"Oh. That's why it's so nice and cool in here."

"But Roger," Iker said, "we have been asked to save money on our energy costs. Such a machine must be very expensive to run."

"I don't think the administration is too worried about the A/C costs, Iker. Have you been up to the Student Retention Office?"

"No kidding," Rodge chimed in. "Feels like a morgue up there."

"So Rodge, where are you draining the water?"

"No need. This bad boy has dripless condensation removal."

"I didn't know that was an option. You know, I've been looking at portable air conditioners, but I thought I'd have to hang the drip hose in the trash can and empty it out in the bathroom every night."

"Nah. This is real low maintenance. Just evaporates."

Iker stood quietly, a faintly disapproving expression on his round face. I'd have to keep this conversation going by myself.

"Something's different about your cabinet," I said.

The top of Rodge's wooden cabinet was crowded with wooden bowls, figurines, and glass jars, as always, but something *had* changed.

"Nah. It's the same old same old. Guess it's about time for me to go traveling again soon, add a few things to my collection."

"Well *that's* new, right? The little statue. It's cute." I stood, went over to the cabinet, and picked the figurine up without thinking. "Are these acrobats?"

I took a closer look and set it down quickly. Now what? Right, stick to the original plan. Ask about student evaluations.

"So, those are your student evaluations? You don't mind if I take a look, do you?"

"Sure. Go ahead."

I took another look at Rodge's curio cabinet. It wasn't just the new figurine. Something else was different. Rodge gathered his evaluations into a stack and handed them to me, and I sat back down on the uncomfortable sofa.

"Cool prof," I read. "Fun and easy. Best class. Wow, this looks great, Rodge."

"Well, it's all about the students. Hey Iker, you're making me nervous standing there. Ya wanna sit down?"

"I am comfortable in the standing position," Iker said evenly.

"Actually, speaking of teaching evals, I was wondering if you had any tips for me. As far as teaching?"

"I haven't even had time to get through all of my own evals yet. There are *so many* of them. You know they had to move my class into the big classroom, right?"

"Yes," I said. "I heard."

"And even after raising the course cap to the room capacity, my Human Potential class *still* has the longest waiting list on campus."

"That's great, Rodge." My gaze wandered back to the top of Rodge's curio cabinet. The wooden bowls were there, along with the collection of voluptuous Shiva statues, and some other items I would rather not examine too closely.

Then I realized what wasn't there. The bottle of pills, with the cheongsam-clad temptress on the label, was gone.

"Your turn, Molly," Rodge said." I showed you mine, now you

show me yours!"

"What?"

"Your student evals."

"Oh. Right. I don't usually like reading these on an empty liver, but sure. Here we go."

Iker was pacing behind me. I wondered if he was making note of important details in Rodge's office, or just waiting for me to finish. I tore open the envelope and pulled out the evaluation forms. The first one was filled in with an angry black scrawl.

"Let's see—nope, can't read *that* one out loud. How about this one? '*Way to hard she should chill this isn't harverd.*' Why do they talk about me in the third person? They know I read these. I tell them that every time. Here's another one. '*Doesnt she know we got stuff to do she expects us to do work at home.*'"

"Sounds like you're giving 'em homework," Rodge said.

"How much homework do you give them? Say, in an average week?"

"Oh, I don't really give graded assignments, per se."

"So the whole grade is the midterm and the final?"

"I don't really do midterms or finals either."

"You can *do* that? So what do you tell them your grading policy is?"

"I just tell them that if they make a decent effort, they'll get an A. That way they don't get fixated on grades. It's really improved the mood in the classroom."

"I can imagine."

"It makes teaching fun again when you don't have to worry about the bureaucratic stuff, like tests, and writing assignments, and textbooks."

The "bureaucratic stuff" was what the rest of us spent our time and effort on so our students could get some kind of real education. While we were doing the heavy lifting, Rodge conducted supervised play time.

I couldn't let my annoyance show, though. I had to keep up the facade of collegiality.

"Aw Molly, don't give me that look. Today's student is different from you and I. Linda told me that. You know Linda from the Student Retention Office? Sharp lady."

"Yes," I said. "I know Linda."

I heard Iker sigh heavily.

"Anyhoo." Rodge seemed eager to direct the conversation away from his shortcomings and back to mine. "What's the next one say?"

"*She should do something about her hair.*'"

Rodge shrugged. "Did they tell you what you should do?"

"No."

"What else ya got?"

"*Luv watching her walk in that red skirt you know what I*' Yeah, not helpful. Next one: '*Way to strick about riding. Give up now if your not a riding genus.*'"

"It's all about confidence, Molly. You get your confidence up, and everything falls into place. Whaddaya say about that, Iker?"

Iker was examining a framed poster on Rodge's wall, an eighties-style graphic of a woman with white skin, black hair, and purple lips.

"There is a proverb." Iker muttered something in a language I didn't understand.

"What does it mean?" I asked. "Was that the one about the beard?"

"It is not easily translated. Molly, you are an honest and dedicated teacher. I do not like to think any person of seriousness would listen to these impudent ravings."

"I'm sure there's some good ones in there," Rodge said. "Lemme see."

I handed him the envelope, self-consciously smoothed my skirt, and sat back down on the uncomfortable couch.

"See, here's a positive one right here. They said…Looks like another vote for your red skirt. Is it the one you're wearing now?"

I decided that we'd had enough chit-chat about student evaluations.

"Listen, Rodge, you know what I was wondering? I never saw anything about a memorial service for Kent. Why is that?"

CHAPTER FORTY

The metal rail in Rodge's futon was digging into my backside. How did anyone manage to sit on this awful couch for more than a few seconds at a time? I sat and suffered, not wanting to risk cutting the conversation short by standing up.

"I did ask if the university could have a memorial service for Kent," Rodge was saying. "He didn't have a family. I mean, there were his exes, but…Kent's life was here, in the university."

I nodded.

"Anyway, they told me they couldn't do anything."

"Why not? We only have a few summer classes going on. It's not like it would be hard to schedule a room."

"It is not beyond the ability of our university to offer a memorial event," Iker said. "Recall it was at the distinguished and pompous award ceremony where Kent met his fate."

"Well, Kent was only a part-timer. They told me they didn't want to set a precedent."

"What? Oh, you mean if they do it for Kent, the next lecturer who dies is going to demand a nice memorial service too?"

Rodge sighed and slumped in his chair. "Pretty much."

"I'm so sorry Rodge. I know you two were good friends."

"Please accept my condolences as well," Iker added.

"At least I have some good memories. Did I ever tell you about the time we went to the all you can eat salad bar at Gavin's? It was classic Kent. You know Gavin's, down on Mamo street?"

I shook my head. "I don't think I ever heard the story."

"Iker." Rodge sounded jovial again. "Come siddown. You're making me nervous pacing like that."

Iker relented and sat down next to me. He shifted uneasily as he tried, without success, to find a comfortable position.

"Gavin's has a salad bar?" I asked. "I didn't know. I haven't been able to find a salad bar since I moved to Mahina."

"Well, I don't think it's there anymore. Aw, I don't know if you want to hear the whole story."

"Sure. I like stories."

I felt a pang of pity for Rodge. He'd described Kent as someone who didn't have much of a life outside of work, but it seemed like a pretty good description of Rodge himself. His students appreciated the fact that he didn't make them think too hard or do any homework or otherwise impose on their busy schedules. With Kent gone, was there anyone left who really enjoyed Rodge Cowper's company?

"It was kind of late for lunch, and Kent and me were both hungry, so we thought we'd try Gavin's. We heard they had shrimp at the salad bar. So Kent had all these plastic sandwich bags in his pockets."

Rodge had picked up my stack of student evaluations and was fanning himself with them. I reached out and pulled them from Rodge's hand.

"I can take these."

"Paper cut," Rodge yelped.

"Oh, I'm so sorry. I've got disinfectant in my office. I'll be right back."

I sprinted over to my office and grabbed the jumbo vodka bottle with the spray nozzle on top. I mostly use it to spray wrinkles out of my clothes and to clean up the occasional spill, but it's a pretty good disinfectant in a pinch.

Back in Rodge's office, Iker sat impassively on the couch watching Rodge clutch the wrist of his injured hand. A bead of blood welled up from the webbing between Rodge's thumb and forefinger.

I aimed the spray nozzle and squirted Rodge's injury. He

opened his mouth in a silent scream.

"No, no, no," I tried to soothe him, waving my arms around in a sort of dance of appeasement. Our slapstick tableau was interrupted by the sound of voices coming down the hall.

"Even during the summer," said a woman in clear, accentless tones, "our faculty members are working on their research and preparing for their classes."

"Marshall Dixon," Rodge hissed through gritted teeth. He was hunched over, clutching his wrist so tightly I could see his fingers turning purple. "Hide the air conditioner."

I quickly unplugged Rodge's portable air conditioner and rolled it behind his desk, out of sight.

"We're going to meet Rodge Cowper, one of our *best* teachers," wheedled a voice I recognized as Linda from the Student Retention Office.

"Booze," Rodge hissed.

"What?" I stared at the giant vodka bottle in my hand, as if noticing it for the first time.

"Oh, I tried signing up for his class last semester but there was a *huge* waiting list." This was a girlish voice, a student, I guessed.

"Well, Skip, let's say hello," Marshall Dixon said, her voice getting closer.

"Skip Kojima. I can't go into the hallway with this bottle." I panic-skipped back and forth in the tiny confines of Rodge's office, student evaluations in one hand, vodka bottle in the other. Rodge, still writhing in pain, managed to point to his bottom file drawer. I yanked it open, which set about half a dozen liquor bottles clanking and rolling. I pushed them back to make room for one more and slammed the metal drawer shut just as Marshall Dixon rapped on Rodge's door frame.

CHAPTER FORTY-ONE

Iker, Rodge, and I stood at attention. I quietly let go of my stack of student evaluation forms. They dropped into Rodge's trash can with a thunk. Rodge's evals were once again spread out proudly across his desk.

Linda appeared in Rodge's doorway first. She looked a little wilted in her long-sleeved muumuu. Next was Marshall Dixon, sleek in expensive beige separates, followed by a sun-browned man in his sixties. Skip Kojima wore jeans and black rubber slippers (or flip-flops, if you prefer). His chocolate brown polo shirt sported the Kojima Surfwear volcano-and-rainbow emblem.

Bringing up the rear was a petite young woman wearing a Mahina State t-shirt in the official school colors as decided by student vote: red, green, and gold on a black background.

"Hi Dr. Rodge." The young woman gave Rodge a smile and a petite wave.

"Heya," Rodge said. I could tell he couldn't remember her name.

"May we come in?" Marshall led the party into Rodge's office without waiting for an answer.

"It's nice and cool in here," Skip said as the four of them crowded in. "Awful hot out there in the hallway."

"It does get a little warm in the summer," Marshall said. "We have a comprehensive energy-saving plan we've implemented on campus, which includes right-sizing our climate control.

We're making a small sacrifice to save the environment. And to save the taxpayers their hard-earned money."

Linda and Marshall shared a forced chuckle, and then Marshall made introductions. Iker stepped forward to shake Skip Kojima's hand.

"Mister Kojima, it is an honor to meet you. I understand your father was part of the 442nd Regimental Combat Team of the United States Army. The brave American soldiers who fought the Axis Powers in the Second World War, even as their own families were subject to internment at home. It is an inspiring example to me, the 442."

Marshall Dixon smiled and nodded.

"Eight presidential citations and twenty one medals of honor." Skip Kojima's grin was radiant. "Now me, I just sell t-shirts."

"Mister Kojima," the young woman piped up, "my dream is to be a famous fashion designer like you. You're such a great role model."

"Well, the fashion industry isn't all glitz and glamor," Skip said. "I hope you're ready for long hours and hard work."

"Oh, I am. I've been thinking about it a lot, and I have it all planned out. I'm gonna call my line *Tokyo Rose*. I already have an idea for the label. It's gonna have the kanji letters for Tokyo, and a picture of a red rose."

The smile died out of Skip Kojima's eyes. Marshall cleared her throat to get Skip's attention.

"Skip," Marshall said, "did you have any questions for us?"

"I do. Young lady, what is your name?"

"I'm Ashleigh. Ashleigh Ueda."

"Ashleigh, however did you choose a name like 'Tokyo Rose' for your business?"

"I don't know. I thought it sounded pretty. My friends say I have a good feeling for this stuff. You know, fashion. And publicity."

Marshall was wincing. Linda beamed proudly.

"And what is your major, Ashleigh?" Skip asked.

"I'm majoring in history."

181

I heard Iker exhale with relief. Not a business major. She wasn't one of ours.

"You're a history major." Skip Kojima repeated.

"Oh, it's not like a regular history major. It's so cool. We don't get all caught up with boring stuff like names and dates. We get to choose what *we* want to study. It's totally student-driven!" Ashleigh directed this last comment at Linda, who smiled approval.

Skip Kojima remained cordial, but the temperature in Rodge Cowper's office had plummeted, and it had nothing to do with his contraband air conditioner. Marshall pasted on a smile and hurried the party out of Rodge's office, presumably to the next stop on their campus tour.

"This was a very unfortunate woman," Iker said.

"Oh, Marshall Dixon?" I said. "I know. Did you see her expression? It was like she was watching dollar bills flying out of the window." Emma was right about the Student Retention Office. They were a menace.

"No, I do not refer in this case to Marshall Dixon. I mean the one known as Tokyo Rose. She was trapped in Japan during the wartime, forced to do the propaganda broadcasts. She was alone and without friends in a country that was not her own."

"Didn't she get a presidential pardon?" I asked.

"Only many years later," Iker said.

"I still wouldn't bring her up to someone whose father was 442," Rodge said.

"Well, looks like Arts and Sciences won't have to buy new letterhead after all."

Iker and I sat back down on Rodge's uncomfortable couch.

"So Rodge." I smiled. "What did happen at Gavin's salad bar?"

CHAPTER FORTY-TWO

"Roger has many reminiscences about his departed friend Kent," Iker said. By the time we finally left Rodge's office, it was time to head home for the day. Iker was walking me down to the parking lot.

"I didn't see anything out of place in Rodge's office," I said. "Did you?"

"No." Iker agreed. "There was nothing of the ill-gotten gains."

Iker and I paused under the overhang of the College of Commerce building. Out in the rainy parking lot, my Thunderbird looked conspicuously turquoise among the white hatchbacks and black lifted trucks.

"I have to say, nothing that Rodge told us improved my opinion of Kent. Kent hits himself on the head with a golf club and then claims to be injured just to get some free rounds of golf. Kent goes out on a blind date and pretends to be literally blind, because ha ha, blind date, get it? I don't understand what Rodge saw in him."

"Perhaps Roger does not have other friends," Iker said. "To have Kent was better than to have nobody."

"Good point," I said. "But personally? I think I'd rather—oh, look, someone's coming. She's waving. Why does she look so familiar?"

"That is our student, Margaret Adams," Iker said. I recognized her then, from my spring semester business communications course. Margaret was an accounting major, quiet in class but

183

remarkably driven. She used to visit my office almost daily to check on her grade. She needn't have worried. Her straight-A average had survived BizCom unharmed.

"Hi Margaret," I said as she bounded up to us. "What are you doing on campus? Are you taking summer classes?"

"No, I'm working. My shift's starting pretty soon, but I saw you guys and wanted to say hi."

"You are doing the bookkeeping?" Iker inquired hopefully.

"Oh I *wish*. No, just working the cash register. Down at Fujioka's Music and Party Supply. I was lucky to get that, with that new off-island degree thing they're putting in all the want ads now."

"Off island degree?" I asked. "What is that?"

"Oh, they want you to have a college degree, but more and more of the employers think a degree from Mahina State's too easy to get nowadays. So they're looking for people who got their degree from somewhere else."

"You mean they're telling our graduates, 'Sorry, a Mahina State degree's not good enough'? Mahina employers don't want to hire Mahina State graduates?"

"But that is terrible," Iker said.

Margaret looked flustered. "I'm sure you guys will work it out with the employers by the time I get my degree. And I got my foot in the door at Fujioka's. So it's working out okay for me, so far."

"Working at a music store sounds nice," I said. "Do you get an employee discount?"

"There is one, but I don't play an instrument, I don't really throw parties, and I can't afford their jewelry. So it doesn't do me much good. It's kind of fun working there, though. Musicians are interesting people."

"They are," I said. "So then what *are* you doing on campus?"

"I heard the bookstore started getting textbooks in. I want to make sure I get mine before they run out. I don't trust the online thing. I've known too many people who ordered books and didn't have them come in on time."

"This is excellent planning," Iker said.

"It is. I'm impressed."

"So Dr. Barda, I saw you were teaching Intro to Business Management *and* Business Planning. I hope your textbooks aren't too expensive. You know I calculated I spent more on textbooks last semester than I did on rent."

"Did you say Intro to Business Management and Business Planning? IBM and BP are Rodge Cowper's classes. I'm not teaching those."

"Oh." A troubled expression passed over Margaret's fine features. "But the fall schedule has you listed as the instructor. I'll double check at the bookstore. Anyway, have a great summer if I don't see you."

Iker and I watched Margaret trot away in the direction of the campus bookstore. Even Margaret, slim as she was, had to push overgrown monstera and strawberry guava aside to make her way down the walkway. Ever since the administration had laid off most of our groundskeeping staff, the endemic vegetation had been reclaiming the campus, smothering buildings and crowding into the paths that crisscrossed the campus. Back where I come from, coaxing anything to grow up out of the bare dirt is an accomplishment. Here, on the wet side of the island, gardening is largely a matter of beating back nature with propane torches and weed killer.

"What were we talking about?" I asked Iker, when Margaret had disappeared from view.

"We were discussing our visit to the office of our colleague, Roger Cowper," Iker said. "We have heard many colorful tales about the late Kent Lovely. We have seen the careless words of a naive student costing our university a large donation. And you have inflicted a bleeding injury upon Roger himself. Yet we are no closer to finding out who murdered Kent Lovely."

"I wouldn't call it an *injury*. It was a *paper cut*. Injury makes it sound like he needed medical—The pills."

"The pills?"

"The pills, Iker. The ones on the top of his cabinet. The bottle of pills wasn't there today, was it?"

"You are speaking of the pills he hopes are not fertility pills?"

"Oh, he got you too? Yes, those. He's had them sitting out forever, and suddenly he throws them away. Why now?"

"Perhaps it was a joke he shared with Kent, and the memory is painful."

"Maybe," I mused. "But if you missed someone, would you throw away one of the few things that reminded you of that person? I don't think so. You generally hang onto it."

The rain had let up. Out in the parking lot, down the Music portable building, I could see the roof of my T-bird glinting wetly in the sunshine. I hoped I'd remembered to roll up my windows all the way.

"It has been a tiring day. I do not find it restful to be in the company of Roger Cowper."

"Yeah, I'm ready to head home."

"Yes," Iker said. "But I must return a book at the library first,"

"Did you say the library?" I hesitated. "Mind if I go up there with you?"

I remembered the library's computers didn't require a login. I considered telling Iker what I was planning, but I decided against it. I wanted to do this anonymously, and I didn't want to burden Iker with having to keep my secret.

It took me a while to find a working computer, and once I was logged on, the internet connection was sluggish. Happily, the Foundation's website had an online feedback form, so I didn't even have to sign up for a throwaway email account.

We want to hear your feedback. Please type into the box below.

I started typing, and before long I had exceeded the character limit. I went back and edited my statement down to the essentials:

Mahina State has taken Foundation money and made things worse, not better, for our students, I wrote. *The Student Retention Office uses Foundation funds to pressure faculty and administrators to inflate grades, dumb down assignments, and let cheaters go unpunished. Now local employers refuse to hire our graduates. This is in direct contradiction to the Foundation's stated goal of "increasing success in higher education." Being unemployable upon graduation is not "success" for our students.*

Once the Foundation got my message, there would be some changes made. I was sure of it. Maybe they wouldn't believe me about the off-island degree requirement, though. I had to provide solid evidence. I could do that.

I retrieved a copy of the *County Courier* from the periodical section, and opened it to the classifieds. I typed in a list of employers who included "off-island degree required" in their ads. Before long, I bumped up against the character limit again. I edited the message down, looked it over for typos, pressed "send," and went to look for Iker.

Maybe the Foundation will redirect the money to something to actually help students, I thought. *A tutoring center. Some full-time composition instructors. They might even shut down the Student Retention Office. Sorry, Linda, but you and your minions should've chosen a less evil line of work.*

I found Iker at the circulation desk. He politely stood aside to let me push through the turnstile first. (I always go hands-free and push through with my hips, because who knows what kinds of hand germs are living on that metal?) Then he followed me out. As soon as we were outside, I turned to him.

"Iker," I said, "I have an idea. If you don't mind and can spare a few minutes. Can we stop by Natural High? Would you mind?"

"Natural High? The herbolario, with the pungent smell?"

"It won't take long. I just want to check something. It's for our audit."

"It is not an audit," Iker said, sternly. "Only a certified—"

"Sorry. Investigation is what I meant to say. I finally feel like we might be making some progress."

CHAPTER FORTY-THREE

I parked my T-bird at the far end of the bayfront. Iker and I climbed out of the car and headed down the row of storefronts to Natural High Organic Foods.

"I don't know why it's so hard to find parking down here," I said. "I'd like to think it's because business is booming downtown, but the stores always seem empty."

"It is a paradox," Iker agreed.

The bayfront's Old-West-style false-front buildings were gaily painted in pinks, blues, and yellows. Across the street, the ocean lapped on a thin strip of shoreline spiked with tall coconut palms. We passed the 'awa bar, several vacant storefronts, and a new dress shop. Finally we reached the carved wooden sign that hung at the entrance of Natural High Organic Foods. Natural High has been doing business in the same spot since 1972. Neither the store nor the neighborhood has changed much since then.

"Are you sure you're okay with this, Iker?" I asked.

"Yes. It may help our investigation, and so I will do it."

Iker pulled open the wood-framed screen door to allow me to enter first. A musty ginseng scent permeated Natural High's interior. I wandered over to the display of rubber gardening shoes, and watched Iker wander toward the back of the store. He made a show of examining the shelves, and was quickly accosted by a blonde-dreadlocked young woman wearing a green apron. I picked up a basket from the stack next to the front door and went over to the bulk bins, straining to eavesdrop as I pretended to study the tamari almonds. Iker seemed to be doing a fine job. I decided I should pick up one or two things before I followed him out so it wouldn't look suspicious. By the time I finished my shopping, Iker was waiting for me outside the store. I stood and gazed at the sparkling blue ocean on the other side of the road. Six-man canoes zipped along past the breakwater.

"I have learned something today," Iker said, when he realized I was standing next to him. "Do you know that on the sole of the foot and here, in the palm of the hand..." (He pressed his palm with his finger.) "...and at several points beside the ankle, there are points of pressure connected to the kidneys? Allow me, please."

Iker relieved me of one of my grocery bags.

"Do you think someone gave Kent Lovely some kind of ankle death grip? Was someone hiding under his table or something?"

"Many things are possible," Iker said. "And yet nothing is certain."

We started back up the street to where I had parked the Thunderbird. Mahina's famous bayfront looked quaint and colorful from a distance and photographed nicely for travel features in airline magazines. Up close, though, the years of the buildings being blasted by salty air and chewed up by termites became obvious. Paint peeled and blistered. Walls and walkways sagged precariously. A few spaces had been repopulated with various social services and nonprofit agencies.

We had almost reached my car when I heard heavy footsteps behind me. I turned around to see a towering security guard hurrying up to us.

"Excuse me, Professor?"

Was there something in my bag I hadn't paid for? And how did he know I was a professor?

"Yes, Sir." I stopped walking and clutched my groceries defensively. "Is there a problem?"

Iker was still walking toward the car ahead of me, unaware.

"Eh, Professor Barda, I'm in your Business Planning class. In the fall."

"Oh, you're a *student.*" I smiled at the hulking young man.

"Oh yah, sorry." The guy looked down at his chest as if he had just noticed he was wearing a security guard's uniform. "This my summer job. Working loss prevention for Sacred Herb. Saw you guys coming out of Natural High, an' thought I could catch you before you was gone already."

"Did you say Business Planning?"

"BP, yah. Business Planning. I wanted to ask you, we get a textbook or what? I didn't see nothing in the bookstore."

"Actually, Business Planning isn't my class. I teach Business *Communication*. Roger Cowper teaches Business *Planning.*"

"Yah, Business *Planning*. Like a brand-new business."

"Okay, but it's not my class—"

"So check it out, Professor, I got this idea for a private security company, yah? But local kine, wit' *aloha.*"

"Well, that sounds very interesting, but—"

"We could do baby luaus, weddings, all da kine, but get one personal touch. Like uncle get too much to drink at the baby luau, we no whack.'im over the head or t'row 'im out into the road, nothing li' dat. We just get 'im on the couch, sleep it off. So no get all *kapakahi*, yah?"

"Okay."

"Name of my company gonna be *Aloha Security*. Don't tell nobody but. I don't want no one to steal my idea. Eh, Professor Legazpi. Howzit?"

Iker had realized that he'd been walking by himself and turned back.

"Ah, Mister Kawānanakoa," Iker said. "A very good afternoon to you."

"Eh professor Legazpi, I like retake managerial in the fall. Hope I do good this time."

"That is my hope as well," Iker said. "What is the expression, the third time is the most charming?"

"Why does everyone think I'm teaching Rodge's classes?" I asked, when the young man had returned to his post at Sacred Herb. Sacred Herb was a small but thriving specialty shop done up in the same red, gold, and green palette as the new Mahina State school colors.

"You would do a better job at these courses than Roger Cowper, I believe."

"Thank you for saying so, although I'm not sure it's true. I don't have any background at all in business. My doctorate is in literature and creative writing."

"Yes, it is as they say. The old fox sheds its old hair, but not its old habits."

"Well?" I asked. "What did you find?"

"They do not sell the pills at Natural High," Iker said. "I attempted to describe the container. The young lady believes that they were for...the gentleman who requires some assistance in fulfilling his marital obligations."

"So not likely that Rodge used them to kill Kent. Darn. Sorry, Iker, not that I'm disappointed that Rodge isn't poisoning people. But then why did he get rid of them?"

"Perhaps he believed such a display was unseemly during this time."

"I don't believe that for a second. Rodge is the walking embodiment of 'unseemly'. Do you mind if we make just one more stop?"

Iker's forehead creased with concern.

"Molly, we already have the information from Natural High Organic Foods. Perhaps the rest of this is best left to the policemen."

"Well, here's the problem. The policemen already have their susp—um."

Whoops. Iker didn't know about Emma's arrest.

"I'm afraid either Emma or Jonah might fall under suspicion," I said. "In the absence of another likely suspect."

"Yes. I know a police car has been parked near to Emma's house, the one she shares with her husband and her brother."

"Right. I know. Can you imagine living like that? No privacy, police watching everything you do?"

Iker's baby face clouded.

"Yes. I can indeed."

"Just a quick stop at Fujioka's Music and Party Supply. Remember, the place where Margaret Adams is working over the summer? She told us her shift was starting soon, so she's probably there now."

"You wish to go to the music store?" Iker asked.

"If you don't mind. If we hurry, we can get there before they close."

CHAPTER FORTY-FOUR

The rain started to patter on the roof of the Thunderbird as we drove up from the bayfront toward Fujioka's Music and Party Supply. The green jungle on either side of the narrow road gleamed against the grey sky. Dripping black power lines garlanded from one termite-chewed utility pole to the next.

"I am glad for this rain," Iker said.

"Really? Good." I wasn't feeling that glad myself. The trip to Natural High had been disappointing. This whole day had been a disappointment, starting with losing Skip Kojima as a donor. I wasn't looking forward to going back to my empty house to listen to rain drumming on my metal roof all night.

"My orchids were becoming melancholy," Iker said. "Now they will be more cheerful."

"I'm glad to hear it. You know, I really don't mind the rain as much as I thought I would. Everyone told me I'd get tired of it. But it keeps this side of the island cool and green. I think the other side of the island is actually too hot."

"It is said, all sunshine makes a desert."

"Excellent point."

I pulled into the narrow lot and parked beside the low cinderblock building. The worn red script on the street side of the building read *Fujioka's Music and Party Supply since 1949*.

It was painfully cold inside Fujioka's. This is how air conditioners seem to work in Mahina—rattling away ineffectually when it's hot and humid, then kicking into blast freezer mode when it cools down outside.

Margaret Adams stood behind the glass counter, setting out packets of guitar strings for a gray-haired Hawaiian man, whom I recognized as a local recording artist. A selection of guitars and ukuleles were arrayed on the walls, and at the far end of the store was a glass-front jewelry display. A security guard in an ill-fitting uniform stood next to it, hands clasped behind his back. Iker followed me over. On the top shelf, under the streaked glass, was a display of semiprecious jewelry: garnets, opals, pearls, and aquamarines. The shelf below it featured a selection of pricey timepieces. One watch, a gaudy diamond-encrusted model, looked familiar.

"Hey Professor Barda. Professor Legazpi. What are you doing here?"

Margaret Adams approached us, tucking her mousy hair behind her ear, only to have it fall in front of her face again.

"Darn it. I should just get bangs again. So are you looking for anything special?"

"I've started guitar lessons," I said.

"Oh no way, Professor, good for you."

"My guitar teacher was the one who told me about Fujioka's. I haven't been in here before."

Margaret clasped her slim white hands. "Oh, speaking of music teachers, wasn't it terrible news? About our computer music instructor? Professor Lovely?"

"Dr. Legazpi and I were both at the retreat when Kent Lovely collapsed," I said.

Margaret wrapped her thin arms around herself in a defensive gesture. "I heard the other music teacher was the one who did it," she whispered.

"Margaret," Iker asked gently, "where did you hear this rumor?"

"Everyone here's been talking about it."

"Jonah Nakamura is actually the one I'm taking lessons from," I said. "He's my guitar teacher."

"*Oh.*" Margaret's large eyes widened.

"Well, contrary to what you might have heard, I don't think the police suspect *him*. Margaret, did you know Kent Lovely?"

"Sort of. He used to come in here a lot, and I know he bought a lot of stuff, but I never rang him up. Wendell, the owner, is the one who did his purchases. Professor Lovely always used university purchase orders, and Wendell said I should let him handle it, 'cause it had to be done a certain way."

Iker pulled a thick blue binder out of his satchel and set it on the glass display case. He paged through until he found what he was looking for and then turned the binder to face Margaret.

"Margaret, can you tell me please, does Fujioka's sell this item?"

Margaret frowned and traced her finger down the page. "I don't think we have these in stock."

"Iker, you brought all your notes. That's terrific."

"Yes. I find it is always best to be prepared with information."

"Okay, just a minute, Professor Legazpi. Let me check for you."

"What's she looking for?" I asked Iker as Margaret left us.

"It is the synthesizer," Iker said.

I watched Margaret disappear through an unmarked door, then turned my attention back to the glittering timepiece in the jewelry case.

"Iker, where have you seen that silver watch before?"

"I have not seen it before."

"Are you sure? It's this one. Look at it again. What do you think?"

"It is very dazzling in this light," he said.

"There's a rose gold version too. Ooh, it one's even more hid—I mean, goodness, this style is quite eye-catching."

The security guard paid us no attention. He stared solemnly into the middle distance, as if he were a member of the Queen's Guard at Buckingham Palace.

"Molly? You are looking very much at this watch. You wish to purchase it for yourself?"

"What? No. But Iker, Marshall Dixon's been wearing a watch exactly like this one. And I haven't seen anything like it anywhere else in town. Have you?"

Iker's brow crinkled. "But this watch, it is so gaudy. And Marshall Dixon, she is an elegant woman. No, I do not believe Doctor Dixon wears such a watch."

"Yes she *does*. I know I've seen her wearing it. And I agree, it isn't her style. I think it was a gift. You know how someone buys you something, and you feel obligated to wear it? I remember one Christmas my mother got me—"

Margaret returned, cutting our conversation short.

"We sell it," Margaret said, "but it's a special order item. At that price we can't afford to carry it in inventory."

"This is the price for a single unit?" Iker was examining a slip of pink carbon paper Margaret had handed him. I peered at the bottom line. Fujioka's markup was a good twenty percent above the retail price.

"We don't have any transaction matching the number in your records, do we?" I asked Iker.

"No. Such a transaction would require many signatures and approvals, including those of the chancellor. Perhaps Kent Lovely purchased it with his own money."

"On his part-timer's salary? I doubt it."

"Professor Legazpi," Margaret said, "I know this is kind of out there, but what about *parceling*?"

"What's that?" I asked. Iker nodded to Margaret.

"Please," he said.

"Oh, me? Okay, it's when you break up a large purchase into smaller installments, so each transaction is under the amount which requires another signature. So if the approval limit is five-hundred dollars, and the buyer wants to purchase a fifteen-thousand dollar item, they can structure it as thirty purchases of four-hundred ninety-nine dollars and ninety-nine cents at a time. Um, did I explain it right?"

"You are correct, Margaret. I did not believe someone in our university would do such a trick. But perhaps I was wrong. In the event, I will search for a series of small purchases totaling to the amount of the large purchase."

"Margaret, you've been so helpful. I wonder if you could tell us just one more thing. These watches. This one. Have you sold any of them over the last year?"

I felt sure Kent Lovely had bought the watch for Marshall Dixon. The question was, why would she accept such an expensive gift from him without questioning where it came from?

I could think of three explanations. (1) Marshall Dixon had no idea what Kent earned as a part-timer (highly unlikely, considering her position in the university); (2) Marshall realized Kent couldn't afford it but didn't care (completely out of character since she would wonder where Kent got the money), or (3) she truly did not realize how expensive that cheap-looking watch really was (the most likely option, in my opinion). There was a fourth possibility: Marshall Dixon had purchased the watch for herself, but that seemed so unlikely it didn't even deserve consideration.

The door jingled as another customer came in, a rangy fiftyish man with shoulder-length magenta hair, black jeans, and a tight black t-shirt. He shook out his wet umbrella onto Fujioka's grimy linoleum floor and looked around impatiently.

"Oh, sorry," Margaret said. "I have to go help this customer. I'm here by myself right now."

"That's okay," I said. "If you have a chance, though, could you let me or Iker, I mean Professor Legazpi know? Here's my number." I handed her one of my university business cards. She pocketed it and rushed off to tend to her customer. With his skinny, hairy arms, he reminded me of a tarantula. Only later did I realize who he was: a famous guitarist—you'd recognize his name—who had bought a house and settled into semi-retirement nearby.

"Iker," I said, "I think we might be onto something here. This place is full of opportunities to spend money. Look at this."

I led Iker along the wall display of acoustic guitars, electric guitars, and ukuleles.

Iker nodded glumly.

"And what about that last phone call from Kent and Jonah's office. Remember? To Linda Wilson? In the Student Retention

Office? Except it wasn't her office phone?"

We reached the door and paused. It was raining hard outside.

"I didn't bring an umbrella," I said. "Sorry."

"Nor I. We will wait."

"The College of Arts and Sciences records don't have the whole story. We need to see the Student Retention Office purchase records too."

"I believe it would be unwise to annoy Marshall Dixon," Iker said. "Even more so after the incident with Mister Kojima. Perhaps there is an innocent explanation for the phone call. Perhaps Kent was telephoning Linda about the teaching award."

"Okay, but if it was work related, why was he calling her personal number?"

"Molly, a telephone call may be very innocent. I must point out you have just given your telephone number to Margaret Adams."

"But it was my *work* number."

"Does your work number not forward to your personal telephone when you are away from your office? Perhaps Linda has also set her telephone in this way, as you have."

"Fine. I *still* wonder why Kent was doing calling Linda at all. Iker, it was the last phone call from his office. It must mean something. And did you hear what Margaret said about how the owner of the store always had to handle Kent's purchase orders?"

Iker didn't answer. We watched through the glass door as sheets of rain swept across the parking lot.

"I have an idea, Iker. You know, the event tomorrow we're all supposed to attend, where they're going to unveil the remodeled classroom? Marshall Dixon should be there. Maybe I'll just ask her about it there, if you don't want to."

Iker gave me a long, considering look.

"Molly, you say Marshall Dixon wears a watch like this one."

"Correct."

"What answer do you think we will find to this puzzle? Do you propose to accuse Doctor Dixon of participating in a misappropriation of funds?"

"Well, I don't think she *deliberately* misappropriated anything."

"I have learned if one asks the question, one must be prepared to hear the answer. Perhaps there are answers you do not wish to know."

"No, Iker. There's nothing I do not wish to know. I *do* want to know the truth."

"There are discrepancies in the purchases of laboratory supplies for the Biology Department," Iker said. "Do you wish for us to investigate those as well?"

"Well I don't know if we need to go *that* far—"

"You see, sometimes we do not wish to have every question answered."

CHAPTER FORTY-FIVE

Emma knocked on my office door the next morning, ten minutes before the start of the search committee meeting. I quickly shut down my computer. I had been doing an online search for Rodge's missing potency pills. I knew our campus IT guy could see all the traffic on our network, but I wasn't worried. The great thing about being a business communication professor was that I could justify just about any online shopping expedition by explaining that I was researching internet marketing tactics for my class. What I had found was that far from being deadly, most of the products were merely ineffective.

"Are you coming to the grand opening later?" I stood and slung my bag over my shoulder.

"Of what?"

"Our new classroom."

"You mean the construction mess downstairs? They're done already?"

"Today is the big reveal. Oh, I hope they put in working air conditioning."

"Dream on," Emma said. "Your whole building's AC is totally bus' up. They're not gonna fix it for just one classroom."

"Yeah, you're right. Well, maybe they replaced those rotted out ceiling tiles."

Emma gave me a "yeah, right" look.

"Or at least cleaned the betel nut spit stains off the floor," I said.

I pulled my office door shut to make sure it was locked. Emma and I started down the dim hallway.

"Molly, how come your college got a remodeled classroom anyway? You know my teaching lab's falling apart. I got less working microscopes every year and no replacements."

We exited the College of Commerce building and headed up the overgrown walkway. I shielded my eyes against the sudden sunshine.

"Be careful what you wish for, Emma. I'm not sure you want the Student Retention Office messing with your lab. Especially not while Linda's in charge. The woman can hold a grudge."

"Yah, I know I probably shouldn't have cc-d everyone on that email. But seriously, how could Linda not know the difference between Gregor Mendel and Josef Mengele?"

Emma pushed open the door of the classroom. Down in the front, Candidate Number Two was already making his presentation.

CHAPTER FORTY-SIX

"The presentation started already," Emma stage-whispered to me. "Shh."

Pat Flanagan was sitting alone in the back row. I pushed ahead of Emma and sat right next to him. Instead of sitting next to me, Emma squeezed by me, then by Pat, and sat down on his other side.

For his job talk, the second finalist for the position of Associate Dean of Learning Process Improvement was conducting a question and answer session. This was not the usual Q&A. The candidate both posed the questions and answered them.

"I interpret the question differently," the candidate was saying, apparently in rebuttal to himself. "It seems to me essential to reframe the question to problematize the inherent assumption therein that there is such a thing as a 'correct' answer, when the construct of the job interview, an institutionally sanctioned act, carries with it an implicit system of legitimation or exclusion..."

Emma nudged me. "I don't think Linda's gonna go for this one. He's using way too many big words."

"Don't be too sure. This guy has a lot of common ground with the Student Retention Office. Notice how he's making quote marks with his fingers every time he says the word *knowledge*. Doesn't it sound a lot like, '*There's no such thing as a wrong answer, only different ways of knowing?*'"

"Molly's right about the common ground," Pat said. "It's at the corner of *Grading is Inherently Hegemonic* and *Trophies for*

Everyone."

"Ladies? Patrick?"

Linda was twisted around in her seat, glaring at us from the front row.

"Did you have a question for Dr. Barnes?"

We all shook our heads. Pat kept his head down and typed on his laptop.

"No class participation points for you two," Pat muttered.

When the presentation was over, the candidate was whisked away to his next appointment. Betty Jackson rushed off to her stats class, and Pat, Emma and I headed to the cafeteria.

"So are you two gonna vote for him?" Emma asked.

"Why would we?" I asked.

"Cause you're all English majors?"

"You think we have some kind of disciplinary loyalty or something?" Pat said.

"Seriously Emma, where did you get that idea?"

"Why *is* there so much infighting in the English Department?" Pat asked. "I'm kind of out of it 'cause I'm a part-timer, thankfully. It doesn't sound like you guys over in College of Commerce are constantly at each other's throats."

"Our mutual hostility is pretty well repressed," I agreed.

"Biology's pretty stable," Emma said. "Know why? 'Cause we're scientists. We're not ruled by emotion."

"Nice try, Emma," I said. "Two words: Physics Department."

We had reached the cafeteria's double glass doors. Pat reached out a long arm and pulled the door open for us.

"You can't count the Physics Department." Emma tapped her temple as she walked into the cafeteria. "They're *meshuggah*."

We purchased our lunches and reassembled at a table in the corner. I had the pasta special. Emma had decided to roll the dice on a bento box, and Pat had selected the daily vegetarian option.

"So Emma." Pat dipped a plastic spoon into a bilious-looking carrot soup. "Heard you got arrested."

"Molly, you blabbermouth." Emma glared at me.

"Me? I didn't say anything."

"Don't blame Molly," Pat said. "Someone I know saw you getting processed down at the station. Anyway, it's out on the coconut wireless now. So. Did you do it?"

I was stunned, both by Pat's directness and by the revelation that Emma's big secret was out. Emma, too, seemed taken aback at first, but she recovered quickly. She fired off a litany of unflattering (and unprintable) assessments of Pat's loyalty, friendship, character, ancestry, and general value as a human being.

"And no," she concluded, "I did not 'do it'."

Pat, thick-skinned crime reporter, remained unfazed.

"I still can't figure out what they think they have on you," he said mildly. "What would Kent's toxicology tests have turned up to point to you?"

"How should I know? My lawyer's already asked them to hand over—why am I even answering this? Molly, do you *believe* he's asking me this?"

Thankfully, my phone rang at that moment, saving me from having to choose sides.

"You gonna get it?" Pat asked.

"Oh, nah, she's gotta make 'em wait," Emma said maliciously. "It might be *Stephen* calling."

It was not Stephen. It was someone calling from the Student Retention Office, summoning me to a meeting with Linda. The central scheduling program showed I was not currently in a class or a meeting, so I was expected to report to the SRO immediately.

"What did you do now?" Emma asked when I'd hung up.

"I don't know. They want to see me right away. We were just in the search committee meeting together. I don't know why she couldn't have just told me then."

"Whoa," Pat said. "Summoned by the Student Retention Office? What leprechaun did *you* kick to have such bad luck?"

"I bet it's about your online reviews," Emma said. "You been getting some really weird ones."

"Oh, yeah, about those—" Pat began.

Emma pulled my plate of spaghetti toward her. "You're not gonna need this if you're going up to the Student Retention Office. They probably don't let you have food in there, yah?"

I gazed sadly at the plate. It was only cafeteria spaghetti, overcooked, under-sauced, and so soggy that it sat in a pool of pink water. But I was hungry, and had been looking forward to eating it.

"Anyways," Emma said, "you know the entrance to their lair is paved with the bones of disobedient faculty members, right? So watch your step, Molly."

"Good luck," Pat added.

They started digging into my waterlogged spaghetti.

"Hurry," Emma said. "You don't wanna be late. Eh, you're not missing much. Spaghetti's not so good."

The receptionist pulled her white sweater tight against the cold and led me through a maze of hallways, depositing me in a quiet room near the back of the Student Retention Office complex. It was both cozy and luxurious, with a gleaming maple floor and vintage-style koa furniture. I sat down on a carved koa loveseat. Its floral cushions were upholstered in a red, green, and tan retro floral print. Across from me, on the other side of the coffee table, was a matching couch. One of these days I'd buy something as nice as this for my house, to replace my cheap leather living room set from Balusteros World of Furniture.

On the koa coffee table lay a stack of about a dozen copies of *Be a Rock Star in the Classroom!* There were no bookshelves, just a low putty-colored file cabinet against the wall. I wondered what was inside it. Probably thousands more copies of *Be a Rock Star in the Classroom!*

Ten minutes went by, and then twenty. Just as I decided they had forgotten about me, Linda swept into the room, followed by her protégé/henchperson Kathy. They seated themselves on the couch opposite me.

I still had no idea why I had been summoned, or what I had done wrong. I braced myself, expecting the worst.

To my amazement, Linda and Kathy had good news. It was

about Bret Lampson, my troubled student. He would not be returning to Mahina State University. He and his shark-tooth club would be withdrawing from summer session to focus on his "personal issues."

"I'm relieved," I said. "And happy for him. It's the best solution for everyone. Thank you so much for letting me know. So what happens when he comes back in the fall?"

Linda and Kathy exchanged a look.

"Bret won't be coming back," Linda said. "He'll be off-island for the foreseeable future."

"He's in California," Kathy added. "He's enrolling in a long-term residential program there."

"Well, I'm delighted to hear he'll be getting the help he needs."

"Yes, this program sounds perfect for him," Linda said. "It's in a little town near the coast. I believe it was a Spanish-sounding name. What was it, Kathy?"

"It was a hospital of some kind," Kathy said. "I think it began with the letter A."

"Not Atascadero State Hospital?"

"Yes," Kathy's tone was encouraging. "That sounds right."

"*Atascadero State Hospital for the Criminally Insane?*"

Linda picked up a copy of *Be a Rock Star in the Classroom* from the top of the stack and offered it to me.

"You'll find this tremendously helpful in improving your teaching," Linda said.

"You gave me a copy a few days ago," I said.

"I know, but we have to distribute all of them by—" Kathy started.

"Perhaps you can share this with a colleague," Linda interrupted.

"Sure." I took the booklet from Linda. "My pleasure. Thank you."

CHAPTER FORTY-SEVEN

When I got back to my office, I found Emma sitting in the good visitor chair, reading a journal.

"Emma, how did you get into my office?"

Emma didn't look up. "Pat and me found your door unlocked."

"I left my door unlocked? Where's Pat then?"

"He hadda leave. I thought I'd hang out for a while. My students would never think of looking for me here."

"Perfect. I have a present for you."

I handed her the copy of *Be a Rock Star in the Classroom!* and settled onto my yoga ball chair.

"Aw, another copy of *Be a Rock Star in the Classroom!?* Molly, you shouldn't have."

"Don't mention it. Hey, do you think I look any thinner since I've been sitting on this ball?"

"What?"

"Yeah, I haven't noticed any difference either."

"Eh, so what did the Student Retention Office want?"

"It was good news, for a change." I related my conversation with Kathy and Linda.

"How'd they let someone like that on a college campus to begin with? Are we so desperate for tuition money? It was a rhetorical question, so no need answer."

I noticed a white spot on the faux walnut grain of my desk. I pulled the vodka bottle out of my bottom drawer, sprayed the spot, and wiped away the remains.

"Eh, what, Molly? Wasting vodka like that?"

"I'm not wasting anything. I was just keeping my desk clea—"

Emma grabbed the bottle from me and aimed a few squirts of vodka into her mouth. I grabbed the bottle back and dropped it into the drawer.

"I can't let you ingest this stuff, Emma. It's basically cleaning fluid. Listen, I have to ask you something. And I want you to be honest with me."

Emma closed her journal. "What is it?"

"You know Iker and I were looking through all of last fiscal year's purchases in Arts and Sciences. Every department. Including Biology."

"So?"

"Iker said some transactions in the Biology Department don't look right. They don't reconcile or something, I don't remember his exact wording. Anyway, they're in your lab. What's going on?"

"What, first you take away my vodka, now you're grilling me about my lab budget?"

"Yes."

"Okay, Molly, I know you're an English major and you never had to worry about getting external funding, but do you know what a grant is?"

"Of course I know what a grant is. I know the entire Student Retention Office is funded by the Foundation grant. And I wish you'd stop calling me an English major. I have a PhD. in literature and creative writing from one of the top ten—"

"But you never got a grant before, right?"

"Well, not personally, no."

"Yah, that's what I thought. They got all these rules about how you can spend the money, and what you gotta spend the money on, and when you gotta spend it. Government agencies especially."

"It makes sense. They don't want to hand money out and have it disappear."

"Yeah, except if anyone really tried to follow all those rules? They'd never get anything done. So when we order something from the supply house, they don't tell us the shipping cost to Hawaii until after it's shipped. And sometimes not till after it arrived already."

"They don't tell you when you place the order?" I asked.

"No. 'Cause Hawaii, ah? We don't get the standard shipping rates. And the grants office won't cover the shipping because they need to have the exact amount in advance, otherwise they won't reimburse."

"What do you mean *they* won't reimburse? Isn't it *your* grant?"

"Yeah. It doesn't work that way, Molly. I can't just take my grant money into SunSport Paddling Supply and buy myself a new canoe. It's what I mean by all those rules. So I had to set up a little da kine, on the side, to cover the shipping costs."

"Emma, you shouldn't have to break the rules to administer your grant. This is money you're bringing in to the university. Can't the university help you?"

"With what money?"

"Well if it's just shipping costs, it can't be much. Can it?"

Emma dug into her backpack, pulled out a crumpled packing slip, and slapped it down on the desk.

"Here's my latest invoice. Cover glass for slides."

I smoothed it out and read it.

"Am I reading this right? The shipping costs twice as much as the actual product?"

"Uh huh."

"How are you supposed to—"

"Exactly. How am I supposed to do my job? Oh, and don't forget, I'm lucky to find a supplier who will ship to Hawaii in the first place. So you gonna turn me in now? Give 'em something to add to the murder charge?"

"Don't be ridiculous. I'm not going to report you. It's just when Iker and I were looking into the university's finances, your lab had these discrepancies. It's the only reason I asked."

"So, you satisfied, Professor Persnickety?"

"Look, I didn't make up the accounting rules. Have you heard anything from your lawyer, by the way?"

"Nothing new."

"This is ridiculous, Emma. No one who knows you would think for a moment you could have poisoned Kent. Poison's not your style. If *you* wanted to get rid of someone, you'd push them out of a window or run them down with your car."

"Exactly."

Dan Watanabe stuck his head in the door.

"Molly, the reception's starting downstairs. We need to get down there. Emma, you want to come? It's open to all the faculty."

"Oh hey, Dan. No offense, but why would *I* want to see *your* nice new classroom? I'm just gonna get all jealous."

"Free food," Dan said. "Molly, you should come anyway. There aren't many of us around in the summer, and we need to show a good turnout for this. Either of you seen Rodge?"

"No," I said.

"Thankfully not," Emma said.

"Dan's right," I said to Emma, when he had gone. "You should come. They might have those brownies."

"Oh, the ones that're all crunchy on top and chewy in the middle? I'm in."

The text alert on my phone pinged as we stood and collected our things.

"Margaret Adams just sent me a text," I said.

"Who's that?"

"She's one of our students. Accounting major. Works at Fujioka's Music and Party Supply. *Two* watches? Now *that's* interesting."

"Molly, what are you babbling about?"

"Marshall Dixon wears this gaudy steel and diamond watch—I don't know, maybe it's just a coincidence. It's not like we have that many different stores in Mahina."

"You're not making any sense," Emma said. "Come on, let's get down there to your glistening new classroom before the brownies are all gone."

"You know the diamond watch Marshall Dixon wears?"

"No," Emma said.

"Well then just take my word for it." I slung my bag over my shoulder. "They sell a watch just like it at Fujioka's Music and Party Supply, so Iker and I asked our student to look into how many they've sold this year."

"Why do you care what kind of watch Marshall Dixon wears? Eh, which way? Stairs or elevator?"

"Elevator's still broken," I said. "We can take the stairs. Wait, I almost forgot my phone. Anyway, remember what we saw at the retreat? With the kiss on the hand?"

"Ew, thanks for bringing it back up," Emma said. "Along with my lunch."

"Anyway, the watch doesn't seem like something Marshall Dixon would buy for herself. Not at all her style. I was telling Iker, it had to be a gift from Kent. You know when someone buys something for you, and you feel obliged to wear it, even if you don't like it? One Christmas my mom got me—"

A brisk knock interrupted my story. Serena, the dean's secretary, stood in the doorway.

"Hey Serena," Emma said.

"We have open house today, Emma," Serena said. "New classroom. Emma, you better get down there before the brownies are gone. Molly, this will only take a minute."

I sighed and put my bag down. I thought of asking Emma to save me a brownie, but she was already gone.

CHAPTER FORTY-EIGHT

"Molly, I'm glad I caught you before you went down. I been trying to get ahold of you—"

Serena paused when she saw the textbooks stacked on my desk. "What are those?" she asked, cautiously.

"I'm still evaluating the Biz Com textbooks. I have them narrowed down to four or five that I like. I know I should be further along by now. But there are so many of them, and it takes so much time to go over each one."

"You're still doing the Business Communication books?"

"I'm trying to find a decent one that'll cost the students less than a month's rent," I said. "I don't know why they have to be so expensive. Look at this one. It's not any bigger than a magazine... What is it, Serena?"

"Well, I'm sure Dean Vogel appreciates you doing all of this work. It'll really be helpful for the future. The thing is, Molly, the dean has been *so* busy, and I guess somehow this fell through the cracks, so I hope you understand. I found out about it just now."

"What is it?" I backed away from Serena and sank back onto my yoga ball. "Am I teaching in the fall? My contract got renewed, right? I'm not fired, am I?"

"No, Molly, you didn't get fired. You're gonna be taking over Rodge Cowper's classes in the fall."

"What?"

"Intro to Business Management and Business Planning. They're yours now. Congratulations,"

212

"I'm teaching IBM and BP? Serena, fall semester starts in a *month*. How am I supposed to—"

"Excuse me?" came a tiny voice from behind Serena.

The young woman looked vaguely familiar: petite, prettily made-up, smooth black hair. Not one of my students. Where had I seen her before?

"Hi, are you busy?" asked the young woman.

"Ah, yes, I am," I said. "I'm in a meeting right now."

"Are you Miss Barda?"

"Faculty aren't on duty during the summer," Serena said. "If you can wait a moment, I'll be right with you."

Serena moved to shut the door, but the girl stepped into the doorway and stood firm.

"I want to talk to a professor. I'll wait."

"So I have to do what now?" I asked Serena. "Why can't Rodge teach his own classes?"

"They want Rodge to teach all sections of HP," Serena said. "It's real popular you know. There's always a waiting list to get in. That's how come the Student Retention Office made us open up more sections. And they told us make sure Rodge was the one teaching it. So with Rodge teaching all those Human Potential sections, we had to give his other classes to someone else."

"Well, great," I said. "I guess I should consider it a vote of confidence, that they can throw two completely new preps at me at the last minute."

My visitor was still standing in my doorway, frowning at her sparkly pink phone as if she weren't listening to our every word.

"So if I'm taking on Rodge's classes, what happens to my Biz Com classes?"

"We're gonna transfer Biz Com to a part-time lecturer."

"Wait a minute. Why not give *Rodge's* old classes to the lecturer and leave mine the way they are? I've already spent most of the summer going over all these books, prepping for fall. Plus, I've never taught BP *or* IBM."

"It was way easier to find a part-timer to take over Biz Com," Serena said. "Alls you need is a PhD in English. There's so many of those who are desperate for work, you know. And Dean Vogel says no one in their right mind would agree to take on IBM and BP at the last min—"

Serena cleared her throat.

"Well, anyway, we know you'll do a *great* job. Okay, let me know when you've decided on a textbook for Biz Com, and I'll pass it along to the lecturer."

"Can I get desk copies of Rodge's textbooks?" I asked. "Since I'm not going to have much time to prepare my *new classes*, I'll just use whatever he's been using."

"Rodge doesn't use textbooks," Serena said.

"Very helpful," I said.

"But if you want to assign textbooks for those classes, make sure you get me the ISBN numbers by the end of next week so I can get the order in to the bookstore."

The young woman watched Serena leave. Then she put away her phone and walked into my office uninvited.

CHAPTER FORTY-NINE

"Hey, Professor." The girl sat down in my visitor chair. "So what are all these books for?"

"I was evaluating textbooks for my fall Business Communication class."

"Oh, but they're giving that class to someone else now, right? I heard what you were talking about. So you did all this work for nothing?"

"Did you have a quick question? I have an important meeting downstairs."

The brownies were probably all gone by now, and the oatmeal raisin cookies probably weren't far behind. If I waited much longer, all that would be left for me would be the horrible banana bread, which is always undercooked in the middle.

"I have to retake Business Planning." She reached into her pink backpack, which matched her pink phone, and pulled out a stack of forms. She shoved my books aside to clear a space and placed the papers on my desk.

"You have to retake Business Planning? You failed Rodge Cowper's class? I didn't think that was—how did that happen?"

"I got a A-minus." She rested her hands on the papers and looked me in the eye. "I have to retake it so I can get an A."

"Well, Rodge won't be teaching it in the fall. The honor, as you heard, falls to me."

"So you're exactly the one I need to talk to."

"Evidently. So how did you manage to get an A-*minus* in Dr.

Cowper's class?"

"Well, I was having a super busy semester, so I wasn't really able to make it to class."

"You didn't show up to class at all, and you got an A-minus? I see. I think your best bet is to work something out with Dr. Cowper. I don't think retaking BP with me is going to get you a better grade."

"Please, Miss, I really want to do this. Not just for the grade. I wanna learn how to write a business plan."

"You want to *learn*?"

I regarded her with renewed interest.

"I want my business to be successful. I'm serious about this. I know I'm gonna be entering a really competitive industry."

"What kind of business?"

"It's a clothing boutique."

And then I remembered why she looked familiar.

"You're Ashleigh?"

"That's right. Ashleigh Ueda." She was beaming now. "Did Dr. Rodge tell you about me?"

"No, you came by Rodge Cowper's office with Skip Kojima. You're a history major, right?"

"Yes I am. Very nice to meet you." She offered a tiny hand. "Marshall Dixon? The vice-president? She wasn't supportive of my business idea for some reason."

"Hm. How did the rest of Skip Kojima's visit go?"

"Okay, I guess. We were gonna take him out for dinner, but he remembered he had to leave early for another meeting."

"So. You want to open a clothing boutique? Here in Mahina?"

I knew little about running a clothing store, but from what I had seen, it wasn't easy. In my short time in Mahina I had seen them appear, with names like Lingerie Lady and Downtown Diva and Beaut-tique, full of optimism and the owner's life savings. Then six or eight months later, I'd drive by, and notice where the shop used to be was now one more desolate storefront with a sun-faded "For Lease" sign propped behind a dusty window.

"I *love* fashion," Ashleigh said.

"I don't think loving fashion is enough, Ashleigh. You'll be running a business. Doing all the—you know, all of the business stuff businesses do."

I had a lot of brushing-up to do before I taught Intro to Business Management in the fall semester.

"Look," I said. "Here's what I do know. I know people here who own their own businesses. Mercedes Yamashiro, who runs the Cloudforest Bed and Breakfast. Tatsuya Masumoto, from Tatsuya's Moderne Beauty. They're always working. It's hard, and time consuming, and risky. The day-to-day seems to be mostly unrelated to doing what you *love*."

"Linda says if you follow your dreams—"

"You'll never work a day in your life. Right. Because that field's not hiring."

Ashleigh blinked.

"But I'm good at it. My friends all ask me for advice on what to wear and stuff."

"Look. I don't know who told you doing what you love was a good career plan, but the person lied to you. The money will *not* follow."

"But Linda says—"

"Listen to me, Ashleigh. Let me tell you what happens when you follow your dreams. You might love language, for example. And writing. You might be really good at it. Good enough to get accepted into one of the top ten literature and creative writing programs in the country. A program so selective, they might admit two students in a year. And you're good enough to stick it out, and make it through, and earn your PhD. Now you have 'Doctor' in front of your name. Fantastic, right? A dream come true. And you know what happens next?"

"No." Ashleigh looked a little worried.

"Nothing. Unemployment. That's what happens."

I took a breath and steadied myself on my yoga ball.

"Where was I? Right. You just got your doctorate. And now you're realizing, a little too late, that a lot of other people love the same things you love, and there's a thousand other poor suckers applying for every job opening you're applying for. And they have fancy PhDs and sparkling CVs and world-famous dissertation advisors, too. So you broaden your horizons. And you apply to places you've never even heard of. And when you finally, *finally* land a job, at the Mahina State University College of Commerce, what does your dissertation advisor say about it? Is he happy for you?"

"I don't know?" Ashleigh hugged herself and shrank back in the chair.

"No, he is *not* happy for you. Because not only do you have to move to the, uh, bottom end of nowhere, I'm paraphrasing here, but you've committed the unforgivable sin of ending up in a *Business School.*"

"But I'm not—"

"So instead of saying congratulations on getting a real job with health insurance, he tells you, 'Teaching a roomful of slack-jawed baseball caps how to pad their resumes is a grievous waste of your fine critical mind.' And all you can say to him is that your 'fine critical mind' is telling you after an entire *year* of fruitless job-hunting, it's time to start earning a living wage."

"But I—"

"A *year*, Ashleigh. Sure, do what you love. But don't *ever* expect to get paid for it. Listen, I have to get down to my meeting."

She stood up, gathered her things quickly, and hurried out of my office without saying goodbye.

"I hope this was helpful," I called after her. "See you in class?"

CHAPTER FIFTY

I hesitated at the door of the classroom. Crowds make me nervous. The fact that many of the people in the room were at some point going to decide on my tenure application pegged the needle on my panic-meter. Linda from the Student Retention Office was there, of course, flanked by a few of her SRO henchpersons. Vice President Marshall Dixon hadn't arrived yet, and the chancellor was a no-show, but I recognized a few of the other administrators. My faculty colleagues were clustered around the refreshment table.

Fortunately, Emma had been watching for me.

"You *have* to see this." She grabbed my wrist and pulled me into the classroom. There was no trace of her earlier envy; she was all *schadenfreude* now.

"Emma, what's going on? Why do you seem so happy?"

"Molly, look at it. Just look around. It looks like a preschool."

I stared around the room, incredulous. She was right. Circular tables had replaced the desks, and brightly colored construction paper covered the walls. Without desks, lectern, or podium, it was impossible to tell where the front of the room was.

Emma shoved my shoulder cheerfully. "Molly, don't look so shocked. What'd you think, the Student Retention Office was gonna do something *good* to your classroom?"

"I don't understand. This was supposed to be—What happened?"

"I'll tell you what happened, Molly. Kindergarten is the last time those SRO dimwits felt smart. So they're trying to make the university just like kindergarten."

"Well that's a provocative hypothesis." I shook my head to clear it. "Are you hungry? I'm hungry."

Emma followed me over to the refreshment table.

"Molly, what I just described is a *theory*, not a *hypothesis*. A hypothesis is a specific, testable proposition."

"Give me a break. I'm an English major, remember?"

"How come you're so late anyways? The good stuff's all gone."

Sadly, Emma was right. Only one crumb-strewn platter with a few slices of sticky banana bread remained. At least there was some coffee left, and it was real Kona, not the ten-percent blend.

Linda materialized next to us.

"So glad you could join us, Molly." This seemed less like a friendly greeting than an assurance that my late arrival did not go unnoticed.

"So where's the front of the room again, Linda?" Emma asked innocently. "Molly needs to know where she should stand when she gives her long, complicated *lectures*."

"Emma, what are you talking about? I don't—"

"There *is* no front of the room, Emma. This is a learner-centered layout. The teacher isn't the Sage on the Stage anymore."

"Okay, wait a minute now. Is there really no desk or lectern for the *professor*?" And would it kill Linda to call us professors, instead of teachers?

"You can probably rearrange things if you need," Emma said. She grabbed the edge of a table and tried to move it, but it was fastened in place. "Oh, wait. No you can't. Sorry, Molly, guess you don't get to decide how your classroom is set up."

This wasn't funny. In a few weeks, I would actually have to start teaching in this classroom.

"The students are all facing in different directions," I said to Linda. "I don't see how—"

"The *teacher* can walk around among the student groups," Linda said, "or join a student group at *their* table. But the focus remains on the students. The teacher is no longer the star of the show."

"So Molly," Emma said, "you're gonna have to walk around the room when you sing 'Wheels on the Bus.'"

"What about student presentations?" I asked. "Or what if we have a guest speaker?"

"Some teachers 'get it' quicker than others. Molly, if you give up your need to control everything, and adapt to this new classroom design, I think you'll really be able to improve your teaching."

"Well, I guess everyone wants *that* to happen," I said.

"Excuse me." Linda disappeared into the crowd.

"Guess she has to go suck up to the vice president," Emma said, and sure enough, Linda had scurried over to Marshall Dixon, who had just arrived.

"It's not even worth it to get angry." I gazed sadly around kindergarten-ified classroom. "They're like Daniel Webster's Jury of the Damned. Our anger only makes them more powerful. They can use it as evidence of our obstructionism and obsolescence."

"You know the SRO doesn't like it when you use those big words," Emma said.

"I know. We have to meet everyone where they are, even if where they are is a third-grade reading level. Where's Betty Jackson? I'd love to get her psychologist's perspective on this."

"She already came and went," Emma said. "She had to leave early to go film our new recruiting video. You know how we gotta showcase our 'diverse' faculty every chance we get. Cause we got so few of 'em."

"Why aren't you in that video, Emma? Doesn't the same thing happen to you? Native Hawaiian, woman in science? How come you're not trotted out at every opportunity?"

"I did one legislator visit," Emma said. "Didn't work out too good. Our marketing office is *so* hung up on all this image stuff. 'Dress professionally.' 'Use your indoor voice.' 'You can't use that kind of language with the senator.' Pfft. Who needs it? Oh look, there's Bob Wilson."

The little bald man in the brown plaid shirt turned toward the sound of his name.

Frankie Bow

"Eh, Bob, good job getting off our search committee." Emma dealt him an approving shoulder punch. "It's one way to do it, ah? Apply for the job yourself."

"Hello Emma. Molly. Do you believe this?" He swept his hand around the classroom. "_This_ is why I'm applying for the Associate Dean of Learning Process Improvement position. We need some sanity around here."

"I was just chatting with one of your majors," I said. "Ashleigh Ueda. I guess she's a product of your new history program?"

"Oh, _Ashleigh_." Bob visibly crumpled. "A product? More like a casualty. If all the Student Retention Office did was to print up those silly booklets, I wouldn't mind them so much. But look at the damage they're doing to our students."

Bob produced an issue of _Island Confidential_.

"Look at this. A complete expose on the student-directed-learning initiative. Just in time for the new school year. I don't know where the reporter got his information, but he really gets it right."

"I thought _Island Confidential_ was anonymous," Emma said. "How do you know it's a _him_?"

"Trophies for everyone," I read. "Interesting headline."

"And do you know about the off-island degree requirement? It's been showing up in the want ads. Employers don't want our graduates now."

"I have heard about it," I said. "It's awful. I hope we can fix it."

Bob Wilson spotted Linda.

"Excuse me," he said. He went over to Linda, placed his hand on her arm, and launched into what looked like an impassioned speech. She absently ran her hand over his bald head.

"Hard to believe those two are married," I said.

"Maybe the conflict spices things up."

"I'll never understand people. Hey, Iker just came in."

"Does he ever not wear a tie? Eh, you guys ever get hold of the Student Retention Office financials?"

"Not yet," I said. "Iker was worried about annoying Marshall.

222

But at least he finally acknowledged we should keep trying. Come on, let's go talk to him."

CHAPTER FIFTY-ONE

"I don't want to talk to Iker Legazpi," Emma said. "He thinks I killed Kent Lovely."

"No he doesn't. He just thinks you're embezzling from the Biology Department."

"You go talk to him. I'll just stand here by myself."

"She can hang out with me," said a voice from somewhere over my head.

"Pat. When did *you* get here?"

"You shoulda come sooner," Emma said. "All the good food's gone."

"Didn't you get an invitation?" I asked.

"Nah. I was walking by and thought I'd crash the party. What *is* this place anyway? A daycare center?"

"No. It's supposed to be a classroom for the College of Commerce."

"Yeah, this just *screams* Future Titans of Industry," Pat snickered. "What's the thing hanging down from the middle of the ceiling? Some kind of panopticon so they can keep you under full time surveillance?"

"Oh, Linda was telling everyone about it before Molly got here. It's the multimedia projector."

"Where is it supposed to project?" I looked around the room again. "There's no front of the room."

"There's a screen on each wall," Emma said. "It projects in four directions at once."

"It sounds kinda cool," Pat said.

"And you're not getting the remote, 'cause there's no secure place to keep it. You gotta use the controls right on the thing itself, so you gotta reach up to turn it on. Glad we don't have it in my classroom. I'd have to stand on a chair."

"Oh, how interesting. I wonder if Linda would demonstrate it for me."

"Good work," Pat said. "You're finally learning to suck up."

"Maybe. I'll go ask her now."

"Well, sounds like you've got business to attend to," Pat said. "I'll just—hey, is that banana bread?"

"It's not very good," I said.

"That's okay. I don't drink, I don't eat meat, and I'm celibate. So even mediocre banana bread is a pleasure for me."

Emma and I watched Pat head to the refreshment table.

"Dang," I said. Emma placed a sympathetic hand on my shoulder.

"What were we doing now?"

"Linda," Emma said grimly. "You wanted to ask her about the projector, for some reason."

"Right. Let's go."

Emma and I sidled through the crowd to the other side of the room. We found Linda straightening out a length of brown yarn stretched between two thumbtacks. It was part of a yarn tree on an orange construction paper background. I wondered what possible educational purpose it served. Maybe to illustrate what trees would look like if they were made of yarn? We waited as she pressed the last thumbtack in.

"Emma just told me you demonstrated the projector earlier," I said. "I'm sorry to bother you, but do you think you could just quickly show me how it works? I'm going to be teaching in this classroom, I should know how to use the technology."

"Well, Molly, you *should* have arrived on time. A teacher has to model personal responsibility."

"Yes, I do realize that. I was on my way down from my office when I had an unexpected visit from a student. Ashleigh Ueda.

225

I believe you know her. She wanted to talk about her Business Planning class, and I didn't want to brush her off."

"Oh, Ashleigh. Yes, you made a good choice. The students come first."

"So would you mind doing a demo for me? Oh, Iker came in after I did. I imagine he could use a review too."

I walked over to where Iker was talking to Marshall Dixon, next to a bulletin board decorated with construction-paper autumn leaves.

"Iker," Dixon was saying, "I appreciate your desire to be thorough, but what you've already done is quite enough."

"It is only that I do not like to do a half-cooked job. If I were able to see the records of the Student Retention Office—"

"Hi, sorry to interrupt," I interrupted, "but Linda's going to demonstrate the new multidirectional projector again for me. Iker, you might have to teach a class in here. Want to watch with me?"

Iker looked like he was about to decline, but his expression changed when he caught my pleading expression.

"Yes, of course. I will watch."

Marshall and Iker turned their attention to the center of the room, where Linda was reaching up toward the ceiling-mounted projector. I realized I was holding my breath. Linda nodded toward me and began her demonstration.

The cuff of Linda's sleeve flopped back on her upstretched arm, revealing a diamond-encrusted watch in a rose-gold finish. Marshall's eyes widened and she looked quickly down at her own watch.

Linda talked about the Foundation's farsightedness and generosity as screens on four walls lit up with colorful stock images of fall foliage, brightly painted houses, and what looked like an Italian coastal village.

"We're all very grateful to the Foundation," Linda concluded. "They're the ones who made this possible. Let's have a round of applause for the Foundation."

The few people who were paying attention managed a

smattering of applause.

"Our friends at the Student Retention Office have really outdone themselves, haven't they?" Marshall Dixon's voice had an edge to it. It could have drawn blood. "Iker, I think you may have persuaded me. No harm in being thorough, as you say. I'll instruct my secretary to message the records to you. Go ahead and tell her what you need, and she'll make sure you get it. Now if you'll excuse me, I have another appointment."

I watched Marshall shake hands with a few people on her way out. Linda was not one of them.

As Marshall left, Rodge strolled in.

"This classroom makes me feel like I'm back in kindergarten," Rodge announced to no one in particular. "I like it. Hey, what's up with Marshall Dixon? She was pulling off her watch like it was on fire."

"She had another meeting," I said.

"Any brownies left?" Rodge asked.

"No," I said. "But there's banana bread."

"Ah, sweet!" Rodge sped to the refreshment table, where Emma happened to be standing. Emma immediately excused herself, and came to join Iker and me.

"Doctor Dixon was telling me I could not have the Student Retention Office records." Iker looked baffled. "But then all of the sudden, she changed her mind."

"I saw the whole thing," Emma said. "Molly, how did you know? Did you see Linda wearing the watch before?"

"No. When Linda reached up to fix the projector, it was the first time I'd ever seen her wrist. But *two* of those watches disappeared from Fujioka's inventory—Iker, Margaret Adams texted me—so I thought there was a good chance Linda had one of them. Remember, Kent's last phone call was to Linda's personal number. And you know Kent. Why settle for just one, when you can have both?"

"So it looks like Linda knew about Marshall, but Marshall didn't know about Linda."

"What do you mean Marshall does not know about Linda?"

Iker said. "I believe the two are well acquainted."

Emma leaned over and whispered something in Iker's ear. His round cheeks flushed pink.

"Iker, how much time will you need to look over the Student Retention Office purchase records?"

"I will make it of the topmost priority," Iker said. "I see the problems may be more widely spread than I first imagined."

CHAPTER FIFTY-TWO

I was at Tatsuya's Moderne Beauty, baking under one of the chrome bonnets with a conditioner pack in my hair, reading *Island Confidential.* It was the issue that Bob Wilson had showed us the other day. I had mixed feelings about the article, "Trophies for Everyone." Of course it was satisfying to witness the dastardliness of the Student Retention Office exposed for all to see. The anonymous reporter described junior faculty and part-timers bullied into passing students, math and writing requirements removed to speed up degree production, employers island-wide closing their doors to Mahina State graduates with the "off-island degree required" disclaimer in their job announcements.

On the other hand, I was an employee of Mahina State University. Anything that made Mahina State look bad reflected poorly on everyone who worked there. Including me. This wasn't simply an issue of pride. It was only a matter of time before some legislator tried to score political points by moving to shut us down.

Tatsuya handed me a cup of tea. The teacup was the Japanese style, with no handle, and very hot. I quickly set it down on the arm of the chair.

"Too warm?" he asked.

"A little." I blew on my seared palms. "Thank you, though. I'll wait for it to cool down a bit."

"I meant the pack." Tatsuya patted his own sleek hair.

"Oh no, my scalp is comfortable. Nice and warm. Tatsuya,

did you see this article in *Island Confidential?* 'Trophies for Everyone'?"

"Yes, I did." He seemed embarrassed. "I'm sure there are good reasons for what they're doing up there. Although using the online ratings to evaluate the professors seems a bit silly."

"They're seriously using the online evals? I didn't think it would really get approved." I picked up the paper and scanned the article.

"I *do* have some experience with online ratings myself." Tatsuya carefully removed the teacup from the chair arm and set it on the magazine stand next to me. "Personally, I would *never* leave nasty reviews for my competitors. It's tempting, but it's not right. Unfortunately, not everyone in our business community feels the same way."

"Tatsuya, how awful. Your competitors are leaving bad reviews for you?"

"Trudy and I can't know for sure who it is. But we have our suspicions. Anonymity is for cowards," he added with surprising force.

"Well, I can see how anonymity could be useful in *some* instances."

Maybe it had been cowardly of me not to sign my name when I submitted that complaint to the Foundation. But I didn't have tenure yet. Until I did, "cowardly" was the watchword.

"I do hope for your sake your university will reconsider their decision," Tatsuya said. "Honestly, people get so ugly online when they know they're not accountable for anything they say. Molly, imagine. What if you have students who decide to hold your evaluations hostage in exchange for a passing grade?"

"Oh, *that* happens already with our in-class evals,"

"But if they go to online reviews, your disgruntled students can get all their friends to gang up on you as well."

"That's true."

"And imagine, when someone searches for you, they'll find those awful reviews."

"I didn't even think about that. I haven't been looking at my online ratings, but now I'm worried. Maybe I should check to see what they say."

I reached up to tip the bonnet back so I could retrieve my phone from my bag, but Tatsuya laid a gentle hand on mine.

"Not here, Miss Molly. This is a place of rejuvenation and rest. You can stress yourself out all you want when you're back in your office."

"I'm actually going to guitar lesson after this," I said.

"Well. Even better. Music can be so healing. And I'm sure your young man will be dazzled by your beautiful, smooth hair."

"It's really not like that with Jonah."

"Well, why not?" Tatsuya settled into the bonnet chair beside me. It was a Wednesday morning, and I was the first and so far only customer. "Is it because he's much younger than you?"

"Jonah's not *that* much younger than I am. I just don't think of him as a romantic interest."

"He's a sweet boy," Tatsuya said. "You could do much worse."

"Now that no one thinks he's a murderer anymore."

"No one really believed that," Tatsuya shook his head.

"So what are people saying about Emma now?"

"I will tell you what *I* think. After reading this story? I think there's something going on at your university, and I'm not sure it's fair to pin it on Emma Nakamura. Although I do see why she might attract suspicion. She has that quick temper, you see. Here. I think your tea's cooled down now."

I walked out of Tatsuya's with my hair soft and gleaming. (The effect would last for about three minutes in Mahina's muggy weather.) I had a few extra minutes before my guitar lesson. Not enough time to go all the way home to shower and change, but enough so, if I drove directly, I would arrive at Emma's house too early.

I started my car, moved it to a shady spot, lowered the windows and turned the engine off. Then I took a deep breath as I pulled up that professor rating site on my phone. My stomach churned with foreboding, and the agonizingly slow connection didn't help. When the page finally loaded, I had to stare at it for a few seconds to make sure I was reading it correctly.

My average rating was 4.9. Out of five. Encouraged, I gathered the courage to read the comments. My numbers were high, but my reviews were...inventive.

She shot a man in Reno, just because he asked for extra credit.

The lectures and the textbook have nothing to do with chemistry. And forget trying to do experiments in class. Worst chemistry class ever.

Hard class, not the best if your just hear to get your ticket punched.

Where had I just seen that? About students who are in college not to learn, but to "get their tickets punched—"?

It was in the *Island Confidential* article I had just been reading in Tatsuya's Moderne Beauty. The exact phrase. Was the mysterious muckraker behind *Island Confidential* a student of mine?

I browsed through the ratings. There were pages and pages of them. All with high numbers, all posted within the previous ten days, and most of them weird. Who was creative and determined enough to leave all those ratings? My troubled ex-student Bret, logging on from whatever accommodations the State of California had provided him? I was about to check Emma's ratings when I realized I'd already killed more than enough time. I got into gear, backed out, and headed up the hill for my guitar lesson.

CHAPTER FIFTY-THREE

As I approached Emma's front door I could hear an argument in progress. A male voice—Emma's brother Jonah? Her husband Yoshi?—grumbled indistinctly, in counterpoint to Emma's yelling.

"Yah, so?" This was Emma. "There's still the *Federal* laws, you dummy. I'm in enough trouble already, in case you never noticed. You live under my roof, you gotta respect my rules."

Jonah, then. I could see this argument going on indefinitely if I didn't interrupt them. I knocked on the door. It flew open, and Emma stood there, scowling.

"Your hair looks weird." Emma stomped away, leaving me to close the door and follow her inside. Jonah got up from the kitchen table when he saw me, and quietly led the way to the laundry room.

The guitar lesson was uneventful. Jonah was even less talkative than usual. I knew Tatsuya had meant well when he suggested Jonah as a romantic prospect, but I couldn't see it. And besides, as much as I love Emma as a friend, I'm not sure I'd want her as my sister-in-law.

When the lesson was over, I came out of the laundry room to find Emma at the kitchen table. She was sitting in front of a nearly empty bottle of wine. I found a coffee mug in her cabinet, sat down next to her, and poured the rest of the bottle out for myself. Jonah retrieved a beer from the fridge and joined us. The three of us sat at the kitchen table and drank quietly.

"They wanna do a plea deal," Emma said, finally.

Jonah inhaled as if he was about to say something.

"Shut up, Jonah."

"What are they offering?" I asked.

"Twenty-five hundred dollar fine."

"Well, maybe that wouldn't be too—"

"And ten years in prison."

I thought I'd misheard her.

"You didn't just say ten *years*?"

"Yeah. That's what I said."

"Ten years in prison? Emma, what about your career? How do they think you're supposed to keep your research program going without access to your lab? Will the university let you teach your classes online?"

Emma glared at me.

"Okay, I guess those aren't the most important things. What does your lawyer say about all of this?"

"Feinman thinks I should take the deal."

"He does?"

Emma nodded glumly.

"But you didn't do it, Emma. You didn't kill anyone."

"Doesn't matter," Emma got up to get another bottle of wine from the cupboard. "Nobody cares."

"But they don't have any evidence at all to point to you. I don't understand—"

"Someone heard her threatening him, that's why," Jonah said. "There's a witness."

"But Emma didn't threaten anyone. I was right there with her. Right, Emma?"

"Alls I said was I hoped he choked on a waffle."

"I remember. But it was a wish, not a threat. I wonder who ratted you out? Emma, I don't have class today. Do you want to—"

"I just wanna be alone."

Jonah stood up from the kitchen table, dropped his empty beer bottle into the recycling pail, and disappeared into his room.

"Sorry, Molly." Emma closed her eyes and propped her forehead on her hand. "I'm not good company today."

I scooted the chair back and stood up.

"I can leave if you'd rather be by yourself."

I didn't believe Emma genuinely wanted to be alone right now, but I wanted to show her I respected her space.

"Nah, don't go," she said. "Sit down. Have some more wine. Distract me. I see you got your hair done at Tatsuya's today. Any beauty parlor gossip?"

"Not really. Here's some interesting news, though. Remember the plan to use our online ratings to evaluate us?"

Emma took a big gulp from her wine mug.

"Is this supposed to make me feel better about going to prison?"

"No, listen. I was worried about it, and I just checked my ratings. I have a whole bunch of five out of fives."

"Really? I thought your online ratings were horrible."

"They were. I don't know what happened."

"What about mines?"

"I don't know. I didn't have time to check yours."

Emma stood up, left the kitchen, and came back holding a small tablet computer. She tapped on the surface, knit her eyebrows, and then tapped some more.

"I have a five-point-oh." She sank back into her chair, looking dazed. "A freakin' five out of five."

"You have a perfect five? I only have a four-point-nine. Emma, that's great."

"Yeah, lotta good it's gonna do me now." She flicked her finger on the screen to scroll down the page.

"Wait, what? I do *not* dissolve students in acid! Not that I— whoa, this is so weird, Molly."

"I know. It's bizarre. But remember, the plan to use the online evaluations for our pay and promotions? They're only going to use the numbers, not the comments. And the numbers are high."

"So who do you think wrote these?"

"I don't know. I thought it might be one of my students, but then why would they do yours too? You know what, though. We should have been doing this for each other all along."

Emma sighed.

"Yeah, those five-star reviews are gonna be super helpful when I'm rotting in prison."

"I'm working on that," I said.

"You are?"

"Yes. Iker and I, we'll fix this."

I had no idea how. But I didn't tell Emma that.

CHAPTER FIFTY-FOUR

Iker sat across from me at my newly cleared desk, his binder open in front of him. He looked glum.

"So Linda Wilson was in on it," I said. "Is that what you're telling me?"

"It appears to be the case." Iker sighed. "It seems our colleagues have colluded. It is a great disappointment."

"More than a disappointment. One of them ended up dead. Dividing up the big purchases into smaller ones, what was it called?"

"Parceling." Iker's tone was mournful. "Sometimes it is called bundling."

"It doesn't seem like something Kent could've cooked up by himself. It must have been Linda's idea."

"To join a conspiracy of thieves is dangerous. We know of two. Perhaps there are more."

"Any thoughts about the watch?" I asked. "Linda must have known about Kent and Marshall. Maybe Linda was jealous. What's the term you guys use? Information asymmetry?"

"Please," Iker said. "That is the economists. I am an accountant."

"Oh, sorry."

"Either Marshall Dixon or Linda Wilson might have had the motive of jealousy," Iker said. "And let us not forget, there are also the husbands."

"Good point about the husbands. Oh, this is hopeless. Just about anyone could have a motive."

"That is not so. You, Molly, do not have a motive to kill the music instructor Kent Lovely."

"Well, Kent was annoying. He wouldn't stop with the gross innuendo, and he insisted on speaking Italian to me, even though I kept telling him I'm Albanian. And you—well, I actually can't imagine you killing anyone, Iker. So I guess you're off the hook."

"This idle speculation is not useful. We are not officers of the law, Molly."

"No, but Emma Nakamura is my best friend. And the way things are going, it's going to be bad for her."

"You do not trust justice to be done?"

"No, Iker, I do not. Maybe you don't know yet. They arrested her. It's ridiculous. Emma is not a monster. I don't care what her students say."

"I did not realize it had come to this point." Iker paused to absorb the information. "Molly, what if Emma is indeed the murderer of Kent Lovely?"

"Emma is not a poisoner. I'm one hundred percent sure. If she were a murderer, she'd be more the I-want-my-face-to-be-the-last-thing-you-see-before-you-die type."

"Yes. You are correct. Poisoning is not in Emma's nature."

"You know what? We need to talk to—" I jerked my thumb at the wall separating my office from Rodge Cowper's. "He was sitting right next to Kent when it happened. And last time we tried to talk to him, we were interrupted. Let's go, Iker. Let's talk to him now."

Iker looked up, startled.

"But we have already spoken to Roger Cowper. I do not understand the reason for this disagreeable suggestion."

"Please. Come with me. Before I lose my nerve. Otherwise I'll have to go by myself. There's one thing we never asked him about. The missing pills. Do you really think that he got rid of them because of his sense of propriety?"

Iker sighed.

"Yes. I too am curious about this. Very well. Let us go."

Rodge greeted us cheerfully, and invited Iker and me to sit on the lumpy metal-framed futon couch. I sat, but Iker walked to the curio cabinet to examine the assortment of carved bowls and heathen figurines. He did not touch any of it.

"Doctor Cowper, you have many curiosities displayed here. But one item is not in evidence." Iker paused, perhaps to let Rodge sweat a little. And I noticed Rodge really was sweating.

I couldn't see Iker's expression. He was facing the curio cabinet.

"You are a jocular fellow." Iker was still turned away from us. "A man who enjoys a humorous story. You use this small bottle of pills as a starter of conversation, and you are fond of telling the tale of its purchase abroad. You do not consume the contents, however. You use the thing as a prop, an amusement only. But after Professor Lovely's death, the pills are not there. We must ask ourselves, why does Doctor Cowper no longer wish to display his humorous pills?"

Rodge fidgeted. "They were past their expiration date."

"The bottle was sealed," I said. "It was just a conversation piece. Even if there had been an expiration date—and there wouldn't necessarily be one, if you really bought it overseas—why would it matter?"

"Why are you so sure the bottle was sealed?" Rodge challenged me.

"It *was* sealed. I picked up the bottle. I remember."

"How do you remember something like that?"

"Perhaps you should tell us what you have been keeping secret," Iker said.

CHAPTER FIFTY-FIVE

Rodge opened his mouth and then closed it again. He ran his beefy hands through his thick grey hair, which left him looking more, not less, rumpled.

"Rodge, Kent was our colleague, but he was *your* good friend. Aren't you even a little curious about what happened to him? Unless you know what happened to him, and you aren't telling anyone."

"'Course I wanna know what happened. I think about it all the time. Hey, you think Dixon did it? She's kind of a hard nose. Maybe when she found out about all that financial stuff—"

"Doctor Marshall Dixon..." Iker gave a reflexive little bow of respect as he spoke her name. "...is responsible for safeguarding the good name of our university. Are you intimating in this capacity, might she have wanted to eliminate Kent Lovely in order to defuse an embarrassing situation?"

"Yeah, that's what I'm saying. Dixon has a motive."

"But for Doctor Dixon to commit this murder?" Iker said. "This does not make sense. Dr. Dixon is a shrewd woman. If the story in the newspaper is an embarrassment, one does not keep this story at a high profile by poisoning the miscreant in public. One avoids taking action, and trusts the fickle readers of the newspaper will soon turn their attention to a different scandal."

"Well," Rodge countered, "who else wanted to get rid of Kent?"

"Perhaps you believe it was Emma who avenged the apparent injustice inflicted upon her brother, Jonah?"

"What? No," Rodge protested. "Not Emma."

"She has a knowledge of biology, and she can easily acquire chemicals. Hers is not such a gentle nature. Perhaps Emma Nakamura could be capable of such a thing, as the policemen believe."

"What policemen?" Rodge apparently hadn't heard about Emma's arrest.

"But Emma did not do this thing," Iker said. "Even she does not have such a hot head as this. Committing such a murder would not help her brother, even if someone had conspired to deprive him of his livelihood."

"And no one even conspired against Jonah," I said.

"No indeed," Iker agreed. "Jonah's courses were cancelled shortly after he reported Kent Lovely's wrongdoing, but this was merely a coincidence. In fact those courses had insufficient enrollment. Standard policy was followed in this case. The newspaper report was incorrect in that regard."

"Well, poisoning is a woman's crime," Rodge said. "That's how come I thought of Marshall Dixon."

Rodge had been Kent's patient sidekick. Maybe he was more fed up with Kent than anyone knew. On the other hand, Rodge genuinely seemed to miss Kent. Heaven only knows why. I couldn't believe Rodge thought it was funny, the way Kent had ransacked the salad bar at Gavin's. It was just like Kent. Barging in like he owned the place, taking far more than his share. The same way he loaded up his plate at the retreat with the last of the *haupia* cake. And dallied with not one, but two married women.

And then I realized what was going on. Rodge hadn't killed Kent. Rodge was protecting Kent.

"I have an idea." I raised my hand. "Rodge, I think Kent did it to himself."

"What?" Rodge looked pale.

"He opened your bottle and took the pills. Just like he loaded up at the salad bar, taking more food than he could possibly eat and ruining things for everyone else. I think you warned him not to do it, and he didn't listen."

I was bluffing. But I had also never been more sure of anything in my life. I watched Rodge stare at his desk.

"Well?" I normally would never be this confrontational, but my best friend was facing jail time for something she didn't do. And it was all because Rodge had refused to tell the truth.

He sat and breathed heavily for a few moments before he finally spoke.

"At the retreat," Rodge said, "when we were about to start eating? Kent said if he lasted more than four hours, don't seek medical attention, just call the Guinness Book of World Records."

"I can almost hear him saying it," I said. "Why did he take them on that particular day, after all of those years they've been sitting out in your office?"

Rodge sighed and crossed his arms.

"Kent knew he was gonna get the teaching award. And he wanted to, you know, celebrate after. He had, uh, um, two dates planned for that night."

"Kent had planned to get the teaching award?" Iker asked Rodge. "How could he be certain of this?"

"Iker, Linda chairs the award committee, so draw your own conclusions. And the press release, which came out right after the retreat, announcing the awards? It had clearly been written in advance, remember? It said Kent accepted the award. Rodge, you knew it was rigged? It didn't bother you that you didn't have a chance at the award?" Rodge shrugged.

"Did you know about the watches?"

"The watches?" Rodge repeated.

"Two ladies' timepieces purchased from Fujioka's Music and Party Supply," Iker said. "They were the identical model. One was a platinum finish and the other—"

"Okay, yeah, I guess I knew about the watches."

"So you knew about Kent's relationship with Linda Wilson, the person who more or less chooses who gets the teaching award. And about his parallel relationship with Marshall Dixon."

"Well, I...I don't want to answer that."

"I understand," Iker said. "You wish to be discreet."

Rodge, pale and fearful, gestured at his lap.

"Molly, Iker, if this gets out, Dixon'll have my—"

Iker went over to Rodge's office door, and pushed it shut.

"It's hard to keep a secret in Mahina," I said. "People know. Count on it."

Serena knew what Kent was up to. Now I knew what she meant when she said, *you play with fire, you gonna get burned.*

"Kent was gonna have a quick—um, appointment with Marshall right before her dinner with Skip Kojima, and you know Linda's husband, Bob Wilson, was off-island at that historians' meeting, and so Kent was gonna go on and meet Linda afterward."

"So Marshall was the one who authorized Kent to approve the purchases for the Music Department," I said. "And Linda is the one who helped Kent figure out how to game the system to get goodies for himself. And her."

"Purchasing authority should not have been delegated to a temporary contract worker," Iker said. "It is not sound practice."

"But remember, the Music Department doesn't have any full time professors left. They only had Kent and Jonah. Two temporary contract workers. And now I suppose Mahina State doesn't have any Music Department at all."

"That is a very sad news," Iker said. "It is inconceivable to me, how our university has let the Music Department perish."

"Know what's sad?" Rodge looked from Iker to me. "Kent was out before they even announced the award. He never got a chance to hear his name called. So how did you two figure it out?"

"I examined the financial records," Iker said. "But Molly was the one who unraveled the rest of the puzzle."

"Once you think about it, it's obvious. Kent was greedy, selfish, reckless, and stubborn, and not really good at thinking about the consequences of his actions."

"Whoa, easy there, Molly."

"Sorry, Rodge. I know he was your friend, but let's be honest. It's completely in character for Kent to do something risky and greedy and dumb, like taking those pills."

"Yes," Iker agreed. "For Kent Lovely, it was a sport to take more than his share. It is so with the pills. If an ordinary man takes two pills, Kent Lovely takes four pills. It is like that."

"An ordinary man's actually only supposed to take one pill," Rodge said. "Why are you so sure it's the pills, though? Why not his sports drink? Maybe it was that."

"Iker and I did some research," I said. "At Natural High, you know the health food store?"

"I was at first reluctant," Iker said, "but Molly was right to insist. It was an informative visit. I asked the young saleslady this thing: a man who is in middle age, who wishes to recapture the vigor of his youth, what are the herbs he might take to achieve this? And these herbs, what is their effect in the body? Can they also carry some dangers? Indeed, yes. They can raise the blood pressure, and cause the kidney to fail."

"Kent's hair color should have been the first clue," I said.

"His hair color?" Rodge looked confused.

"His hairstylist warned him not to go too dark," I explained. "But Kent ignored the expert's advice, and insisted on the black tint."

"I know Kent had high blood pressure. I shoulda—"

"Rodge, you couldn't have stopped him. Kent wouldn't listen to anyone. Not even you. For crying out loud, I don't know how many times I tried to tell him I don't speak Italian."

Rodge looked miserable. "I can't do anything about it now."

"Yes you *can*. You can call Detective Silva. Why didn't you say something right away?"

"I thought he was gonna make it. And then when he didn't... You guys knew him. Do you think he'd want everyone to know he died of an overdose of...he died like that?"

"Rodge, if you don't tell the truth, someone innocent is going to be blamed for this."

"They'll never arrest Jonah," Rodge said. "He's just a kid. I don't think even *they* think he did it. They're just keeping an eye on him for show. Give it a couple weeks. It'll die down."

"You're right. They're not going to arrest Jonah. Remember, *Emma* is the one with knowledge of human biology, and access to chemicals."

Rodge's ragged features tensed. "You think Emma could be in trouble?"

Emma would kill me if she ever found out I told Rodge about her arrest, but I couldn't think of any other way out.

"Do I think? Rodge, Emma was *arrested for the murder.*"

"What? That's impossible."

"Believe it. How would you like it if Emma went to prison for ten years because *you* wouldn't tell the truth?"

Rodge stared at me as if he'd been pithed, like one of the unfortunate frogs in Emma's first-year biology lab. I picked up Rodge's office phone, dialed a number, and asked to be connected to Detective Silva. Then I handed him the receiver. Rodge hesitated, and then took it.

CHAPTER FIFTY-SIX

Emma and I were having lunch in the cafeteria, sharing a copy of the latest issue of *Island Confidential*. The cover story was a full feature on the Kent Lovely case. It was probably going to be a collector's item. By midmorning, the newsstands around campus had been cleaned out, and the *Island Confidential* website had crashed, overwhelmed with page hits.

I had finished reading to the bottom of the front page, and stopped to wait for Emma to catch up.

"So Rodge never really threw the pills away?" Emma asked.

"He did throw them away. But the police were able to get another sample for the toxicology tests. You know where it turns out he got them? Right here in town."

"So you mean he didn't buy them from some exotic far-off land? I knew it." Emma snorted. "What a phony."

"Yeah, not unless you count the strip mall next to Galimba's Bargain Boyz as an exotic far-off land."

"Oh, *that* place. Lucky Golden Fortune? I bought a wok there. Friggin' thing rusted through before I ever got a chance to use it. You already done with your breakfast?"

"Yeah, I should've gotten more than just a little bag of nuts."

"Want a bite of my Spam *musubi*?"

Emma picked up the *musubi* and waved it in front of my face. I was still hungry, and it smelled good.

"Sure. I think I will have some." I took it out of her hand.

"You're gonna eat Spam? No way. I'll believe it when I see it.

Go ahead."

I closed my eyes, wrinkled my nose, and took a bite.

"Oh, that's not bad." I managed another bite before Emma grabbed it back.

"It was actually edible."

"Yeah, that's how come I was eating it. Buy your own."

"Maybe I will. Okay, I'm going to turn the page. Ready?"

"Oh, now we're getting to the good part." Emma traced her finger down the column as she read. "The popular herb is toxic at high doses, but easily purchased in any health food store. The analysis found additional stimulants and vasodilators as well as a chemical compound derived from the blister beetle. This substance can cause severe damage to the—"

"Stop. I read ahead. I don't want to hear any more."

"Fine." Emma pulled the paper away and read silently for a few seconds. "I wish they wouldn't give this much detail. People might get ideas. Ooh, *this* looks like a bad way to go. So Molly, do you know every cell in your body—"

"No. Seriously. Please don't read any more. It's too horrible."

"Really? Not as horrible as Kent Lovely going around nailing our married administrators. I still can't get my head around it."

"I don't want to think about it either," I said. "I'll just sit here and think nice, G-rated thoughts about sunshine and flowers."

"G-rated? You know flowers are the genitals of plants, right?"

"You have to ruin everything, don't you? Have you ever considered maybe *genitals* are the flowers of *people*?"

"What?"

"Never mind. I just made it worse. Emma, there's one thing I still can't figure out. The code in Kent's notebook in the office. Remember, the hearts with 12 and 13 written on them? Did that have to do with the pills, or his purchases, or his busy social calendar, or something else?"

Emma pondered a moment.

"Oh, I know. thirteenth letter of the alphabet is M. So that must stand for Marshall. Then the twelfth letter of the alphabet is L, for Linda. It musta been Kent's super-secret code for him having dates with Linda and Marshall that day."

"That must be it. How did you come up with it so fast?"

"I dunno. That thirteen equals M thing just popped into my head. I must be a natural, what's it called? Crypt keeper."

"Cryptologist."

"Whatever. Eh, so Jonah. Since everything's cleared up, his guitar students are coming back. So thanks, ah?"

"He's a good teacher," I said. "I think I'm already making some progress."

"Too bad he's still not making enough to be able to afford his own place yet. Hey, Molly, weren't you saying you missed having a roommate?"

"I did say something about having a roommate. I believe my exact words were, 'The best thing about getting a real job after grad school was never having to have a roommate.'"

"Come on, Molly, you and Jonah get along, right? And think about it, he could pay rent with guitar lessons. You wouldn't have to pay money anymore. Barter. It's super sustainable. No, seriously. And know what? He totally likes you. And I know you like him too, right?"

"Don't you need the rental income to pay off your lawyer?"

"Nah, we already paid Feinman. Cleaned out our savings. Know what though? If I had a sister-in-law with a nice, steady job in the College of Commerce, it'd be a load off my mind."

Emma continued to badger me as I watched a familiar figure come through the doors of the cafeteria.

"Oh, look." I waved. "He doesn't have anyone to have lunch with. He should come sit with us."

"Who are you talking about, Iker? Pat? Who?"

"*Rodge*," I yelled across the mostly empty lunch tables. "Over here. Come sit with us."

Emma shot me a hard stinkeye. But she let the Jonah thing drop.

CHAPTER FIFTY-SEVEN

Jonah Nakamura is no longer staying with Emma and her grouchy husband, Yoshi. Jonah has moved to the Pacific Northwest, where he's helping a friend operate some kind of medical dispensary. I had no idea Jonah had any interest or training in medicine, but Emma tells me he's helping out people with conditions like glaucoma and loss of appetite, and he's making bank besides.

I don't have time for guitar lessons anyway. Fall classes have started, and it's all I can do to stay one chapter ahead of my students in my newly assigned courses, Intro to Business Management (IBM) and Business Planning (BP).

I haven't met the lecturer who took over my Business Communication classes, nor am I likely to. He took the job on the condition he be allowed to teach exclusively online. And instead of choosing the course textbook from my painstakingly assembled short list, he assigned his own self-published book to the class, a tactic that falls somewhere between "deplorable" and "I wish I'd thought of it."

With budget cuts in the air and Skip Kojima of Kojima Surfwear no longer interested in making a donation to the university, the administration has decided not to replace either of our music instructors. This has effectively killed our music program. The dilapidated Music portables are being rented out to a commercial test-prep center that caters to local parents who hope their children will end up somewhere better than Mahina State.

About Pat Flanagan: He is *Island Confidential*. It's not common knowledge, so I probably shouldn't say anything, but you, discerning reader, would have figured it out already. Pat also owned up to being the one behind the mysterious evaluations on the online ratings site. Upon learning of the scheme to tie our personnel decisions to our online ratings, he decided to do all of us a favor. I don't know why we never thought of it before, but we've started uploading five-star reviews for one another. Pat Flanagan, Emma Nakamura, and I are now the three highest rated instructors at Mahina State.

My attempt at whistleblowing did reach the upper echelons of the Foundation, although the result was not exactly what I had hoped for. The chancellor's secretary sent out an urgent email to the entire faculty, warning us that faculty members are not under any circumstances permitted to make direct contact with the Foundation. All communication must go through the designated liaison in the Student Retention Office.

The chancellor's secretary may not have realized the original message from the foundation chair to our chancellor was attached to that email: *Bud: Looks like someone in your shop isn't a team player. We don't need your people going off the reservation. Let's keep an eye on this.*

Having failed in reforming the university, I set my aspirations a little lower, and set about improving my workspace by installing a new coffee machine in my office. Sure, it's pushed back my student loan repayments by a month, but it's improved my quality of life (and energy level) immensely. Emma now spends more time than ever in my office, as does our new friend Patrick Flanagan, whose coffee addiction puts ours to shame.

So I'm teaching two new preps, I don't really have any romantic prospects, and I don't even have a real office chair. But I do have two good friends now, and a rewarding job. I live in one of the most beautiful places on earth, and I have excellent coffee whenever I want it.

The Kent Lovely situation was stressful, of course, but I've put it behind me. I mean, this is quiet little Mahina. What are the chances I'm going to be involved with something like that again?

An excerpt from... The Musubi Murder

CHAPTER ONE

Our guest of honor, Jimmy Tanaka, may have been "The Most Hated Man in Hawaii," but he was also the biggest donor in the history of the College of Commerce. We were in no position to be picky about the moral character of our benefactors. Not after the latest round of budget cuts.

I had never seen the cafeteria this dressed up: white tablecloths, a wall-length refreshment table laden with stainless chafing dishes and platters, and extra security. I felt out of place, a drab little sparrow (and a sweaty one) in my dark wool suit. Everyone else sported Aloha Friday wear, cool cotton prints with colorful hibiscus or monstera designs. Something was making my neck itch. It was either the humidity or the plumeria-spiked floral centerpiece.

I was the only professor at the table. We had been evenly dispersed around the cafeteria to encourage (force) us to mingle with our Friends in the Business Community. The arrangement had the added benefit of keeping Hanson Harrison and Larry Schneider separated. Our two most senior professors are like fighting fish, flaring their gills at each other when they get too close.

I'm constantly telling my students how important it is to network. What I don't tell them is that I, personally, hate doing it, and, furthermore, I'm not very good at it. Mercedes Yamashiro, the only person at the table I knew, was deep in conversation with the woman next to her.

Bill Vogel appeared at our table, looking even more sour-faced than usual. Put him in a lace mantilla, and my dean could do a passable impression of Queen Victoria. "Mercedes," he barked. "Do you have any idea why Mr. Tanaka would be delayed this morning?"

"Oh, hello, Bill. No, I haven't seen Jimmy since he checked in last night."

He gave Mercedes a curt nod and stalked off without so much as a glance in my direction. I was the only person at the table who actually worked for him, but I was of no immediate use. Vogel would remember my name well enough when it was time to delegate some unpleasant task.

The good-looking man on my right was studying the contents of a manila folder. Even if I had the nerve to interrupt him, I couldn't imagine what I would say. I certainly couldn't open a conversation by telling him how much I liked the way he smelled, although that would have been the truth. He had a pleasant aroma of soap and cedar. Maybe I could comment on the weather. *Hey, have you noticed it's raining outside, ha ha, what are the chances? It only does that like three hundred days a year in Mahina.* He looked familiar, but I couldn't quite place him, and I certainly didn't want to volunteer the fact that I had forgotten his name. I wished that whoever had planned this breakfast had thought of providing name tags. I stared at the exit sign over a side door.

Exit. I dearly wished I could.

A flicker of motion under the sign caught my eye. I thought I saw a flash of baseball caps and sunglasses. I blinked at the empty doorway, and wondered if I had seen anything at all.

A shriek, followed by a metallic crash, startled the entire cafeteria into silence. At the refreshment table, two black-aproned servers stood wide-eyed, staring down at the wreckage of the dropped fruit platter. One held his hands over his mouth; the other clutched a round, stainless steel cover. Something round and white rolled to a halt on the floor, where it rocked gently among the translucent pineapple wedges and flabby melon chunks. Security guards converged on the object, conferred briefly, and sent the skinniest one sprinting out.

"It's okay, Molly." Mercedes Yamashiro patted my arm. "This kine stuff follows Jimmy around. I cannot even remember how many times he's had blood thrown at him, or people make one human chain to keep him out of somewhere. Not your guys' fault that people can be so rude. What *was* that thing? Not a bomb, I hope."

"Look over there," I said. "Our dean seems really upset. This is very unfortunate."

I had been secretly hoping for a minor disruption like this—something that would let me get out of there and back to work as quickly as possible. I could see Vogel now across the room, shouting into his cell phone, his jowly face wobbling like an enraged blancmange.

"Eh, this is late, even for Mr. Big Shot Jimmy Tanaka." Mercedes glanced around, then lowered her voice to a whisper that only a few tables around us could hear. "I wen' knock on his door this morning to see if he wanted to drive up with me but no answer. I left him alone 'cause I thought he got a ride with someone else, but now I think he was probably hungover in his room."

I glanced over at the refreshment table. The spilled food was being swept up, and a replacement fruit platter had already been set out.

"Do you want to call Mr. Tanaka and check on him?" I asked.

"Too late." She shook her wrist to clear a tangle of gold and jade bracelets out of the way, and checked her slender watch. "Even if he left now, he wouldn't get here till after ten. Probably for the best. Eh, Molly, you no like the food?"

Mercedes gestured at the Spam musubi congealing on my plate.

The Spam musubi, Hawaii's favorite snack and Merrie Musubis' signature dish, is a cube of sticky rice topped with a slice of fried Spam, and then wrapped in a strip of dried seaweed. From a distance, musubis look a lot like oversized pieces of sushi. Up close, they're delicious.

Unfortunately, my appetite had been damped by the stench

of our ancient air conditioning mixed with the greasy breakfast smells and cloying plumeria scent. Also, I'm a little self-conscious about stuffing my face in front of attractive strangers.

"Of course I like the food." I stole a sidelong glance at the nice-smelling man, and wondered if I could pocket the musubi without anyone noticing. I could eat it later, in my office. "It's just, I'm not usually up to breakfast this early."

That was a dumb thing to say. This town still runs on plantation time, and no one around here thinks nine in the morning is early. The Farmers' Market opens before sunrise, or so I hear.

The handsome man closed his manila folder and tucked it into the briefcase next to his chair.

"Good idea to have Jimmy Tanaka's restaurant cater the breakfast," he said, with an easy smile. Who was he? He seemed to know Mercedes, which wasn't any help. Mercedes knows everyone.

"I do like Merrie Musubis," I said.

"Really?" The man eyed my untouched plate.

"Oh sure! I think their food is actually pretty decent. Especially compared to most of what you find around—"

"Oh, Molly!" Mercedes interrupted me. "Speaking of food! When are you going to invite Donnie to come talk to your class about the restaurant business?"

Donnie! Now I remembered who he was. I was sitting next to Donnie Gonsalves, owner of Donnie's Drive-Inns, Home of the Lolo Lunch Plate, and the Sumo Saimin Bowl. Merrie Musubis' main competitor.

"Oh!" I squeaked, "That's a great idea! You know my students really—"

"Shh!" Mercedes waved her hand to quiet me. "Here's your dean. He's gonna say something now."

About the Author

 Like Molly Barda, Frankie Bow teaches at a public university. Unlike her protagonist, she is blessed with delightful students, sane colleagues, a loving family, and a perfectly nice office chair. She believes if life isn't fair, at least it can be entertaining. In addition to writing murder mysteries, she publishes in scholarly journals under her real name. Her experience with academic publishing has taught her to take nothing personally.

Sign up for news of releases, giveaways, and events at: bit.ly/SpamMe.

CPSIA information can be obtained at www.ICGtesting.com
Printed in the USA
LVOW08s1622290316

481260LV00001B/153/P

9 781943 476022